THE SPANISH HOUSE

CHERRY RADFORD

An Aria Book

First published in the UK in 2021 by Head of Zeus Ltd
This paperback edition first published in 2022 by Head of Zeus Ltd,
part of Bloomsbury Publishing Plc

9 7 5 3 1 2 4 6 8

A CIP catalogue record for this book is available from the British Library.

ISBN (PB) 9781801103886
ISBN (E) 9781801103879

Printed and bound by CPI Group (UK) Ltd, Croydon, CR0 4YY

Head of Zeus
5–8 Hardwick Street
London EC1R 4RG
www.headofzeus.com

THE MUSIC OF THE SPANISH HOUSE

MUSIC PLAYLIST

Create a free Spotify account and listen to some of the music
in *The Spanish House*.

Chapter 4
'Volver' (Return) – Estrella Morente (Carlos Gardel, Alfredo
Le Pera)
'The Summer Knows' – Antonio Serrano, Federico Lechner
(Michel Legrand)
'Algo Contigo' (Something with You) – Rosario, Niña Pastori
(Chico Novarro)

Chapter 6
'My Defences Are Down' (Annie Get Your Gun) – Howard
Keel (Irving Berlin)

Chapter 9
'Jill's Theme' (Once Upon a Time in the West) – Edda
Dell'Orso (Ennio Morricone)

Chapter 14
'Como Me Duele Perderte' (How it Hurts Me to Lose You) –
Gloria Estefan (Marco A. Flores)

Chapter 16
'Problema' (Problem) - Ketama (Antonio Carmona, Josemi
Carmona, Juan Carmona)

Chapter 19
'Stayin' Alive' – Bee Gees (Barry Gibb, Maurice Gibb, Robin
Gibb)
'They Say It's Wonderful' (Annie Get Your Gun) – Betty
Hutton, Howard Keel (Irving Berlin)

Chapter 22
'Too Much Heaven' - Bee Gees (Barry Gibb, Maurice Gibb,
Robin Gibb)

Chapter 27
'Stars' – Simply Red (Mick Hucknall)

Epilogue
'The March of the Siamese Children' (The King and I) –
20th Century Fox Orchestra (Oscar Hammerstein II, Richard
Rogers)

ONE

The girls weren't even talking loudly. Later, they'd wonder how they were heard, above the clatter of the District Line. They'd explain that all they did was find themselves sitting next to each other, saying hello-I-mean-*hola*, and then chatting in Spanish – as members of South Ealing Spanish Practice Meetup do. In next to no time, it seemed, the lads lurched down the carriage to them and a fag-stained finger was wagging inches from Juliana's face.

'Stop that fuckin' stupid language! You're in *England*!'

Juliana looked up to meet the half-closed eyes of tall and swaggering Fag Finger and his potato-faced sidekick. 'Sorry if it bothers you,' she said. 'We're getting out soon anyway.'

'We go to a Spanish practice group – we're just *learning*,' Nadia put in, managing to hide her Polish accent.

Fag Finger's mouth dropped open. 'You *what*?'

They looked a bit thick and stank of weed, but they didn't seem to be doing too badly, with their big white trainers and crisp haircuts.

'Na, na,' the chap beside him started, jutting his big chin

forward for a better look at Juliana. 'No *way* this one's English. Go back to your own country! Too many of you spics round here.'

'This *is* my own country,' Juliana said, hoping she wouldn't have to go into how she was half Spanish.

'Then why you look like, like…' He scratched his jaw as he looked her up and down.

Turnham Green. Two more stops. But Nadia had taken her arm, probably thinking they should get off earlier.

'…Pocahontas!' He nudged Fag Finger, and was chuffed to make him laugh. Bent double, they were, the idiots. Then Fag Finger swooped down and pulled her up by her plait.

'Get off me!' Juliana shouted, her heart thudding in her chest.

Two black guys in football gear who'd been poring over a phone looked up.

An older guy in a suit got up and came over. 'Now that's enough.'

Still holding her plait, Fag Finger turned on him. 'Oh yeah? Who says?'

There was an intake of breath from the old woman opposite, and then the suited man's eyes widened, his cheeks quivering, as he looked down at Fag Finger's other hand. Something flashed in the harsh light.

Nadia had stood up, linking trembling arms with Juliana.

The other one laughed at her. 'Now don't you worry about your friend,' he said to Nadia. 'She's coming home with us to play cowboys and injuns, aren't you, gorgeous?' He grabbed Juliana round her waist. A sickening smirk spread over Fag Finger's face.

The train stopped dead, throwing the boys into each other. Something clanged to the floor.

A small knife.

Fag Finger grabbed it and pointed it at the suited man. 'Keep back! You might be the big man at the office, but *I'm* in control here.'

The old woman started whimpering. The footballers got to their feet. Then the train sped forward again and stopped abruptly in the station.

'Not now, you're not,' one of the black guys said with a grin, putting away his phone and pointing to the policemen waiting to board the train.

———

Juliana climbed the stairs to her bedsit. Her two housemates, standing in the doorway of one of their rooms, stopped chatting as she went past.

'I'll be having a very, *very* long bath,' she told them.

The shared bathroom was a bubbling source of disagreement, so she was surprised to see them exchange glances and nod. Perhaps they could see something was wrong, but didn't want to hear about it.

She shut the door of her room behind her, leant against it while glancing around at her English life: the six o'clock tea mug and Weetabix bowl on the sink, the David Nicholls novel she'd left behind on the bedside table, the Handel on the music stand. Half Spanish? She had a rusty A level, devoid of rolled 'r's; she didn't like ham, seafood or olives; had only one seldom-seen Spanish relative; and hadn't visited Spain for years. Boyfriends thinking her exotic had been hugely disappointed. When the genes were handed down to her, they somehow managed to create a totally English woman trapped in a dark and incongruous Spanishness. A Spanishness that came from nowhere – or so it felt, having not seen Mama since the age of seven.

3

And yet... she slipped off her rucksack and shoes, flopped onto the bed and rested her eyes on the crowd of baby cacti on the windowsill. And yet what she knew of Mama – the courageous departure from her family's village to get involved in the Sergio Leone Sixties western, *Once Upon a Time in the West* – had stayed with her. As had Mama's wide smile, and the 'Hooli' sound of her name in Spanish.

From the chest of drawers, the Woody cowboy doll from *Toy Story* grinned down at her. A present from Toby when they had been an item. *Cowboys and Indians*... A 'Pocahontas'. Of all things, those idiots saw her as that. Not that she hadn't been one before. She'd been most things, over time. Including a horrified person on a number of modes of transport, and more times than she could count, a minority ethnic policewoman. Native American, South American, Hawaiian, Latin, Asian – she'd played them all. That's what happened if you worked full-time as a television and film extra for... well, thirty years. Since she was a baby, in fact. Nadia, bless her, had told the police her Meetup friend was an actress. *Supporting Artiste*, she'd had to correct them – and don't worry about the 'e' on the end; there's seldom anything glamorous about it.

She pulled herself up and went over to her laptop. Yes, there it was: instructions for the next day's shoot, which was going to be more of being one of several crime scene officers finding body parts in wheelie bins, but in a different street. It felt like more than half her work was to do with crime. Bodies. Weapons. *Knives*. No wonder she went into some kind of daze on the Tube, as if waiting for the director to yell 'cut'. There were other emails asking about her availability for jobs – and not just from Dad's extras casting company – but she didn't want to think about work now. Her phone was as bad, and after sending a night-night message to Nadia through the Meetup group's WhatsApp, she silenced it.

She washed the Tube boys from her hair, then lay down with water up to her chin in the bath. Wonderful. Like a big hug. Like the hug from Kelvin, one of the football guys who'd looked like he didn't care, but had been secretly calling the police. Arty type, designed furniture. Told her to be proud of her Spanish half. Unfortunately, he was wearing a wedding ring. How wonderful to have a man like that. She sighed. If she couldn't find an arty, hugging man of her own, she could at least get a *bath* of her own. Time she rented her own flat, however tiny. Perhaps if she started making money from her blog; maybe there were companies who'd want to advertise in *Views from a Human Prop*.

Back in her room, she got under her duvet, blanket and fluffy dressing gown ; she was outnumbered regarding the house heating level, her PE teacher housemates seemingly born without cold receptors.

She plugged in her phone. Took a vitamin pill. Turned out the light. Tried not to keep seeing those hooded, mean eyes, and the knife…

Her phone lit up. Maybe poor Nadia couldn't sleep. A number she didn't recognise. It had called several times. She scrolled down… about *ten* times. *A Spanish number*. It had to be Uncle Arturo. *Or his housekeeper*. It was very late; maybe something had happened. Please *no*… She pressed the number.

'Hooliana?'

'Hello, are you all right? I'm sorry I missed—'

'Are *you* all right, Hooliana? You not answer my email. You have read my email?'

'Er, no, I…' She went over to the laptop and turned it back on. He started saying something else, but in Spanish – or rather, Andalusian, with all those missing 'd's and 's's.

5

Croaky Andalusian; he was sounding older than a year ago. 'I'm sorry, I didn't understand that,' she said in Spanish. 'I'm a bit tired. I can't see an email… ah, unless…' Unless he's sent it to the dodgy old email address that she'd stopped using because it didn't work on her phone. She opened it up. It was very long, and in Spanish.

'You read it now, then you call me, *vale*? *No te preocupes.* Don' worry. Is good thing for you. Is what you need, but don' know it, *te digo.*'

Te digo. I tell you. Yes, he was always good at telling her things. *"Stop with this Toby boyfriend." "What? We broke up eleven years ago!" "Yes, but he never go, no' really"* (as he tapped her head). It usually made her laugh, but this email was in ten bullet points and she'd seen the words for *paint, house* and *ninety days*.

'Okay. I might need to look up some words… I'll call you back.'

'*Perfecto.*'

She started translating – as well as she could, in her excitement. When she started gasping, eyes darting from one bit to another, she printed it out.

My dear Juliana,

For two years now, I don't visit the summer house in San Rafael. I have been renting to friends sometimes, but they are now older and prefer hotels. It is time for me to say goodbye to it.

As I told you, my Miguel is busy with the fashion business I have passed to him. He doesn't like San Rafael. He and Susana prefer their life in Madrid and travelling for holidays of golf. Even when he visits me here in Almería city, he doesn't want to drive there. He prefers places more fine.

But you like quiet, and need a place your own, and to understand more about your Spanish inheritance. So I am thinking, my dear, that if you can accomplish these conditions, within the ninety days you are allowed to stay in Spain, starting this 1st May, the house will be yours. I have consulted my lawyer and, in the event of my death, he and an executor I have chosen for this will determine if the conditions have been done. Don't worry, I will explain you how all the expenses will be paid, you will have a car, and the conditions are easy and you will enjoy.

1. *Paint the front of the house and inside (yourself, because it is the only way to make acquaintance with a house); form a cactus garden (best for semi-desert here); and replace the boiler (using the man I recommend), the crockery (they make it beautiful in village Níjar), kitchen equipment, bedding and towels et cetera as needed.*

2. *Get on well with your neighbours.*

3. *Make a weekly visit to your mother Antoñita's nicho in the cemetery. Talk to her.*

4. *Visit Fort Tabernas Studios, where your mother and I worked with costumes for Once Upon a Time in the West back in 1968. Explore, stay the night in one of the holiday cabins, take the horse-and-cart ride. Do all these things.*

5. *Take part in the municipal amateur production Annie Get Your Gun at the end of July. They start auditions and rehearsals in May. I used to do this every year. It raises money to pay for music, drama and dance classes for children of parents who cannot pay for them.*

6. *Attend at least one of the monthly concerts at Cactus Garden, Níjar, where also you can buy cacti for the terrace.*

7. *In the city of Almería, visit the music shop for things for your flute.*

8. *Visit the Central Market in Almería. We are the tomato capital of the world, and you have to eat our special and divine Raf tomato.*

9. *Use the car to visit all fifteen accessible beaches between San Rafael and Cabo de Gata.*

10. *Take photos, stick little things in a book, write a diary or start a new one of your blog. Note everything.*

In the house I will leave all the local details you need, and my lawyer's card. I say again, don't worry. You can do it. But this plan is our secret. It is best you do these things without help or hindrance from other people. Say I have paid you to improve the house and look after it for three months. Later they can know it is yours and you can tell them about the conditions you met.

I need details of your passport so that I can buy your flight for 1st May, and bank details for expenses. Answer me soon, that I am not good with the waiting.

A strong hug,
Your Uncle Arturo

'Oh my God!' Laughing tearfully, her heart tapping away, she looked round the room to make sure she wasn't dreaming, then read it again. Picked up the phone and put it down again. May the 1st. Six days. 'Breathe! Think!' Dad was always saying she made decisions too quickly. But how could she say no? The decorating and the amateur dramatics would be a tiny price to pay for... her own house in Spain! She'd be able to escape, any time. No more endless cold, damp winters. No more painful dreaming of swimming in a warm sea. She could rent it out for part of the year, so she could afford to rent something better here – with her own bath.

But... a horse-and-cart ride and a tomato as part of the conditions? Had he really put these crazy requests through a lawyer? Maybe he hadn't, and was losing his mind, poor chap. But what was the worst that could happen? She'd miss a lot of work, maybe the expenses wouldn't be quite enough, but he wasn't going to let her starve. Three Spanish months. Time with Uncle Arturo, with whom there'd always been a spark of fun and affection.

She scrolled through her calendar. It would be great to get out of the family's party for her twin stepsisters' birthday, and she doubted she'd be missed. The evening with her friend Lucy planning the writing of this year's summer play for Lucy's Year 6 class could be brought forward and continued on FaceTime. The Spanish restaurant date with Toby – who was still seeing that actress in the series – would only leave her pointlessly pining again. There was really nothing to keep her here. She picked up the phone.

TWO

DAY 1

Bear in mind that San Rafael is a sad, crumbling ex-goldmining village – which your mother couldn't wait to escape. Why couldn't she get Dad's Sunday lunch words out of her head? She leant against the window full of French clouds and closed her eyes. Admittedly that's pretty much what she and Toby thought of it when they'd driven over from Mojácar to have a look: the hulking concrete remains of the hillside mine looking down over the village, the streets of old miners' cottages in ruins. But that was eleven years ago.

'It's changed, Dad,' she'd said. 'There's this beautiful old building from the mining days that's now the office for the nature reserve the town sits in, it's got a botanical garden, and the village has become a bit of an artists' hang-out.'

'Is it near a beach?' one of her twin stepsisters had asked. Their primary interest in the Mediterranean was to get brown and even more golden – usually between modelling shoots.

'Yes. Several.'

Her stepmum Olivia had given her an extra hill of mash,

as if she were about to starve crossing a desert. 'I know it's an adventure, and goodness knows we're all fed up of months of wind and rain, but will you be safe in this place, on your own?'

'I've lived as good as on my own for five years,' she'd said, 'and at least I won't be using the…' She hadn't told them about what happened on the Tube. 'Can't be as dangerous as London. I haven't had a proper holiday in years – can't wait!'

Dad had looked at her and sighed. *Again.* She'd started wondering how she could cut the visit short and go back to Lucy's earlier. The whole morning, Olivia had fussed about which cupboards and drawers could be used to store her belongings from the bedsit, and things like whether she'd packed Imodium, while Dad had just been maddeningly doom-and-gloom about the whole thing. 'I worry you're expecting too much of this,' he'd said, finally. 'Arturo's a strange chap. And…' he'd lowered his voice '…you're not going to get any answers.'

Answers as to why, aged seven, visiting Spain with her mother, Dad had had to fly over to bring her back to England, because Mama had decided to stay there. He was right there; it was unlikely there'd ever be an answer to that.

———

She woke as the plane landed with a bump at Almería's little airport. It was more like arriving at a station or – when within minutes she was through arrivals with her bag and out into the car park with its giant cacti and succulents – a garden centre. She took off her cardigan; ten in the morning, and there was already the heat of an English summer – but here it came with a dry breeze and the aroma of baked, rusty earth.

A lady in an Indalo Parking sweat top was waiting for her at the car park kiosk, waving like a long-lost friend. 'Hooliana? Arturo sen' me photo!' She showed it to her; it was the selfie they'd taken last year at Kew Gardens. 'Hello! Here is your car,' she said, handing over keys and pointing behind her at a silver Fiat Panda.

'Oh!' When he'd spoken of a car he 'doesn't really use anymore', she'd imagined an old man's vehicle, something outdated and too big.

'Remember, you can park any time free when you take a flight – jus' email us. You have parkin' for the year.'

Year? The car was only hers for ninety days. 'Thanks.'

She'd never driven on the right before, so after leaving the car park and going through a series of tiny roundabouts, she turned into a residential area for some practice. At least the controls were the same as her old Fiat 500 at home.

She parked in a square and had a coffee and a jam *tostada* among Spaniards wearing jumpers or jackets in the heat. Perhaps this felt cool to them, compared to the summer heat to come. The house painting was going to need doing before she was living in an oven.

She programmed the satnav, took a deep breath and set off. It started just as Arturo had described – a quiet country road alongside a sea of such deliciously deep blue that it was hard to keep her eyes on the road. Eventually she was taken inland through some tatty *invernaderos* – ugly plastic greenhouses that produce vegetables for Europe and have boosted the economy of an area that used to suffer widespread poverty. Arturo said their added benefit was that, hearing about them – along with the barren semi-desert landscape – kept most British holidaymakers away or hurtling straight down the dual carriageway to the resort of Mojácar. Just as she was beginning to understand why, a sign announced she was entering the *Parque Natural de Cabo de Gata-Nijar*.

The greenhouses and agricultural buildings suddenly gave way to pastures of luminous yellow and purple wild-flowers and spiky agaves, between ever larger, rounded hills. The sort of hills a child would pat into shape with their hands on a beach, or draw with a crayon and then cover with tufts of grass. That's what these hills had – clumps of tough grass dotted over them, making distant and larger hills delightfully fuzzy in appearance. One hill had a scampering herd of white goats – or maybe they were sheep with short coats; even driving slowly past a herd by the side of the road, she had no idea. Here and there, a few white houses huddled together on a slope, shaded by chunky fan palms and the occasional tree. People could keep their pine forests and lines of palm trees; she liked this gentle, lunar beauty, and couldn't wait to take some walks over it.

She was back at the sea, passing a hamlet with a sandy beach and a small hotel before the road started rising along cliffs and snaking round the curves of the mountains. When did a hill become a mountain? Another thing she didn't know. She'd spent far too much of her life standing around in clothes of the opposite season, waiting to be filmed doing practically nothing. Higher and higher she drove, the rocky coastline and cobalt-blue sea below her – and yet according to the satnav, she was only five minutes from the house.

An abrupt curve inland rose up to a blind summit. She crunched the car into second gear. Then first. When she reached the top, she gasped.

A huge valley of yellow-flowered pasture was spread below her, surrounded by rocky mountains, except for at one end – where the sea, between two hills, looked like it had been poured between their slopes. Not far from there, on the opposite slope, was the white village of San Rafael. Her home for the next three months.

She crawled down the steep road. She and Toby never saw this; they had approached from the other side. Even so, she still couldn't understand how she hadn't noticed the beauty of this volcanic *caldera* – 'cauldron' valley. Perhaps, at the time, she'd been too obsessed by *Toby*'s beauty to see it.

Turning off the road into the village, she started to feel oddly nervous about meeting the house. She wasn't sure she believed Arturo's difficulties with sending a photo – after all, he'd managed to send one to the Indalo Parking lady – so was there, as Dad suggested, some reason he didn't want her to see the house before she arrived?

After the bridge over a dry riverbed she turned right into the village's main street. It was still a road of mainly single-storey white buildings, many with neatly painted borders of blue, russet or deep yellow around their windows, but there were now not just one but several restaurants and cafés; a place displaying ironwork and colourful rugs, another with woven beach mats and inflatables; a couple of small grocery shops; a smart little pharmacy; a *ferretería* hardware place that she hoped would stock paint. And everywhere she looked there were wall posters from 'Grupo Rafaelarte', presumably some kind of artists' club, featuring everything from dark abstracts to turquoise seascapes.

Then there it was, the fork to the right – *Calle del Campo*, her road. Her heart started beating madly as she drove down towards the lower numbers. Through breaks between the even-numbered little houses on her right, she could see they overlooked the dry riverbed, a wild area of cacti and fan palms on the other side, and then pastures stretching away to the mountains in the distance.

Number 4. Second from the end. She parked outside its

narrow front yard and put a hand to her mouth. Arturo had chosen the gorgeous but now faded blue for the door and the surrounding of the windows; ornate window bars matched the ironwork of the fence and gate; and the white walls rose up one storey to a curved, Christmas-cake-like edge at the top, before the blue sky took over. It was the prettiest house she could imagine.

She was about to get out of the car when she noticed a solidly built old woman standing in the doorway of a house opposite and shaking a finger side to side at her; maybe she didn't like her parking here. She reversed into the space next to the house, and that seemed to do the trick; the woman disappeared.

The narrow front yard needed sweeping and cheering up with some pot plants. Close up, she could see the house needed a coat or two of paint, but wasn't nearly as bad as she'd feared. She couldn't wait to see inside, and put one of the big keys in the door. It wouldn't budge, so she took it out, dropped the ring of keys in her hurry, and then put the other one in. It wouldn't budge either. She pulled the door to with the handle and tried again. No difference. Damn. She fought off further worries about Uncle Arturo's sanity, wondering for a moment if he actually owned this house at all. She looked at her phone to check the address she'd been given. Tried yet again. Out of the corner of her eye, she thought she saw the woman at her window; how the Miserable Bag would be loving this. Time to try the back door key.

She took the path at the side of the house leading to steps going down to a lower level on the slope down to the riverbed. Aha – she was wondering how the little one-storey house could have two bedrooms. Brilliant – the small key on the ring opened the big iron gate, so this *was* the right house.

What a wonderful terrace! But… she was not alone on it.

Standing in front of the back door like he owned the place, fixing her with rectangular pupils, was a white goat. Or possibly sheep. He looked over at the terrace next door – or maybe the tumbled wall between, as if to explain himself – and back at her. Then took a few steps towards her, hooves clicking on the terracotta tiles, and lifted his chin as if to check her out.

She took the laptop flight bag off her shoulder. 'Shoo! *Shoo*!' she said, swinging her arms forward at him, but then worried about his curly horns and stepped back instead.

He didn't even blink.

'Gawd. All right, mate, I'll deal with you later.'

She retreated and closed the gate. It was tempting to leave it open in case he followed her and could then be shut out of the terrace – at least on this side – but releasing a goat into the road could have been something the neighbours she was supposed to be getting on with might never forgive.

Back at the front door, she tried one of the keys again and it turned easily. In her excitement, she must have tried the wrong one twice. She dashed back to the car, returned with her suitcase, and opened the door. Flicking the electricity switch, she heard a fridge buzz into life in the kitchen alcove to one side, and helicopter-like ceiling fans whirred into welcome action. She opened all the dark wooden shutters, letting in sunshine and the view of the valley.

It was a homely room of old sofas covered in orange and blue cotton throws with elephant designs, a scratched and ancient dark wood table, tall bookshelves and cupboards, and a fireplace with a wood burner. On the mantelpiece over it were a few old photos – including one of teenaged Arturo and Mama, with what looked like a puppet theatre. Did she really have to change anything? But he wanted it repainted white, and the walls *were* a bit tatty here and there...

She checked out the dark wood kitchen, small utility room and loo, then took her suitcase down to the terrace level. On one side, there was a bathroom – with a bidet she could use for those sandy beach feet – and a single bedroom with pretty blue tiles as a headboard. She opened the final door. Her bedroom! A wooden double bed, cupboards, a chest of drawers, a table near the window that maybe she'd use for her laptop... She grinned, pushed the maximum button on the stand fan, kicked off her Crocs and flopped down on the bed – which was positioned for the best view of the distant mountain, the area that would be her cactus garden... and the goat. He was looking in at her through the sliding doors, the cheeky bugger.

Maybe she should let her neighbours know. She was going to have to introduce herself soon anyway. She decided to knock on their front door later. Then she noticed something on the terrace... Good God, she'd left her laptop bag there. She needed to retrieve it before her hoofy friend stamped or peed on it.

She closed the bedroom door – damage limitation in case he dashed past her into the house – unlocked the back door and crept out. Yelping as she collided with his warm, soft coat, she rushed over to the bag, and in one movement flung the strap over her shoulder and the laptop onto her back. '*Not* for your lunch,' she said to him. They stared at each other. 'And now, I know you're quite handsome, but can't you just sod off?'

The goat twitched his ears and looked behind him, over the wall. She followed his gaze – to a man on the next terrace. Staring at her, wide-eyed.

'Oh! You made me jump!' she said.

He was no more responsive than the goat. Tall, with a mop of mad, wavy hair blending into a thick beard to give a bear-like face. A circus bear, perhaps, because he was wearing clown-like loose patchwork trousers with his dark jumper.

'Your goat is on my terrace,' she said in Spanish.

In a low voice he said the goat wasn't his, and waved a hand at a goat-sized gap in the fence the other side of his terrace, suggesting he was one of the herd there. Then he added something about 'Chica' being 'her own goat'.

Should a girl goat have horns? But then these Almerían sheep-goats were a bit peculiar.

'Then we need to repair the wall,' she said, hoping he'd offer; it matched the one at the front of his terrace, so was obviously his.

Instead of answering, he started calling 'Chica' and holding out a hand to her. The goat deftly scrambled over the wall to him, then leant her body against his as he sat down on a bench and put his arm round her, scratching her gently between the ears as he whispered to her.

Juliana found herself smiling. Chica, as long as he – *she* – was the other side of the wall, was really rather cute – and just for a moment, so was the grisly man.

'I'm Juliana. The niece of Arturo Fernández who owns this house,' she said, putting out her hand.

He stood up and looked at her hand. Of course, Spaniards would normally greet each other, even on first meeting, with the kiss-on-each-cheek thing – but she could hardly do that over a wall and a goat.

He nodded, maybe to indicate that he knew Arturo, or maybe even to acknowledge that he'd known she was coming, then took her hand awkwardly and mumbled, 'Hosemigarsia.'

José Migarsia. No, it would be *García* – a Spanish surname as common as Smith. Josemi García. A Joey Smith.

He let go of her hand and asked if she was English.

'Half English.' It seemed odd saying it that way round.

'Speaking half-Spanish,' he said, still in Spanish, with not a twitch of a smile. A bit of a cheek, given her efforts. Then he said he had to work and, having adjusted a plank in the fence to encourage Chica to jump through to the paddock to join her friends next door, disappeared indoors.

Not entirely happy with this exchange, Juliana went inside and started unpacking. She looked Spanish, didn't she? So why did both the Miserable Bag across the road and the bear man next door look so freaked at the sight of her? She picked up the printed email with the 'Conditions'. *Get on well with your neighbours*: how was she to qualify for that? Would just being on correct parking and monosyllabic non-sequitur speaking terms do?

One of many questions for Arturo when she saw him tomorrow, because… She looked round her bedroom with all her belongings, shoved the suitcase in the under-stairs cupboard out of sight, went up to the kitchen and made a black tea to drink on the squishy sofa while she gazed over at the fuzzy hills… She'd love this house to be hers.

THREE

DAY 2

Juliana sat on the terrace's wooden bench and hosed down her sandy legs and the pebbles she'd brought back from the early morning beach – a collection of white, blonde, streaky grey and the rare, silky-smooth russet. As she arranged her favourites on one of Arturo's chipped plates, the rest in a small tin bucket that she'd use for a bedroom doorstop, she thought about the lunchtime meeting with him.

She wanted to arrive having already made a start on the conditions: one of the beaches ticked off, the gas boiler man booked, and a scrapbook started about her ninety days in the Spanish house. She took out her phone and put the pictures for her diary – and new blog – into their own album. The windows with their shutters and bars; a sunset shot of the dry riverbed; the wild, sandy beach; a before-and-after of the wall – broken, with a lucky shot of Chica posing on it, and then piled-up again, with the help of a pair of Arturo's old gardening gloves. After her shower, she was going to take photos of her first visit to Mama's grave in the cemetery.

The scent of coffee came to her over the wall. Josemi had come out with a mug, and was steadfastly gazing over at the mountain. If he looked her way, he'd see a wind-blown woman with yesterday's plaits, yesterday's skirt and a near-identical navy T-shirt. Of course, she didn't really care what he saw – but he could at least say good morning.

She called out a *buenos días*, wanting to point out how she'd mended the wall.

He nodded and mumbled something, but laughed and shook his head when he looked over at the bricks. What was that supposed to mean? He said something else she couldn't catch, and went back inside. She waited in case he'd gone in to fetch something – some cement to finish the job properly, perhaps – but no, that was it. If Arturo asked about the neighbours, it might be better to concentrate on the couple the other side of the three-car parking area, who she recognised yesterday as the friendly Dutch lady and her Spanish husband who ran the bakery with the homemade cheese-and-spinach *empanadillas*.

She showered, pulled on a white tiered skirt and a pink T-shirt, and wondered if all full-time supporting artistes found themselves with an entire wardrobe of comfortable footwear and non-patterned, non-logo clothes.

In the little bakery, she learnt it would only take fifteen minutes to walk to the cemetery, and bought some orange *bizcocho* cake. 'I think we're neighbours... I saw you—'

'Oh, when you said yesterday you were looking after your uncle's house, I should have known – you're Arturo's niece.'

'Yes. Juliana.'

'Elise,' she said, pointing to herself. 'And have you met Josemi the other side?'

'I have. Although I think he'd rather I wasn't there.'

She laughed. 'Oh, he's not so bad. Both he and his mother can be a bit...'

'Grumpy?'

'Yes! Wonderful English word.' She looked pensive for a moment. 'Somebody told me there was some accident when he was a child... his sister died, I think.' She smiled again. 'But what I say is, there's always something good about a man who likes sweet things – and he *loves* that *bizcocho*!'

Juliana took a mouthful. '*Mm*... better not tell him I took the last piece, then.'

She took the unmade road with the *Cementerio* sign that she'd seen forking off from the main one out of the village. After a hot walk through the rolling countryside, she came over a hill and there it was below her: a white-walled square corral with an earth car park. She picked a bunch of rough-stemmed yellow flowers that looked like gorse and went down. There were no cars, and the ironwork gate looked seriously locked – but wasn't. She pushed it open and went in.

She and Toby had looked up Spanish burial traditions once, after a cemetery scene in an Almodóvar film. It turned out that the Spanish didn't put their dead in the ground, but in a *wall*. Remembering this, the odd spelling of *cementerio* – with its 'cement' content – began to make sense. In front of her were narrow walkways between burial walls a little taller than her. The end-of-coffin-size recesses in these walls had black or white marble fronts with inscriptions, religious symbols, plastic flowers and a glass-protected photo of the deceased – if occupied. Others were empty, with just a sad, scribbled number – because the *nichos* were rented for a certain number of years, and then, when there were no relatives left, or nobody wanted to pay, the remains were taken away to some common burial ground and the *nicho* rented by another family. She couldn't decide whether this was gruesome or sensible.

She made a start down the first aisle. Nearly every plaque had one of her Mama's surnames; it was going to take ages. The second aisle had a middle-aged man in front of a plaque with his head down, so she moved on. Dizzied after scanning all the plaques, she was about to sit down on the stone bench near the entrance, when she saw it. Just a few *nichos* along from where she'd come in.

Antoñita Fernández García… at the age of 46, rest in peace. And like nearly all the other plaques, it ended with *your family won't forget you.* Mama's parents hadn't remembered her for long, because they'd both died the following year. Although really, they'd lost her to England long before that, only seeing her once or twice a year. Arturo remembered her, of course. As for herself… She stared at the faded photograph of Mama – her big, downturned eyes, her delicate, pretty face – trying to feel sad, but mainly creeped out by the thought of the bones behind the angel-decorated black marble.

The flowers were sweating in her hand, already half dead; she could now see the point of the plastic ones. She shared them out between the two integral flower vases on the plaque, and went over to the tap by the gate for some water for them. Where was a discarded plastic water bottle when you wanted one? A Coke can. The cellophane wrapper to a fag packet. Anything. Damn. She cupped her hands under the tap, gathered a pathetic amount, went back to the vases and dribbled it in. Repeated. It was going to take a while, but it was doable – even if it made her look like Mr Bean. Which could have been exactly what Miserable Bag from across the road was thinking, glaring at her from further down the aisle. Juliana took a photo of her efforts, prompting a definite 'tut' from the woman, and left.

Climbing up the hill back towards the village, it occurred to her that the woman couldn't be as old as she looked, if she walked this far. She stopped to see if she was following her. Then looked back down at the cemetery and told herself, *Mama is down there* – and just briefly, heard Mama's voice saying 'Hooli!' as if pleased to see her.

———

'So, you found your way all right?' María José asked in Spanish, possibly for the second time. Juliana had been waiting in Uncle Arturo's beautiful *salón* overlooking the smart Almería promenade and sandy beach for some while now, without any real explanation from his kindly housekeeper.

'Yes, I kept to the easy road by the sea that Arturo told me about.' She put her hand in her bag again to check she'd remembered the printout of the conditions, and considered revisiting the immaculate marble bathroom. She thanked María José for the second glass of peach juice, and nervously looked over at the doorway. She felt like Dorothy waiting to see the Wizard of bloody Oz.

'Ah!' María José put a hand over her mouth, looking troubled. 'I forgot. We have e-algre.'

'Sorry?'

'E-algre, English.'

'*Earl Grey*.' Uncle Arturo. Like he'd arrived in a puff of smoke. He was smaller and even more dapper than she remembered, more circus master than phoney wizard. As he came closer, he looked older around the downturned eyes that were so like Mama's, his beaming smile pulling his face taut. 'Also I have here some cups and saucers, Royal Dol-ton, and Beatles, Bee Gees...' he said in English, coming towards her with open arms. 'Hooliana...'

The double kiss was followed by a hug that squeezed away some of her anxiety. 'How are you, Uncle?'

'Good, good. *Especialmente* now you are here. Come.' He linked arms with her. 'We can go to the market for lunch – and complete one... maybe two of the *condiciones*,' he said with a wink.

They took the lift down and came out between two busy cafés. He waved a hand over the palm-tree-lined promenade, a huge sculpture of a man reading in a deckchair, the gardens and port further along with their backdrop of mountain. 'What do you think?'

'I didn't know a city beach could be so gorgeous. I parked in the first car park and walked down to your building. By the way, I love the Panda!'

He smiled. 'Good. Is like your Fiat *Quinientos*, no?'

They took a taxi that careered through some scary roundabouts and then down a wide avenue of trees with heads clipped into pom-poms.

'The best shopping street – although I know clothes no' interes' you.'

'True!'

They got out at a grand entrance to what looked like a theatre, but had 'Central Market' in large letters over the door. Inside, under the ancient high ceilings, were rows of stalls with beautifully arranged and supersized fruit and vegetables, olives of every hue, gaping fish... Her uncle explained that they were going to choose what they wanted for lunch and then the market café outside would prepare it for them.

'So are you enjoying San Rafael?' Arturo asked, once they were sitting with coffees at a table under a tree. He'd decided to switch to Spanish, as if entering a more serious part of their meeting. 'It was a wonderful place to grow up.

Your mama and I were very lucky, despite the family not having much money and living in a small house.'

'I *love* it. Is the family home still there?'

'Barely. It's one of the ruined ones in the fenced-off area. By the time they get round to renovating it, there'll be nothing left.'

'Oh… But I'm glad to hear Mama was happy there. Dad said she couldn't wait to leave San Rafael, when she was eighteen.'

Arturo put down his coffee. 'He didn't say why?'

She shook her head, and wished she hadn't mentioned this; there was no place here for Dad's negatively skewed agenda about Mama.

'Well, I'm sure she wouldn't mind you knowing…' He then said something about Mama having had a thing (relationship?) with some important mining gentleman's son. There'd been a scandal, and the opportunity to work at the Tabernas Film Studios as an assistant in the costume department couldn't have come at a better time.

'Why couldn't he have told me that? I mean, it was before they met.'

Her uncle went very still for a moment. 'There are many things your father has said – or *not* said – that I cannot explain.' She waited for him to continue, but he seemed to want to move on. 'Now, Hooliana, do you have any questions about the conditions?' he asked with the encouraging smile of a teacher.

'Well, yes, I might.' She pulled the piece of paper out of her bag and unfolded it onto the table. 'Let's see… Paint the house. I helped a friend paint her parents' cottage in the Lake District once – that's no problem.'

'I remember. You had come back from there when I last came over.'

She scanned through the rest of the paragraph. 'Cactus garden… I can't wait! The crockery: do I *have to* replace it? We seem to both love blue and orange.'

He laughed. 'But you wait until you see the crockery and ceramics in Níjar. There are also shops in nearby Campohermoso, for getting new fans or anything else…' He tapped the end of the paragraph. 'Look – it says *as needed*, which means, as you like.'

Did it? How many of the other *condiciones* could be fulfilled as she liked? She gazed at the next point about getting on well with neighbours, and tried to think of a way of asking him – in Spanish – how that was to be defined. But his finger had slid down to number 5, *Annie Get Your Gun*. Perhaps inspired by the title, he was suddenly back in English. 'I think you don' like, but remember, says only "take part", so you can be no' actress but…' He rolled his hand, expecting her to finish the sentence.

'A person giving out programmes?' He either wasn't amused, or didn't understand. 'Costumes?' The hand continued to roll. 'There's an orchestra?'

'*Eso.*' That. He smiled and nodded. She wasn't going to sing for her supper, but she'd be piping for her present. They had only covered two conditions, and it already felt like a game of charades rather than the instructions for acquiring a property. Then he said something about how he would take her to the music shop later, so that would be two conditions already met. Two? Presumably the other condition she was going to meet – literally – was the Raf tomato. *Jesus*.

'I've already made a start on the conditions,' she said, as she'd planned. 'I've discovered the beach, booked Juan Luis to come and look at the boiler next Tuesday, made my first visit to the cemetery, and I'm planning to visit the Tabernas Film Studios on Monday afternoon. Oh, and I'm keeping a diary, with photos.' She took out her phone and flicked through the album of the best ones.

He glanced at them – disappointingly briefly – then looked at her steadily and went back into Spanish. 'You've been to the cemetery.'

'Of course.'

'And found your mama.'

'Yes.' He seemed to be waiting to hear more. 'It was… very nice. I'm going to buy some artificial flowers for next time.'

He sighed, for some reason. 'And your neighbours? How is it going with them?'

'Well, Elise is lovely and seems to like speaking English for a change. Josemi is busy, but we've spoken a few times.' Twice, to be exact, and not very successfully. They needed to move on down the list.

'This is always a busy time for him, getting everything ready for the summer.'

'Really? He seems to be home most of the time.' His van was nearly always in the car parking bay. 'Maybe he's working on his *own* house.'

Arturo looked puzzled.

'Rather than fixing other people's,' she added.

'Juliana… he's working *in* his house, not on it. He's an *artist*.'

'Oh. His van looks like… Oh.' Why hadn't Josemi said anything, instead of keeping that – and everything else about himself, other than his love of Chica – a huge bloody secret?

Why wasn't *Arturo* saying anything? She thought she'd done well, for a day and a half. He was looking round for the waitress, and as if responding to a signal, she appeared with Juliana's *tortilla*, a mixture of squiggly seafood for Arturo, and a bowl of tomato-dominated salad. Sliced, except for the centre-piece tomato, that appeared to have been buffed to a shine. He picked up the 'Raf' with two elegant fingers, twisting the deeply crinkled dark green-and-red fruit in his hand. Apparently, it was unique to Almería, something to do with tolerating salty water. He added that it ripened from the inside out, whatever that meant – and a seriousness in his eyes suggested it looked like she was supposed to understand what that meant on more than one level.

Couldn't they just eat now? The heat, the hunger and the sheer weirdness of it all was making her light-headed. She looked at the comical *special and divine Raf* he was still going on about. It was a tomato, for heaven's sake – and not even a looker.

'If I don't eat it, I don't get the house? Really?' An unladylike guffaw came from her, followed by the shaking of silent laughter.

He waited for her to stop, unamused.

She took it from him and bit into the firm skin. Inside, the juicy sweet-and-salt flesh was a flavour explosion; this was a tomato that came ready seasoned. 'God. It's… unbel*iev*able.'

He nodded, but still looked unhappy with her. About a *tomato*. What would he do if she put the rest of it on the ground and squished it with her foot? She put a hand over her mouth, because she was doing what she used to do in her first (and only) year at drama college: no matter the seriousness of the scene, no matter how cross the director, she could be taken over by manic hilarity. When he started to look weary with her, she took a deep breath and stopped.

'Hooliana. You are not going to complete the conditions if you merely see them as a list to tick off,' he said in slow Spanish. 'Josemi is a person, not just a man with a van; the cemetery is where your mother lies, not a film set; and I have written clearly that you have to spend the *night* at the Tabernas Studios attraction, not just book an afternoon, to understand its significance. Maybe even more. You are not an "extra" here in Spain. It's not enough to just turn up; you have to start involving yourself – ripen from the inside out like the Raf. Only then will your time here be truly special – and the house become yours.'

FOUR

DAY 4

It was only half ten and already too hot outside for any more scraping and sweeping up of loose paint. She went down to the terrace and flopped onto the sunbed with a Diet Coke. The re-crumbled wall taunted her – she was going to have to do something about it – but Josemi seemed to be out again today, so it was unlikely Chica would come over and make her jump out of her skin.

She closed her eyes, exhausted; she hadn't slept well the two last nights, thinking about what Arturo said. Today she was due to tick another condition off the list: a concert at the Cactus Garden place. Not that she was supposed to be seeing any of them as just 'things to be ticked off'; it seemed they were each supposed to have some kind of added value or meaning. What the heck was the meaning of a jazz concert? She didn't like jazz, so the chance of some kind of epiphany was somewhat remote. Cacti, however, were another matter; hopefully she could slink off early to concentrate on them.

She went in to shower, but stopped in the second bedroom, which she was using as a study, to see if there were any responses to her new blog. Hopefully some of her *Views from a Human Prop* followers had dreams of a place in the sun and had already leapt over to last night's *90 Days in an Andalusian Village; Could I Live Here?*

She looked at the title uneasily. Of course she couldn't live here; where would she work? She was fully unqualified to do anything useful – especially in a country with high unemployment. One of her stepsisters had suggested she put herself forward for supporting artiste work at Tabernas Studios, but even before she could answer, Dad had tersely explained that it was mostly just an amusement park these days.

There were a dozen or so 'Likes' and a string of questions – mainly about how far Almería was from Malaga or which 'costa' it was on. For Pete's sake, she'd explained where it was, and it wasn't on one of their 'costas' – which was the whole point. At the same time, however, she felt a bit guilty letting on about Almería, and particularly little San Rafael; maybe her next post should be about the ugly plastic greenhouses on the way from the airport, before planefuls of Brits invaded the area.

She scrolled down further… and her heart thudded with maddening predictability: *Toby* had commented. '*Sounds wonderful. When can I visit?!!*' This was followed by the usual flurry of fans wanting to engage with Toby Campbell-West, whose profile picture, lest they should forget the full-on effect of his sculpted and blonde gorgeousness, showed him in his latest incarnation as the title role in *King Arthur*.

She knew he wasn't really going to visit, any more than she was going to live here; actors and bloggers are both prone to exaggeration. But it did give her an excuse to send him a little message.

She picked up her phone and noticed that she'd last

WhatsApped Toby three days short of two months ago, and the message before that was exactly a month before that. It was odd that *three months* should be her minimum goal for both the gaps between contacting Toby and the length of her relationships – as if she was allowing herself to contact him in between each failed romance. The truth was, she hadn't been making progress with either goal – unless she gave herself credit for the absence of any relationship whatsoever for well over a year.

Last seen today at 11:05, his profile said. Five minutes ago. Saturday: getting ready to go to the gym, or maybe still in bed with the girlfriend... She wiped out that last image and tapped out a cheery *hola!* They'd always shared a love of Spain – that holiday in Mojácar, the long weekend in Seville, the pop-flamenco Ketama album, the Almodóvar films; he'd think it odd she *hadn't* shared this with him.

Toby is typing.

'Jules!' popped up on the screen and sent her into an uncontrollable grin. *'90 days doing up that house? Looks more like 7 days, followed by 83 enjoying a life of beach, tapas and flamenco!'*

'Rather more than that, I've got quite a list of things my uncle wants doing. But I'm not complaining!'

'A LIST? Why doesn't he just get a builder in?'

'He's a fussy so-and-so. And he's kind, thought it would be nice for me.'

'Hm. I think he's seeing if you should inherit it.'

What?

'Gay fashion guy isn't he? No kids.'

Toby always was a bit of a stereotyper. *'Arturo is a widower with a much-loved son.'*

'Then why isn't the son sorting out the house? I tell you, Jules, you're IN there.'

Good God, how the hell had he guessed? She picked up

Arturo's lawyer's business card; *this* was who she should be talking to about this, if anybody; not Toby. '*Don't be ridiculous! Anyway, I've got to go now.*'

'*To get on with the list? We need the list on the next blog post! Come on, we all want to SEE!*'

'*No! That's NOT what the blog is about.*'

'*Ah, so there's the blog, and there's what's REALLY going on,*' he wrote, with a winking emoji.

She started punch-tapping out that *nothing* was going on, but it just made it look even more like something was.

'*So what else is on the list? Acquainting yourself with the lure of the area, finding employment, a Spanish husband?*'

'*No! Just stuff for the house. And things he must think would be good for me.*'

'*Wouldn't a Spanish husband be good for you?*' came back at her, with a tongue-out emoji. '*Okay, maybe just a Spanish amorío... a small price to pay... And then he'll change the will.*'

Her smile dropped. '*That won't be necessary. He already has. In fact, if I complete the list, the house will be mine in 90 days' time.*'

She stared in horror at what she'd sent. It was Toby's fault, the patronising suggestion of what he thought would be *good for her*, that did it; she had to shut him up. She'd promised Arturo she wouldn't tell anybody, but Day 4, and she already had. *God.* She looked at the lawyer's card again, then outside at the terrace – which she should be filling with cacti today. She interrupted Toby's string of congratulatory emojis. '*I'm not supposed to tell anybody, okay? It's a secret. Promise you won't mention this again.*'

A surprised emoji, then the one with the zipped mouth.

'*I mean it. Promise me.*'

'*I promise. Don't worry.*'

Having rushed to get away from Toby on the laptop, she reached Níjar half an hour early. It was the county town, as you'd say in England, but just a pretty, hill-hugging white village slightly larger than the others dotted around the countryside. Accustomed to a network of choked and confusing roads back in West London, getting around in this area was like driving a toy car over the treasure-hunt-style local map. Even going to Almería city, she could ignore the dual carriageway and just trundle along the old coastal road. She took the turning to *centro urbano* for a quick look, and was soon driving along the main street.

'Wow!' The car slowed down so much, as her eyes darted around in amazement, that the van behind her beeped. She put a hand up to apologise, and pulled in – wondering when she'd last been able to park on a high street. When Arturo had told her about this place, she'd expected it to have no more than the mild appeal of craftwork in other Spanish villages; she was no shopper. She got out of the car and walked along. Among the banks, post office, groceries, cafés – and unexpected small paddocks of ponies or deliciously scented orange trees – there were numerous shops selling glazed, richly coloured ceramics and thick, shaggy rugs called '*jarapas*'. She only spent a few minutes in two shops, but came out with a bedside rug, a bath mat, four Moorish egg cups with matching saucers, a lizard-design mug and the certainty that she needed to come back and spend a day among all these beautiful but inexpensive essentials.

Back in the car, the satnav took her over the bridge spanning a dry riverbed and on to the Cactus Garden at the edge of the village. She took one of the last spaces in the car park, got out and wandered around. The garden centre part – selling pots, cacti and succulents at prices that looked like they were missing a zero – was small compared to the

terraced cactus garden. She followed the meandering path –
and the aroma of spices and cooked tomato – to where it
turned, on arriving at a sharp drop into a valley, and took
you to an amphitheatre. While a small band of musicians
tuned up, people paid for their tickets, milled around greeting
each other and then sat down with laden paper plates and
glasses of beer from the tables on one side.

She often went to concerts on her own in England, but
being surrounded by so much loud and friendly chatter made
her search for a known face among the crowd. If Arturo was
such a fan of these concerts, why wasn't he here? She should
have asked Elise; perhaps she could have switched shifts with
her husband. She was glad Toby couldn't see her now, the
silent singleton.

It was her turn in the queue for food. There was the usual
surprised look when the clumsy non-native Spanish left her
mouth. She'd asked about the contents of something resembling a spring roll, and wasn't doing too well with the reply,
when a girl about her age with freckles and a bob of light
brown hair tapped her arm.

'You're English?' the girl asked.

'Yes.'

'It's got *pisto* inside – a sort of Andalusian ratatouille. If
you're looking for something else veggie, they also do mush-
room *croquetas*…' she said with a slight northern accent,
pointing at a plate.

'Great, thanks.'

Juliana sat down with her lunch and a Coke on the end
of a stone bench and smiled at the people a little way along
from her – a smartly dressed young man with glasses and an
older woman, presumably his mother.

Somebody on a microphone was introducing the musicians. It looked like they'd herded up whoever they could

find: an elderly American man on piano, a diffident Spanish teenager with a curtain of black hair over his face on guitar, a tattooed biker-type percussionist, a bulging fifty-something who looked like she'd be singing and a bass player who'd only just turned up. But never mind, the food was tasty, she'd soon be buying cacti, and it was better than sitting at home mulling over the Toby messages.

'Ah! Hello again.' The English girl sat down next to her, then giggled and slapped the young man's hand when he tried to steal her ham. 'Good?' she asked, pointing at Juliana's plate.

Juliana nodded and smiled. 'You're a regular here?'

'Yes − I usually finish work at half twelve, so it's perfect. You on holiday?'

'Sort of. I'm house-sitting my uncle's place in San Rafael for a few months. Ooh, looks like they're starting.'

There were some instrumentals to begin with. It was jazz-flamenco. Flamenco-jazz. A bit of a mix, like the band, but… all the more beautiful for it. Then the singer stood up, and with a voice that was simply expressive but also had the florid flights of flamenco, she sang about a past love being unforgettable, someone being an *Obsesión*, and a woman waiting for the day some guy might love her − but from the jaunty rhythm it went into, you could tell she knew she was kidding herself. She thought of Toby. Songs were always about Toby. Then came the song from the Penelope Cruz film *Volver*, all about wanting to go back to someone − but unwisely, from what she could understand. The audience needed little encouragement to join in with the chorus. *Volver*: perhaps it could also mean going back to a place, or thinking again about someone who's gone… Next to her, the Yorkshire girl sang along with her boyfriend and smiled at her.

A guest singer was beckoned on, and given a microphone. No, not a singer; the tall, ponytailed man was holding a harmonica. She didn't catch his name. The way he quietly nodded to appreciate the encouraging applause reminded her of Josemi. In fact, he was like a clean-shaven Josemi, hair tied back, in normal jeans and a black T-shirt... She put a hand to her mouth. The large, fiery eyes; the cheekbones; the prominent nose...

The English girl noticed her surprise and leant over to whisper. 'Bit of a hunk, isn't he?'

'I dunno... He's my neighbour!'

'You're joking!'

There was an eerie piano introduction to something she half recognised, then Josemi started to play. A simple three-note tune, but developing, and achingly sad... it was 'The Summer Knows', theme to an old film she couldn't remember. His eyes were almost closed, he was totally inside the music, swaying, fingers twitching sensitively.

There was loud applause, a couple of people shouting out his name. He thanked the audience and smiled. *Smiled.* Had she seen him smile before? Perhaps that was why Arturo wanted her to come here, to see another side to her gruff neighbour. To make her wonder at how he could play like that.

'Amazing, isn't he,' her new friend said through the applause.

'I'd no idea...'

'Didn't he tell you he was playing?'

'No! I've only twice had a few words with him, and mainly just about the broken wall between us.'

'Ha! I suggest you get it fixed – or taken down. On the other hand...'

A guest female singer was introduced to join in with the final song, *'Algo Contigo'*. 'Something with You'. Another number about unrequited love – with a solo in the middle for Josemi – but a song for women strong enough to survive it.

It was the end, and much as the audience had loved it, they all seemed to have somewhere to go and were leaving quickly.

'What were you going to say about my wall?' Juliana asked.

'I was going to say, there'll probably be a wall there anyway; he's twice been bitten by English girlfriends who've buggered off back to Blighty, poor guy! One of them was my fault – a lass who used to come to the Friday expat club in San José, who I persuaded to come to one of these concerts.' She shook her head. 'Actually, why don't you come to the club? I'm Kim, by the way.'

'Juliana.' *He's had English girlfriends.* 'And you work in Níjar?'

'I've got an English school here. But I live in San José – need the sea.' She pointed to her boyfriend and the lady. 'Carlito and my mum.'

'Ah, hello!' She exchanged nods with them.

Kim delved in her bag and brought out a card. 'Look, give me call if you'd like to come to the expat bar. I've got to dash – got a meeting with the director of the drama society's play. *Annie Get Your Gun*, would you believe, and the songs are in English so they want me to translate—'

'I'm doing that! They want my flute in the orchestra!'

'Brilliant! I'll see you at the rehearsal on Thursday then. Now, I suggest you go and say hello to your neighbour, or he'll think it's odd if he spots you. And you need to get on with him, because he usually gets roped into playing clarinet.'

'No, really? Oh God!' They laughed and said their goodbyes.

She finished her drink, wishing she didn't have to do this.

Would Josemi really care if she just went off to buy cacti? Last time she looked, he was chatting with the band members and two girls who'd been in the front row. She took her plate to the rubbish bin. Then she helped one of the organisers pick up a barrier that had been knocked over by some of the audience when they were leaving.

'Hooliana… always trying to put up walls.' His low, Spanish voice.

She turned. He threw some paper cups in the bin, and smiled at her. Not quite like the smile he'd given the audience – she was English, after all – but a smile nonetheless.

'Your playing was…' She couldn't think of the word. It would have been hard even in English.

He gave a nod. 'Thank you.' He laughed. 'I think?'

She grinned. 'Yes! I loved it… I loved the concert a lot.' This wasn't coming out right. 'I'll have to come every time.' Oh dear.

'Why not? Except soon you will sometimes have orchestra rehearsals on Saturdays,' he said, then put a hand to his face and scratched his chin.

'Yes…' How did he know that? 'Have you heard me on my flute then? I thought I was playing when you were out,' she said, although the Spanish tenses might not have been right.

'Don't worry, it sounds good,' he said, but looked over to where his fellow musicians were chatting and packing up. Conversation over.

'I'm going to buy cacti. Would you like a little one? Something not too prickly?'

FIVE

DAY 7

'Hello, Mama. Look what I've brought you.' Juliana pulled the plastic flowers out of her cloth bag. 'Oh hang on, let's get rid of these…' She took the shrivelled wildflowers to the cemetery's bin and came back again. 'There you go. Purple… lavatera? Hibiscus? I dunno, but they're your colour.' She had a memory of laying her head against Mama's soft purple jumper, and there'd been a summer dress, maybe from Laura Ashley, with a grape design… *Was* purple her favourite colour? Dad probably wouldn't even remember. 'And I've got *lots* of others too – I'll change them each week, mix them up, give you a surprise…'

She became aware of two elderly men further along in front of a huge plaque for multiple family members. One was tapping a photo and saying something to the occupant; the other nodded at her, as if giving permission to continue with her transcendental tittle-tattle.

'Say hello to Yayo and Yaya from me.' All she could recall about her grandparents were pats of affection and – even though it was a summer visit – plates of worrying stew.

'I love your village. Quiet and cactusy, friendly shops, and what a beach – can't wait until the water's warm enough to go swimming. Ah, and I'll be going to Tabernas Studios in a few weeks' time; I'll let you know how it goes.'

One of the old boys was fanning himself with his hat and saying *que humedad*.

Humidity? What? Juliana looked at the sky. Okay, for the first time in a week there were a few clouds, but the señor had *no* idea; he should try a few days in London.

She turned back to Mama's plaque. 'Dad said you couldn't stand the weather in England anymore, bad for your asthma. But… I could have visited *you*. I don't know why Dad never brought me over. He kept saying he would, but two years later… Well, then you were here, in this wall. Anyway, I'm here now. Oh…' She looked at her watch. 'Gotta go, gas boiler man's coming.'

———

Fanning his sweating bald head with Arturo's laminated gas installation certificate, Juan Luis took her to the brick cubbyhole at the side of the terrace and pointed to two large orange bottles of gas. She'd not really understood much of his inspection of the boiler – other than that he would have to take it away to work on it and return with either it or a replacement – but it looked like he wasn't going to leave until she'd successfully demonstrated she could understand how to turn these bottles on and off and change them.

'You can take an empty bottle and exchange it for a filled one at the Repsol garage, but they're very heavy,' he said in his very Andalusian Spanish, aided by hand movements. 'Better to watch out on Thursdays for the lorry that comes through the v... finger to his eye...

'Ah, okay.' S... they a bit... dange... making explosion har... her Spanish.

He laughed and sho... follow the warnings on the... paper in her hand. 'They are... we have here. I've been working... have been no house fires in the a... ...ne where they say a drunk woman w... with a cigarette...' He didn't illustrate that, ...ed sad for a moment, but then looked up again ... a smile. 'Don't worry.'

He gave back the certificate, asked her to sign the inspection sheet and then continued to fan himself with it. '*Que humedad!*' he said, just like the old guy in the cemetery.

While he went on to say something about rain, she looked up and saw that the clouds had thickened. 'Feels okay to me. Still beautifully warm, and clouds are nice for a change. Are you sure you wouldn't like a drink of something? I've got—'

'No, no, thank you.' He looked up and down the two-storey back wall of the house. 'My brother did a good job of this.'

'He painted it?'

'Yes. I see now that Arturo was leaving the front for you to do!' He pointed to her scraper and painting stuff.

'Yes!'

He looked over at Josemi's identical back wall. 'And Arturo asked him to do your neighbour's too – when he was out, as a surprise!'

...y the neighbour is an artist and
...turo a painting. A painting for a paint-
...paintbrush movements then drew a square in
...aybe you'll find the painting in the house.'

'Oh! I'll have a look.'

'Is Friday good for me to pick up the boiler?'

She said it was, thanked him, let him out of the big
terrace gate, and dashed inside and upstairs to the living
room. It had to be one of those moody seascapes... but no,
they were by Alberto something. It wouldn't be the ancient
still life paintings of edible stuff in the kitchen. The flamenco
dancer on the landing? No. She went downstairs to the
bedrooms. Surely not... It was too small, too... *patient*. She
went through to her bedroom and stood in front of it. A
beach – clearly the San Rafael one, despite the impressionist
blurring. She'd liked the translucent blue waves of course, but
otherwise not given it much attention. For the first time, she
noticed the people. Just a few, in winter clothes. Hugging
themselves, or defiant and laughing, against the breeze.
Thinking of warmer days to come or, perhaps in the
stooping old lady's case, the past. How he cared for his
people, these daubs of paint that somehow, just with a lean
here or a stance there, were so... human. She was so
absorbed in it, she nearly forgot to look at the signature. Just
his first name, surprisingly small: Josemi.

Was it a picture Arturo had admired, or had he chosen it?
What made Arturo decide to have the back of his neighbour's house painted? How well did they know each other?
Better, it would seem, than her uncle had been letting on.
Then there were the conditions asking her to get on with
neighbours, be in the show with him, go to a concert where
he regularly guested... Maybe Toby was right, he wanted his

through the village; the man will change it for you.' He put a finger to his eye and pointed up towards the road.

'Ah, okay.' She looked at the orange monsters. 'Aren't they a bit… dangerous?' Taking his lead, she found herself making explosion hand movements and noises to accompany her Spanish.

He laughed and shook his head. 'No, no. Not if you follow the warnings on the sheet,' he said, pointing to the paper in her hand. 'They are very good, it's cheap – and all we have here. I've been working forty years with them. There have been no house fires in the area. Oh, except a tragic one where they say a drunk woman was sleeping in bed with a cigarette…' He didn't illustrate that, and looked sad for a moment, but then looked up again with a smile. 'Don't worry.'

He gave back the certificate, asked her to sign the inspection sheet and then continued to fan himself with it. '*Que humedad!*' he said, just like the old guy in the cemetery.

While he went on to say something about rain, she looked up and saw that the clouds had thickened. 'Feels okay to me. Still beautifully warm, and clouds are nice for a change. Are you sure you wouldn't like a drink of something? I've got—'

'No, no, thank you.' He looked up and down the two-storey back wall of the house. 'My brother did a good job of this.'

'He painted it?'

'Yes. I see now that Arturo was leaving the front for you to do!' He pointed to her scraper and painting stuff.

'Yes!'

He looked over at Josemi's identical back wall. 'And Arturo asked him to do your neighbour's too – when he was out, as a surprise!'

'Really? That's very kind.'

He nodded. 'Apparently the neighbour is an artist and insisted on giving Arturo a painting. A painting for a painting!' He made paintbrush movements then drew a square in the air. 'Maybe you'll find the painting in the house.'

'Oh! I'll have a look.'

'Is Friday good for me to pick up the boiler?'

She said it was, thanked him, let him out of the big terrace gate, and dashed inside and upstairs to the living room. It had to be one of those moody seascapes... but no, they were by Alberto something. It wouldn't be the ancient still life paintings of edible stuff in the kitchen. The flamenco dancer on the landing? No. She went downstairs to the bedrooms. Surely not... It was too small, too... *patient*. She went through to her bedroom and stood in front of it. A beach – clearly the San Rafael one, despite the impressionist blurring. She'd liked the translucent blue waves of course, but otherwise not given it much attention. For the first time, she noticed the people. Just a few, in winter clothes. Hugging themselves, or defiant and laughing, against the breeze. Thinking of warmer days to come or, perhaps in the stooping old lady's case, the past. How he cared for his people, these daubs of paint that somehow, just with a lean here or a stance there, were so... human. She was so absorbed in it, she nearly forgot to look at the signature. Just his first name, surprisingly small: Josemi.

Was it a picture Arturo had admired, or had he chosen it? What made Arturo decide to have the back of his neighbour's house painted? How well did they know each other? Better, it would seem, than her uncle had been letting on. Then there were the conditions asking her to get on with neighbours, be in the show with him, go to a concert where he regularly guested... Maybe Toby was right, he wanted his niece to have – well, *Algo Contigo*, as the song went, with his young friend Josemi. He couldn't put it in the conditions – she'd looked up about wills, that kind of thing wasn't allowed – but he could try and make her fall for him.

She wandered out onto the terrace in a daze. The painting – along with memories of Josemi's expressive harmonica playing and the handsome smile on his de-bearded face – had filled her with a heady confusion she didn't want to name. Toby's stupid suggestion of a fling that would be 'a small price to pay' for the house flitted through her mind. But what about her promise to herself that there would be no more relationships of hurtfully less than three months? Besides, imagine the awkwardness each time she came back to the house, if it became hers. There was also the small matter of his seeming to not want to be in her company for as much as five minutes at a time.

On the other hand, he had started to mend the wall, even without her mentioning it again. Maybe, while he was out and she could still easily get onto his terrace, she could copy Arturo and give him a little neighbourly present. He'd looked tempted for a second when she offered to buy him a potted cactus, and after her second trip to Níjar, she now had so many.

'So, what d'you fancy, Mr Grumpy?' She ran her eye over the huddle of plants in the corner, the line of them along the low terrace wall, and the two either side of the back door. The fig and the yucca in their huge terracotta pots that Elise's husband had helped her with were obviously out, and even the middle-sized bonsai-looking thing would be difficult to get over the wall. It was a question of choosing one of the coloured pots.

'So let's see, what's *you*…' The prickly big boy cactus, for sure – but the shape of it! She smirked, imagining his face.

He might have liked the coral-like folds of the red-tipped kalanchoes, but they too had started to look suggestive… It was going to have to be a friendly blobby-leaved crassula.

'Let me guess your favourite colour…' The pots were typical Níjar shades: faded orange or blue, with the odd mustard and moss green. She looked over at his terrace. All it had was an enormous yucca and an aloe in ancient terracotta pots that had probably been there from before he moved in, or was even born. 'What you *need* is orange, but okay, you can have blue.'

She picked it up and started towards the wall, but then remembered the path she'd been creating on the bank sloping down to the riverbed, through the rocks, *palmitos*, esparto grass, thyme and clumps of yellow-flowered *albaida*. To create a gentle zig-zag descent, she'd taken the path over to the area in front of Josemi's terrace, and Chica, taking a liking to it, had hoof-flattened a connecting path to the low wall of Josemi's terrace.

She made her way down, smiling to herself as she breathed in the hypnotic spicy scents, and then went up and over into Josemi's terrace. 'Oh!' What she'd thought was some kind of easel in the corner next to their wall was in fact a table with bowls of shells and pebbles. So maybe it *had* been him that she'd seen the other side of the beach the morning after the concert, picking things up and putting them in a rucksack. The blue-potted crassula looked like it had always been there on the corner of the table. Then she saw that some of the pebbles had been painted: sometimes just a few lines to make a face out of the markings, other times, all over. A pointed one had been made into a wild boar's face. Another had an intricate ant on it. There was a blue jellyfish. One of those crimson daisy things that seemed to be a natural ground cover plant in the area. Oh – a purple lavatera like the flowers that she'd given Mama – after leaving them on her outside table for a day... he'd copied them? She picked it up, the white stone smooth and fitting her palm as if made for it. The she heard the sliding door open behind her.

'Hello, I was just...' It wasn't Josemi. Staring at her with the same horrified face that Josemi had on their first meeting, was Miserable Bag from across the road. There were other similarities: the fiery eyes, the prominent nose, the thickness of the grey hair that fought to escape her pinned-up hairdo. Elise had spoken of Josemi and his mother both being a bit grumpy. *Frightening* was more the word at that moment, as the woman glared at her, waiting for an explanation.

'I was just bringing this pot round to thank him for building the wall. Or *starting* to...'

'You are English?' she asked in deep, throaty Spanish.

'Yes, but my mother was Spanish.'

The woman nodded with a touch of impatience. 'Your father is English, or part English?'

Jesus, what was it to her? Okay, her son had been bitten by two English girlfriends, but asking for Juliana's pedigree – before even exchanging names – was a bit much.

'He's a blonde Englishman, hundred per cent.' She considered adding a reminder of the dominant inheritance of brown hair and eyes, but the woman was now jabbing a finger towards her right hand and asking something.

'I'm sorry?'

'Are you *taking* that?'

She still had the lavatera pebble in her hand. 'No, no, just admiring it.' She put it back with the others.

Now she was saying something about telling Josemi, and how it would or wouldn't be a problem.

'Well, I've got to go. Nice to meet you. I'm Juliana,' she

said, forcing herself to smile but not making a move over to the woman for an unlikely physical greeting.

The woman said something about *dolor* – pain – which Juliana would later interpret as actually being her name, Dolores. She mumbled something else about Josemi and then, watching Juliana go over towards the low wall to the little path on the bank, added *cuida'o*.

Cuidado. Juliana wondered if that meant be careful with the steep path on the bank, or careful with her son.

SIX

DAY 9

Rain was different here, Juliana thought, as she walked along pavement tiles washed to a pearly blue. The drops were bigger and warmer, initially plopping like broken eggs on your head, and then forming into rain that wasn't English 'cats and dogs', but *a cántaros*, by the jug. In an Andalusian rainstorm, it was by the barrel.

She'd gone out when it was briefly returning to a plopping-eggs phase, unable to resist Elise and Eduardo's bakery for a third day.

'Juliana! You don't have an umbrella?' Elise asked, laughing and shaking her blonde head.

'No umbrella, no raincoat. Never mind.'

'It's true you are unlikely to need them again for many months... But I could give you a coat? I'm sure my daughter left one here years ago.'

'Well, that would be great. So you have a daughter? How old is she?'

'About to be thirty.'

'Really?' She was astonished, as she'd thought Elise herself was only about forty. 'Same age as me.'

'She lives in Granada, maybe she'll visit while you're here.'

There was a roar outside, the rain barrelling down again. 'Oh no. Lovely to see the river filling up though, isn't it?'

'River? There are no rivers down here! The Spanish call it a *rambla* – every town and village has at least one – a channel to take storm water away, sometimes only once a year. Some of them are also roads, but our *rambla* would be too dangerous for that. We'll see how fast and high it gets – and from our terraces, we have the best view.'

'Great!' Juliana bought some *empanadillas* and a selection of little cakes with fig, honey and almonds that had come from Eduardo's uncle's *tetería* in the city. 'I'm going to need some energy; I've got the first orchestra rehearsal today.'

'You should ask Josemi if you can go with him; it's silly you both driving over to Níjar.'

'Not sure he's coming; he's been away for a few days.' Five, to be exact.

'Oh. Probably gone up to Madrid. He stays with his uncle there, delivers commissions, probably catches up with old friends. But don't worry, he'll be back soon, won't want to let the orchestra down.'

Juliana tried to look like she couldn't care either way.

'Anyway, I'll drop the rain jacket round when I close at one o'clock, so you don't have to arrive soaked.'

'Thanks!'

Back at the house, Juliana put on a dry T-shirt and sat down to keep up with her diary and finish off a comic blog post about this morning's orange gas bottle lorry.

Then she worked on the little play she was writing for her friend Lucy's Year 6 class. As usual, she could hear Dad telling her how she'd never make any money writing bespoke plays for kids in low-achieving schools like Anderton Moss Primary. Toby, on the other hand, was ridiculously glib about her chances of becoming a famous children's playwright. Neither could see that it helped her make sense of the years she'd spent in Saturday drama school and summer drama camps – not to mention her disastrous first and only year at musical theatre college, after Dad had spent an arm and a leg on private coaching for her to get through the audition. She liked to pass on the enjoyment of drama that she once had, before all that pressure and expectation.

This Year 6 play was even more ambitious: *The Wizard of Moz*, with multiple friends for Dorothy. Or rather, the *three* Dorothies, because the enthusiastic middle Dorothy had Asperger's – or autism spectrum disorder – and could be overwhelmed at the last minute, her lines having to be shared out between the other two. Juliana groaned and chuckled at a WhatsApp from Lucy asking for 'The Plastic Man' – very unbendy, and thinks he has no sense of humour – to have a few more lines and to become identical twins. It was a shame she was going to miss the show, but at least the Parents' Association was getting a professional video recording done this year.

She went upstairs to watch the rain and the *rambla* from her living room window and eat her delicious lunch on one of her new fish-design Níjar plates, but somehow, as the time to leave for the rehearsal approached, her appetite started to disappear. She'd been through the flute parts she'd been emailed by the friendly-sounding music director, and she'd looked the place up on the map, but... 'There's *no* business like *show* business like...' she sang, knowing she was going to want to gag every time she had to play the show's main song in the next two months. It was that old nervy can't-do-it feeling she'd had every day at college – even though she was just in the orchestra.

———

She was going to be late; she'd forgotten Elise had mentioned something about road works in Níjar. As a supporting artiste, she was always on time; it was one of the few professional requirements – along with wearing appropriate clothes and not talking to 'the talent'. But she'd long ago noticed that she was uncontrollably late for anything involving large social groups – as if, the longer she put it off, the greater the chance something would happen to stop her going altogether.

Having found the road blocked, she'd had to go back over the Níjar *rambla* bridge and look for where she could cross it again further into town. This involved taking the poor Panda through a maze of quaint but scrape-risking narrow streets until she finally reached a church with a square, where she could park and WhatsApp Kim for directions.

The gleaming white Performing Arts Centre looked like a quadrangle of one-storey houses around a square that had been bought up to allow music, drama and dance 'houses' to interconnect. She made her way to where she could hear instruments tuning up, and opened the door.

Expecting something like her old secondary school orchestra, she wasn't prepared to find what easily looked like fifty people in the room. Musical director Enrique – whose emailed gratitude about her participation seemed hard to understand now she could see there were already three flautists sitting there – welcomed her and introduced her as their visiting English friend joining the band this summer. There were stares but mostly nods or smiles from the very mixed-age orchestra, but she noticed a clarinet player more interested in fiddling with his reed. Josemi.

Maybe it was just as well; it gave her a chance to shed Elise's daughter's pink raincoat with little rainbows before he saw her in it. She sat down between two teenage girl flautists. Rather than being practically next to him as she'd imagined, she was a row behind and further along; she was just going to get occasional views of his appealing profile when he leant over to the lusciously ponytailed oboist beside him.

Well… Good. She needed to concentrate on the music; some of Irving Berlin's loveliest songs were in the show, and anyway, she was here to earn her Spanish house. She smiled at her fellow flautists and put her flute together. The rehearsal began. Was this really the first one? Apart from the odd missed entry, and perfecting the timing of the sloweddown bits, the first number – 'There's No Business Like Show Business', as she'd guessed – was nearly there.

Then came 'My Defences are Down', the song the Wild West sharpshooter Frank sings after meeting feisty tomboy shooting competitor Annie. It was deliciously sentimental, and it was fun playing the flute part's teasing commentaries between what would be the singer's lines. She couldn't help wondering what Josemi thought of it; he didn't seem like a person who ever let his defences down. It was *her* with the dismantled barriers, having exchanged the cold and complex realities back home for this simple and colourful life, the dream of a Spanish house, and the softening warmth – and now sultriness – of this climate. They moved on to 'I've Got the Sun in the Morning', Annie being happy with her lot.

At the end of the rehearsal she saw Kim beckoning her over from the doorway. She packed her things away and went to her.

'Did you have fun?' Kim asked.

'I did! I can't believe how good they are.'

'Told you.' She lowered her voice and winked. 'And don't worry, your drama training secret is safe with me.'

Juliana bit her lip. What had possessed her to tell Kim so much about herself? She'd WhatsApped Kim about the expat group, even though she wasn't that keen on the idea, and before she knew what was happening, they were chatting for ages on Zoom, Kim recounting her dreary work and love life in Leeds after a lower second Geography degree, and Juliana feeling honour-bound to assure her she hadn't fared any better, with her extras work after a curtailed Musical Theatre degree. Kim, of course, with her English school and engagement to Níjar accountant Carlito, was full of the advantages of leaving miserable Blighty behind.

'But I need your help. The actors need me all at the same time, and one of the pianists – very sweet, by the way, but also very married – is tearing his hair out with the kids.'

'Kids?'

'You know, Annie's siblings and their singing of "Doing What Comes Naturally". Could you just hang on for a bit and go and help him? Explain the verses to the kids so they understand about the song? Pedro's English is practically non-existent.'

'Oh Gawd, I'm no good with kids.'

'What? You're writing a play for a school! Come on, I'll take you for a coffee and pancake after.'

'Ah. Now you're talking.' Juliana let Kim take her along the corridor and round to where practice rooms were filled with singers going through songs. There was a snippet of the duet 'They Say It's Wonderful'. 'Oh! That sounds good.'

'Husband and wife. They're always embarrassed to be given leading roles every year, but they're so brilliant, nobody can resent it. You're about to meet one of their kids.'

Kim took her into a room and left her with a smiling but rattled-looking Pedro at the piano and five children of between about ten and fifteen larking about riding chairs or looking at phones. Pedro handed her a piece of paper with the words. 'Please tell us what this is about!'

'Well…' She glared at the children and waited for them to be quiet, like she'd seen Lucy do in her class. There was no effect, so she gave them an English *hey, shush will ya?* which was so weird for them that they were stunned into silence. 'I'm going to tell you about this,' she continued in Spanish, flapping the paper about. She went through each verse, in which Annie was describing how various relatives were as happy as could be without any 'learning' – having no need of it for stealing chickens, singing out of key while milking cows and avoiding tax. All they had to do was repeat the 'Doing what comes naturally' each time Annie sang it at the end of a verse.

'Ah, thanks,' Pedro said. 'Any chance of you singing Annie for them?'

'Er… okay, that would probably help.' It was a very silly song, but she could hardly refuse. She sang the verses, miming the meaning of the words where she could – getting an increasing amount of laughter and enthusiastic chorus line from them as the song went on.

When they got to the end, there was applause all round. Two people in the doorway joined in: Kim and – Juliana couldn't believe it – *Josemi*, with the ludicrous rainbow-covered pink mac over his arm. She must have left it behind in the orchestra room.

Pedro thanked Juliana, standing up and giving her the two-cheek kiss.

Kim patted her arm. 'Look, I'm sorry, I'll have to take

you to the pancake café another time; Mum's just called me, not feeling well. It'll be nothing, but…'

'Oh, you get off, we can go another—'

'I'll take her,' Josemi said.

Juliana's heart thudded.

'Would you? Brilliant!' Kim said for Juliana.

There was the usual round of Spanish goodbyes, even from the children, and then she was walking under an umbrella with Josemi, trying hard not to bump into him.

They stopped at Café Nido where she'd been for coffee during her big ceramic and rug shop. 'Oh, I've *been* here, I love it!' she said in Spanish.

'So do I. We'll only have half an hour, but it's just enough.'

They ordered coffees and crepes with chocolate and bananas. 'I love the village cafés here,' Juliana said. 'In England they close halfway through the afternoon – exactly when you want cake – whereas here, that's when they open.' She sipped her cappuccino. 'Mm… and the coffee's better. Thanks for this.'

He nodded and smiled. 'You deserve it after this afternoon. But I don't understand, given your profession, why aren't you *acting* in the play?'

Who told him her profession? She tried to explain but, not knowing the Spanish for 'supporting artiste', her roundabout description made her sound like it was about being a person who not only had no voice but little brain either.

He shook his head and chuckled. 'But you have had acting training.'

'I told Kim not to tell anyone!'

'She didn't tell me. It's obvious.'

'I had one year at musical theatre college. Basically, I was too shy and not really good enough.' She couldn't remember ever putting it that succinctly, even to herself.

He was nodding. 'I understand this. Last year they asked me to play Jesus in *Jesus Christ Superstar*. I thought of standing there, you know...' He put his arms out, Messiah-style. 'I tell you, the shyness would have killed me long before the crucifix! I like to perform, but only with an instrument – a harmonica or a paintbrush!'

Your body is your instrument, they used to say in drama classes. It was quite something that this chap who'd been given such an appealing instrument wasn't in a rush to show it off.

'I know. I always used to think, where do I *look*?' She made rolling around movements with her eyes to demonstrate.

He laughed. 'Exactly that!'

The pancakes arrived, beautifully garnished with fruit. 'Wow.'

'I think if you spend most of your time working alone, you can't cope with these things,' he said. 'I take a lot of persuading even to go to a party.'

'Me too!'

'It is the same for you with your writing, I suppose.'

Her writing? How did he know about that? 'My blog?' She must have been looking confused.

'Arturo told me. He was laughing to himself on the terrace once, and explained that his niece had written something funny about the arrogance of actors at lunchtimes on a shoot.' He shrugged. 'I don't know why I remember that. He hadn't yet said you were coming to San Rafael.'

'But... he did tell you I was coming?'

He started fiddling with the flowers in the blue ceramic vase between them. 'Of course,' he said, quietly.

It was no good, she couldn't resist asking. 'Then surely he would have mentioned that his sister married an Englishman, that I was coming over from England, and... you shouldn't have been so surprised, when you first met me, to find out I was English?' She was going to add that his mother had reacted in the same way, but he already looked quite perturbed by her question. 'I mean, I know I don't *look* English, but...'

The café owner was going around politely reminding people they were closing soon. Why did she have to go and spoil their time there with that stupid question?

He wiped his mouth with the serviette, paid the bill and refused to let Juliana contribute. Then he looked at her and gave a weary half-laugh. 'I think Kim has been telling *you* things about *me*. Please, I don't hate the English, okay? The English, or the half-English.'

'Well, that's good to hear.'

Then he quietly said something she couldn't quite grasp about her heritage – or maybe inheritance – being something for her to understand or deal with. What was that supposed to mean?

'Hooliana, we've had a good chat and fabulous pancakes. Now we must go.'

SEVEN

DAY 10

Juliana flicked through her phone between mouthfuls of Spanish Special K, then came back to the translations of 'heritage' and 'inheritance'. Even if she could have decided between the two words, she didn't know whether Josemi had told her to cope, manage or understand it. If only she'd asked what he meant at the time – and why it seemed to be important to *him*. Maybe she could talk to Arturo about it when she saw him next week.

Flick, flick... She was startled to find a somehow missed WhatsApp from Toby. *'Have fun at the rehearsal! I'll never forget you as Sitting Bull in Stageclub's* Annie Get Your Gun*! What were we, 13?'*

That sounded about right. By that stage, most of the boys had given up, and she'd played a number of male roles. She remembered an unflattering pair of tasselled trousers, an itchy headdress and lots of lines in which she had to be kind to the blonde and bitchy girl playing Annie to Toby's Frank.

Then, in typical Toby style, he'd jumped to something

quite different. '*I'm thinking of buying a Spanish place to do up! Three more episodes, a couple of weeks filming a small role in a drama, and then I'll have time before the next series to have myself an adventure! I was thinking of the Alpujarras, but that's sort of been done by the* Driving Over Lemons *bloke. Maybe somewhere near Vejer de la Frontera in the Gulf of Cádiz. I'll be picking your brains!*'

'*Sounds great!*' she typed, then deleted. Did it? She couldn't help feeling miffed that in this too he was no doubt going to do better than her. She tapped a few surprised and happy emojis and closed the phone. It was time to get on with things.

She was an arm-aching third of the way through the living room ceiling when the doorbell chimed so loudly, with her right by it, that she had to grip onto the ladder to stop herself falling off. She got down and opened the door.

'Ah, *buenos días!*' She'd forgotten Juan Luis was coming to pick up the boiler today.

He said good morning, then pointed at her paint-splattered hair and made hair-washing hands with his scant grey wisps. 'Oh dear, you'll be needing a shower later, sorry! Maybe one of your neighbours—' he said in Spanish.

'No, no; a cold one after all this will be fine,' she said, wiping her forehead. 'You'd think the rain would make it cooler…'

'Ah, but better now than in a month. You carry on,' he said, tapping the ladder, 'and I'll get the boiler.' He went downstairs, and she got back on the ladder and started painting another section.

When he came back with the surprisingly light-looking contraption, the doorbell rang again.

'Don't worry,' he said, and opened the door. She could hear him talking to someone with an unmistakable low, fast voice and then the two of them chuckling.

Josemi came in and looked up at her. 'Hooliana. Don't go on the bank today to play with your little mountain garden. Or to get closer to watch the water in the *rambla*. It's dangerous. D'you understand?'

She stopped her paintbrush mid-air. She'd have been touched by his concern, if he hadn't been coming across like a *guardia civil*.

'He's right,' Juan Luis said, then turned to Josemi. 'Although it looks like she'll be busy today.' Then he tapped the machine under his arm. 'Maybe she can use your shower.'

'No, no,' she said.

Josemi shrugged his shoulders. 'She only has to ask,' he said, as if he knew she wouldn't.

The two men exchanged what sounded like a few comments about the weather, said their goodbyes to her and then were gone.

It occurred to her that Josemi still hadn't mentioned the crassula pot she had put on his terrace table. Maybe he thought his mother had given it to him, or else he just hadn't noticed it. Maybe, if he kept making patronising comments, she'd take it back.

By lunchtime – Spanish lunchtime that was, at about three – she'd finished the ceiling, washed her hands and face and sat down to salad and supermarket *tortilla*. The rain was finally easing off, and she watched Josemi down on his terrace giving Chica something to eat and a scratch between her ears before disappearing back inside to answer his phone.

She opened hers. Toby was asking what she knew about the cultural merits of Cádiz. What did he think she was, The Lonely Planet Actors' Guide to Andalucía?

Back outside, Josemi was closing the fence to keep Chica

in her paddock, probably giving her the same warning as he'd given her.

She was going to pack it in for the day but, remembering she was seeing Arturo on Tuesday, she thought it would be nice to be able to tell him she'd finished the living room. It was doable; there was no gloss work, the doors and window frames being natural wood, the skirting boards just a row of terracotta tiles that needed re-fixing here and there. She could nip out and get some masking tape from the patient old guy in the *ferretería* – or maybe Arturo had some in the baskets of bits in the lean-to shed.

She went downstairs and out onto the terrace, happy for the light rain to cool her down. Once at the lean-to, her eyes met rectangular pupils. 'Chica! What are you doing here?'

Chica pushed her head against her shorts – either for affection or to dry her head. Probably both. Juliana put her arm round her warm-haired body. 'You've got your own shed in your paddock, you silly girl. Much more fun with your friends. Your dad obviously thinks that's where you are; he's closed the fence.'

She called out his name. All that happened was Chica, expecting to see her adored Josemi, came out of the shelter, looked over at the empty terrace next door, and then back up at her.

'Come on, over we go. I'll try and figure out how he opens up that gap in the fence for you. Or maybe he'll get paint out of his ears and come and help us.'

Chica considered the wall. Maybe the puddles of water in it made it look slippery and unappealing, because goaty eyes looked up at her for a solution.

She put a hand on her neck, and called out Josemi's name again – but instantly wished she hadn't; it was too much for Chica, and after a glance suggesting Juliana must be daft, she dashed over to the low wall of the terrace, jumped over it and onto the bank path.

'No… No, no… Chica! Come back!'

The noisy tumble of water was so high that it was just a couple of metres beneath Chica's tail.

'Up! Up!'

Her hooves were trying to bring her up, eyes fixed on her little path up to Josemi's terrace, but it was muddy, her back legs sinking down, further and further, and then the poor thing looked behind her and lost her balance, tipping over… Back legs landing in the turbulent water, front hooves scrabbling, she bleated desperately, her eyes wide with fear.

Juliana screamed Josemi's name and then went over the wall, edging carefully down the bank, holding on to the bushes, until she was near enough to lunge forward… The third time, she managed to grab a horn. 'Up! Up! Come *on*!' It felt like a tug of war. Chica was heavy. They glared at each other. 'Come *on*!' This close, the water was a roaring beast. Her arm was losing strength. She counted to three and hauled with all her might. Yes! Chica leapt onto a bush, suddenly knowing what to do, but buffeted Juliana, who twisted, groped the air…

The torrent of angry water was on her, with its branches and debris, her hand reaching for the sharp rocks of the bank, feet trying to keep the stony ground… She stumbled and went under, was swept along, found her feet, grabbed a bush of needles on the bank, but was pushed under again… An arm grabbed her front, taking the breath out of her, pulling her onto the bank, pushing her ahead, but holding her until slowly, somehow, they'd climbed the bank. He lifted her over onto the terrace. They stood there breathing hard. She caught the white shape…

'Chica… fence…'

There was an angry response, but he let go for a moment, and patted the goat through. She still couldn't breathe – she was fading, as if waking from a dream, or going into one…

Then he helped her inside and put her on a bed, a towel over her, another wiping her face. A blanket. His face was above hers, saying heaven knew what, but calmly, as if the water anger that had possessed him had left.

'Is okay, breathe.' English. Josemi-but-English.

She couldn't stop shaking, her teeth chattering.

He opened a wardrobe, pulled out a fleece jacket and put that over her too, tucking it round her.

'Are you hurt?'

She shook her head. After a while, the spangly stars started to disappear.

'*Bueno*. Hot drink or bath. Which first?'

She couldn't seem to answer.

'Drink. I will get it. Don'… *no te muevas.*'

She didn't move. She closed her eyes. She'd now started to hurt: she had overstretched ropes in her shoulder, her head throbbed. She took a stinging hand out from under the covers and it dropped blood and mud.

He was back. 'Can you sit?'

She hitched herself up. 'I'm sorry. Such a mess…'

'Is okay. Can you take this with other hand?'

She took the mug from him.

'Drink, is not too hot, don' wait.'

It was sweet. Like back in Café Nido.

'I'm sorry. Chica…'

'Is me. I was thinking she was in the field… I shut the thing. But look, you don' die for a goat, is *tonta*, Hooliana.'

'I love Chica, I couldn't… Am I dreaming, or are you speaking English?'

He nodded. 'Don' think I do it again.'

She managed a smile.

He was examining her hand and something on her forehead. 'You finish? Now bath and we do these things.'

'Yes…'

'*My* bath, that any-way, you no' have hot water today, no? I put water in bath and find clothes.'

He disappeared. She looked around. She was in his bedroom. Everything white, except a blue-painted chair. Paintings, large and small, all over the walls. Not all of them his, she guessed. One was a picture of a boat, made from wood, string and bits from the beach. She pointed to it when he came back in and he smiled.

'Come.' He was holding out a hand. He helped her to the bathroom and left her there with a towel, a pair of corded bathing trunks and a long-sleeved shirt on a chair.

When she came out, he told her to sit down on the remade bed next to a box of sticking plasters.

'I can do that.'

'On the hand? I think that no.'

He sat down next to her. He'd had a shower upstairs, smelt like the rosemary bush on the bank, and was wearing the clown-hippy trousers he'd had on when she first met him. He was very close, busy putting patches all over her. She wanted to give him a little thank-you kiss on his stubbly cheek, or stroke his shiny wet hair where it curled at his neck, but there was a spell she didn't want to break. He got off the bed and she missed him at once, but then he was back, behind her, gently brushing her hair.

'I can do that,' she said again.

'No.' He combed for some while in silence. 'Your hair is… very Spanish. Not anything half-English.'

She didn't answer. There'd been something she was going to ask him, but she couldn't think what it was now.

'Thank you… Thank you so much. I should go now.'

'Is too soon. Stay until you are all okay, no? We will eat something when you can. Then I go with you, because you don' have a key, no? We will be going over that *puta* wall! But I will help, don' worry.'

EIGHT

DAY 14

'Hooliana. *Buenos días, guapa.*' He was back in Spanish. The *guapa* – gorgeous – was new, but universal round here; the guy in the café, the men in the Sunday market and even the old boy in the *ferretería* called her and every other female that. Josemi popped his head over the new wall, disappeared like a Punch puppet, then came up again with a chuckle.

She laughed. 'I swear you've made that wall higher.'

'Why would I do that? We're just not used to it… Anyway, I've got something for you. Put your hand over.'

'How do I know it's not got a hundred legs?'

'Not that many, I promise.'

'An *abejorro*, then.' He'd laughed his head off yesterday when a gigantic black bee-like thing had drifted by with a baritone buzz and made her scream. How was she to know they were gentle giants?

'No, no. Come on, it's to say thank you for my plant.'

'Which was to say thank you for the mended wall.'

'Which you're now complaining about.'

'Uh…' She put her right hand over.

'Not that one, silly.'

She drew it back, and gave him the one without a dressing over the palm. He put something cool, smooth and rounded in it, and folded her fingers over it. His hands were warm and dry. She needed reminding to take her hand back. In it, was an orangey pebble the colour of the mountain earth, with an intricately drawn, cockily-stanced Chica.

'Oh!' It was beautiful, but somehow she'd expected the one with the lavatera flower that his mother had seen her with.

'You don't like her?' His eyes looked slightly fiery, but she'd learnt not to pay too much attention to that, after a few days of exchanges over the wall.

'Of *course* I do.' She must have been smiling at it, but he still looked perturbed.

'But you want…' He disappeared for a moment then was back again, with the lavatera stone.

'Thank you. It reminds me of my mother. I'm just off to the cemetery now. I'll take it with me.'

'You mustn't leave it there!' he said, rather loudly, eyes in full fire.

*Jes*us. 'No, no.' Although, why not? It would have looked beautiful on the ledge. Maybe it was some cultural thing she didn't know about. She was waiting for him to explain, but he seemed to be waiting for further assurance. 'I'm going to put both of them in my special pebble bowl upstairs.'

'Good.' He ran a hand through his mad hair, scratched his bristly chin; he was in bear-like work mode. Then he looked her up and down, as far as that was possible with the wall in the way. 'It's today you visit Arturo? But should you drive?'

'Kim's taking me. Says she's happy to spend *ages* in the

shops while I'm with him.' She made an eyes-to-heaven look, guessing – correctly, by the look on his face – that they shared a lack of interest in clothes shopping. Then he went inside to answer the front doorbell – almost certainly pressed by his mother.

Mothers: something about hers was inexplicably abhorrent to him, and she wasn't too fond of his either. The aptly named dour-faced Dolores – literally a *pain* – had been round every day since she heard about the accident. Admittedly, when Juliana came out of the house with Elise to go to the doctor, Dolores had crossed the road to ask how she was; but after that she'd had her anti-Englishwomen face back on – probably with additional resentment that Juliana had put Josemi's life at risk by needing to be saved from the flood.

She set off towards the cemetery, and as the goat man waved and the waiters in the café called out something to her, she wasn't sure if she was enjoying her new notoriety in the village. Everybody knew about the daft *inglesa* who'd been heroically scooped out of the *rambla*. The goat man – Diego – had given her some goat's cheese and a bottle of wine for saving Chica; Juan Luis's wife had made her a figgy cake; and the market stall woman with the thin cotton clothes had insisted on selling her two palm-tree shift dresses for the price of one, telling her – correctly as it turned out – that they'd be easier to put on with a bandaged hand as well as being the coolest possible attire for the hot weather.

————

Kim looked over at her when they were waiting at a T-junction. 'Lovely dress. What's this new look about then?' she asked with a wink.

'Six euros from the *mercadillo*,' she said, smoothing the soft cotton turquoise and palm trees over her thighs. 'I've got another in bright green. Can't be doing with buttons or waistbands anymore.'

'It suits you. I look ridiculous in those things – too English pear-shaped for them.'

'Nonsense – you're just a classier bird!' Kim, as usual, was looking stylish in a sleeveless linen number.

'No but really, you should wear bright designs more often. You look fabulous. *Arty*.' Another wink.

Juliana decided not to notice it. Through the cloth bag on her lap, she felt the rounded weight of the lavatera pebble. Rebelliously, she'd taken it to the cemetery to show Mama, told her about what happened. About Josemi. And then, with nobody around, something had made her move along to the plaque Dolores visited. Three relatives – her husband, sister and twelve-year-old daughter – all dead on one day. Must have been a car crash. Poor woman. Could you ever recover from that? How precious Josemi must be to her. Poor creature had every right to be a Miserable Bag.

Kim glanced over at her. 'Penny for them?'

'Oh… Still a bit tired, that's all.'

'It's the shock. I'm not surprised. Carlito had a near-miss with a rip tide a few years ago, had flashbacks and fatigue for ages.'

'Uh, that sounds awful. Yes, I get those.' Although she was also getting replays of gentler memories of that afternoon.

'But you've got to admit, it's pretty romantic to be swept up out of a river by Josemi's strong arms!'

'I don't know about romantic – he was a bit rough, shouty and cross. But he was a very sweet nurse, I have to say.'

'Aw, so…'

'So we're now *friends*, Kim.' She decided to share the other difficult revelation of the day. 'Because, anyway... I think he might have a girlfriend, another artist.'

On her way back from the cemetery, she'd seen an artfully draped and bangled woman get out of an estate car in the main road, start unloading bags and paintings into a smart apartment block, and then fling herself into Josemi's arms. The woman could have stayed there for ages, for all she knew, because Juliana had quickly disappeared down a side road and gone back to the house another way, all the time trying to tell herself that the angular painting style she'd seen wasn't the same as the one she'd noticed in Josemi's bedroom.

'Don't worry. Probably just a friend; it's a big artist club there in the summer.'

'I'm not worried. It's all good. For the best, really.'

'You mean you're not a holiday fling kinda lass.'

'That's right.' She pulled a water bottle out of her bag. 'Hotter than ever, isn't it?'

'Ha – you wait until August. Oh no, you'll have gone back by then.'

As usual, the thought of going back to England – on the rare occasions she allowed it into her head – was a punch in the tummy.

'Unless of course... you decide to *stay*. Couldn't you pack in the TV extras work and just become a blogger?'

'I'm nowhere *near* being able to make an income from that. Maybe in a few years' time.'

'Well... teach the flute, then.'

'Ditto. I'm only grade six.'

'Okay, then it would have to be teaching English.'

'I know.'

Kim glanced over at her. 'You mean, you've thought about it?'

Juliana grinned. 'Well *of course* I have! There are four-week intensive courses in Granada – if I could find the money. But I'm not sure I'd be good with children.'

'What? You were a natural with those kids at the rehearsal last week. And my God, there's plenty of work – I'm soon going to need some help – especially if Carlito and I start a family. Get qualified and come and work for me!'

'Really? Wow! But… supposing I hate it? Maybe I should come and watch you teach one day.'

'Just what I was going to suggest.' She patted Juliana's arm. 'And you need to stop falling into *ramblas* and come to the expat group on Fridays. Honestly, Juliana, this could work for you: renting a nice little flat, teaching and blogging, Josemi seeing you differently once you've shown you're sticking around…'

———

'Hooliana…' Arturo stood up as she approached the table.

'This is lovely!' His local *chiringuito* – a charmingly wooden and informal restaurant on the beach that he'd promised made the best *tortilla* in Almería.

He kissed her, then put a hand on her arm and examined the graze on her forehead, took the wrist of the wrapped-up hand. 'It's all my fault. I should have warned you about the *rambla*,' he said in Spanish. 'When I think what—'

'No, no.' She sat down, encouraging him to do the same; he looked shaken by the sight of her. 'I *was* warned. Josemi had come round specially, earlier in the day.'

He nodded. 'But you couldn't help wanting to save that goat he adores. Promise me you'll never—'

'I've promised everyone, don't worry.' She smiled. 'How are *you*?'

'I'm… good, good.' He ordered *tortilla*, some kind of seafood and a shared salad, then turned to her. 'So, tell me, dear, how are you getting on? Despite your run-in with the *rambla*, you're looking very well, more relaxed and… colourful!' He plucked at the shoulder of her dress. 'I like this on you. But take it from me, whatever it says on the label, wash it by hand!'

'Ah, okay.' She was conscious she mustn't repeat her last visit's mistake of sounding flippant about the inheritance conditions. 'I'm getting on – I *feel* like – I'm getting on well. I'm busy but I'm loving it. Can't believe I've only been here two weeks.' She wondered whether she should tell him that she was already thinking about how she could earn a living here.

He was nodding, as if maybe he already knew.

She pulled the printed-out diary from her bag. 'It's in English I'm afraid.'

He took it from her. 'Good for my brain. I'll read it later. For now, let's see these photos… Ha!' He laughed at the selfie of her looking perplexed by the orange gas bottles; admired the cacti and the Níjar items for the house, and looked interested when she pointed out her friend Kim at the rehearsal and told him about the expat group she might try out.

'The painting's taking much longer than I thought, but I'm enjoying it. Most of the beaches I'm leaving until the water's warm enough to swim in them. And… I've booked a cabin at Fort Tabernas Studios, but it's not until the end of the month.'

'Good, good. I have the DVD of the film your mama worked on, *Once Upon a—*'

'*Time in the West*. I saw! I've already watched it. Is it my imagination, or does the camera catch her face looking pained—'

'It does. She was sometimes an extra as well as helping with costumes.'

'Dad never said.'

He shook his head, as he often did when her father was mentioned.

The food had arrived, and Arturo was taking small mouthfuls of battered something from a small plate. She remembered him tucking into an enormous tuna-and-sweet-corn jacket potato when they went for a pub lunch near her flat in South Ealing.

'You *are* going to help me with this *tortilla*, aren't you?' she asked.

'Only if you try some *chipirones*,' he said, pushing his plate towards her.

'What are they?' she asked, looking at the translated menu. '*Baby squid*. Oh God. At least it's small.' She put one onto a fork, hesitated, then put it into her mouth. It was sweet, slightly nutty, and not as chewy as she'd feared. 'It's nice!' She took another.

'Didn't your dad and his wife ever encourage you to try seafood? In Spanish restaurants, at least?'

'We didn't come to Spain – other than Marbella once, when it tied in with a catalogue shoot my little stepsisters were doing. It was usually Greece or Italy for holidays… and always the same: a big hotel with plenty of English food and childcare.'

'I suppose Spain was painful, reminding him of Antoñita.'

She couldn't remember Dad ever looking pained about her. 'I don't know. But having come each year with Mama,

until I was seven, I didn't make it here again until I was eighteen, with Toby.'

Toby's name also produced shakes of the head.

'I'll never understand why Dad never brought me over to
visit Mama after she came back here. In *two years*. It would
have made such a difference to me to see her, even if she
didn't want to live with us anymore. If I asked, he'd just say
we *were* going, when we could… and then she died.'

He looked shocked, even though she'd probably
mentioned this on most of his annual visits to England. He
usually told her to bring it up with her father, but this time he
put a hand on hers. 'I don't know, but believe me, Antoñita –
your mama – adored you. She was a person who loved with a
fire, and you were everything to her.'

Tears pricked her eyes, and she wanted to believe him.
'I've been meaning to ask you… I know there was a scandal
about her and the mine owner's son, but would people still
remember that? Josemi's mother is unfriendly towards me,
and even Josemi's face drops if I mention Mama. I mean,
you're her brother; did you get this?'

He looked at her steadily. 'No. Not at all. What has
Josemi said?'

'Something about how I had to manage or understand
my heritage – to be honest, I couldn't understand what he
was on about.'

He smiled gently. 'It sounds like he cares about you, feels
your uncertainty, and knows you need this.'

She sighed with relief. 'D'you think?'

'Yes.' He tapped the printed-out diary. 'I see you don't
mention him much in here, but your face tells me everything.'

'What?' she said, laughing.

He grinned and nodded.

a smile. 'Hooliana! Your houses are pushed together, your music pushes you together… it's not me.'

'Hm. Well I hate to tell you, but I think he has a girlfriend, anyway.'

Arturo dismissed that with a flick of the hand; it was clearly not in his plan. 'Now, eat up, because I've realised you're ready for something I've been wanting to give you.'

Back in the apartment, she waited on the shady half of the balcony, with the usual peach juice from María José.

He finally appeared, breathless but happy, and sat next to her. 'I've made a copy for you to keep,' he said, spreading an A4 sheet with a central square of loopy handwriting on the table. 'It's a letter from Antoñita to her old schoolfriend, Teresa. Teresa's husband gave it to me earlier this year, after she died.'

Juliana leant forward.

'End of May, 1968. We'd been in Tabernas one month of the three. She was eighteen, more than an hour from our loving but very critical and Catholic parents, living in a flat with just an easy-going older brother.' He grinned, pointing to himself. 'Escaping the misery of a village that everyone was deserting, with the mining coming to an end. And she was working on a film! Antoñita *loved* films. It was as exciting for her as coming here to Spain is for you. She's also left behind an infatuation and found… well, you'll see.'

Juliana picked up the piece of paper. Having translated it into English as best she could, it read:

Calle del Castillo 18, apto 3,
Tabernas.
28 de mayo del 1968

My dear Teresita,

I'm so happy to hear your news, and will do everything I can to come to the wedding in October! You and Bernardo are made for each other – we always knew this! And brilliant that you're getting out of San Rafael and off to Almería.

*Don't be sorry for me; I haven't given Ignacio a thought since I've been here. Such an unequal relationship would never have worked, and to tell such lies about me… Anyway, I'm learning so much about filming and costumes and acting, and have made such wonderful friends, I haven't had **time** to give him a thought!*

Teresa, one of these friends… he is an angel, I tell you. I'd been asked to mend his jacket – and we got chatting about films and horses and dreams of staying on at the studio after Once Upon a Time in the West *and being in film after film, him as stuntman and actor, me as seamstress and doing a little acting here and there… but we also have such a laugh, because you know how you like my mimicking? He's even better! I never realised how important laughter is to a relationship – something I know you have in yours. Ah, I've written it now: **relationship**. That's what it is. We love each other. But it has to be a secret at the moment. I haven't told Arturo; I don't want him worrying about me again.*

The only thing is: what will happen after the filming ends in July? One of my new mates, Ana María, has some English relatives with an acting and extras agency in London who have invited her to come over to work and bring some Spanish friends. Imagine being in something like Far from the Madding Crowd*! But I really want to stay here with my angel. We will have been together three months by then, and even more inseparable. We need work. He comes from a close-knit Romani family. There are problems with us being together that I won't go into here… It will take courage. I hope I can find it.*

Let's write again soon,

With much love,
   Antoñita

NINE

DAY 28

Juliana sat down next to her bag and read the letter again. What had happened, to make Mama lose the courage to stay with her 'angel'? She couldn't believe she went on to find another angel in Dad. Of course, maybe for some of those twenty years before Juliana unexpectedly came along, Dad was different – not so critical, less of a work and whisky-aholic – but she could barely remember them being in the same room. It was odd that Arturo didn't seem to see how sad the letter was. She put it in the inside pocket of the bag. 'Come to Tabernas with me, Mama; tell me what happened.'

She could still hear her own angel chatting with his angu-lar-arty and bangled friend next door. *Gabi*. They'd been introduced, and every time Gabi had been round – a *lot* in the last two weeks – the woman had said hello, talked to her about her cacti, or offered her a slice of cake; unfortunately, there was absolutely nothing not to like about her.

She turned her attention back to packing. Should she take her laptop? How good would the Wi-Fi be, in the only desert in Europe? But at least she could catch up with her diary and sort out her photos tonight; there wasn't going be much else to do in a log cabin on a closed-for-the-night amusement park. She went through to her laptop and noticed another blog comment from Toby, wishing he could join her on her Wild West adventure. This had inspired a string of comments about how good he would look in cowboy chaps, his likeness to Robert Redford and so on. She rather resented this tawdry dialogue after what she'd thought was a thoughtful piece about hopeful young people from a failing Sixties mining town applying to be film extras. She snapped the laptop shut.

She picked up her phone to put it in her laptop bag, then saw Toby had also sent a WhatsApp. '*Seriously, wish I could come with you. Sounds fascinating and we'd have a laugh!*'

Yeah, right. Anyway, how would that have worked? A family cabin, with a bedroom each? About three years after they'd broken up they'd spent a night together for old times' sake, and it had taken her about another three years to get over it.

She was going to leave by the front door, so as to avoid the possible sweethearts next door, but that was ridiculous when the car was a metre from the terrace gate.

'Hooliana!' Josemi called brightly as she came out, waving a hand.

She turned, laptop bag over her shoulder, hand on her case handle. It was oddly like when she first arrived, except today he was being super neighbourly.

'Where are you off to?' he asked. Gabi was standing next to him, coffee in hand. He should fix her up with a drip, the amount she downed on that terrace.

'Just off for the night. Don't forget to water your plants.'

He looked pleasingly perplexed, but Gabi assured her they'd get the hose out right away.

'Oh, and be an angel and squirt some water over at mine too, would you?'

———

It was as easy as Arturo had promised: the dual carriageway to Almería, but long before entering the weir of scary round-abouts she filtered off onto another road heading inland towards Tabernas. The orange earth gave way to a pale, lunar landscape of eroded rocky hills and canyons.

She drove through the village where Uncle Arturo and Mama had shared a flat during the filming. It had a quaint central square with elegant wrought-iron benches and arbours, and an ancient church, but not a lot going on. Even now, there were just a few cafés, despite its proud promotion of the studios with metal cowboys on some of the walls and a row of sculpted film director chairs – including one for Claudia Cardinale, star of *Once Upon a Time in the West*. Mama and Arturo's *Calle del Castillo 18* apartment building was now a doctor's surgery. She was tempted to climb up to the ruined fortress on the hill for a wonderful overview of the village, studio and desert, but she needed to concentrate on today's condition – which she'd sensed was an important one.

She followed cowboy posters to Tabernas Studios – or *Fort* Tabernas Studio as it was called these days, emphasising its Wild West theme. As she drove up to the entrance, she wound down her window to be welcomed by a weathered cowboy rattling out the times for the shows and asking for a large ticket fee before she surprised him with the printout of her reservation. It looked like it had been a while since a woman on her own had stayed the night there.

She parked and got out of the car into an oven of heat. There wasn't a hint of cloud in that intensely blue sky; perhaps midday wasn't the best time to arrive. The accommodation girl took her through part of the main street of old clapboard town buildings. Even the lightest of breezes was whipping up whorls of sandy dust, and when a mounted cowboy trotted past there was a near-sandstorm. They reached a short row of log cabins near the pool at the back of the grounds. Beyond them, there was nothing but rocky desert as far as you could see.

'Wow, this looks great!' she said, but once she'd been shown round her wooden toy house and was left alone, she flopped onto the bed. Of course, in Mama's time here, there would have been no pool, ice cream kiosks, air-conned cabins and choice of restaurants; you'd have to be desperate or really love what you were doing to be here in the heat and dust of May – let alone June and July. Then she remembered Josemi saying that *he* might forget to water his plants, but *she* would forget to water *herself*. She got up, washed her face and drank a bottle of water, followed by a peach juice from the mini fridge. She was then ready for *Action*, as it were.

A few hours later, she was cooling off in the Saloon with a beer and a pizza, having had a rather good time. She'd visited the Bank, been imprisoned in the Jail, bought boiled sweets from the Drug Store, been to a can-can show, and, from the Hotel balcony, watched some filming going on near the church in the Mexican village area. Some of her fellow visitors – many of them English families on a half-term break – were going around in heavy Wild West costumes that made you sweat just thinking about them. Toby would have loved it. *She* loved it, but she was supposed to be concentrating on fulfilling a condition – and was yet to see the meaning behind any of this.

She went up to the bar and asked the old guy in the saloon waistcoat for a Coke.

He smiled at her and poured it out. 'Enjoying yourself?'

'Yes! Even more than I thought.'

'No friends interested in Spaghetti Westerns?'

'None that could come with me, no.'

A couple of cowboys swaggered past, much to the delight of three ladies at a nearby table; you'd think they were on a hen night.

Juliana felt a sudden need to explain her visit. 'I've always wanted to see the place. My mother worked on *Once Upon a Time in the West.*'

He stopped pouring and looked at her. 'Really? Fantastic! Those were the days… What was her name?'

'Antoñita Fernández. She helped with the costumes.'

He thought for a moment, then shook his head. 'There were so many of us… and it was so many years ago.'

'You worked on it too?'

'Yes. Horse riding, acting. And never left! How crazy am I?' He laughed, found a slice of lemon for her Coke and pushed it towards her. 'On the house!'

'Ha! Thank you.'

He pointed to the left side of the veranda outside the swing doors. 'Pinch a stool and put yourself there; it's the best place to watch the Wild West show. Starts in about ten minutes.'

'Okay.'

Before long, all the verandas and steps of the buildings surrounding the central square were filled with men, women and little boys with toy guns. Music from one of the Clint Eastwood Dollars trilogy was piped into the heavy hot air, and there then followed an inevitable but humorous bank robbery, dust-storm horse chase, jail escape and showdown.

She couldn't understand much of the cowboys' Andalusian drawl, but there was no denying the appeal of their flapping duster coats, the unruly hair escaping their Stetsons, their spurred cowboy-booted sauntering, and lithe legs-apart leaping on and off horses. Her favourite was the Josemi-like quiet, reluctant sheriff.

It was over, and the cowboys stood by the town water well accepting applause, whistles and selfie photo opportunities. She took her stool back to the bar and exchanged a thumbs-up with the barman, then bought her third watermelon ice lolly and settled down on a shady wooden step by the Blacksmith's Forge. She'd left the map somewhere, but as far as she could tell there was just one area – a ranch or something – left to explore. Other than the pool and the horse and cart. Why on earth did she have to stay the night? But then, maybe it was just as well; she'd been so enjoying herself that she'd been forgetting to take enough photos. Noticing her battery was low from videoing the show, she took her phone back to the cabin to charge and went off to the gift shop.

The shop was staffed by one of the can-can girls, who was wincing and shifting from foot to foot.

'Are you all right?' Juliana asked her.

'Uh, it's my hip. And I've still got another show to do!'

'Oh no, poor you. I've got some ibuprofen if you…'

'Oh God, have you? You darling! Yes please.'

She downed them gratefully then started tapping the prices of Juliana's fridge magnets and postcards into the till. 'Ooh, there's one you haven't got. The best, in fact. And it's on the house – literally!'

She pulled down a card of a gloomy dark brown house with a triangular Swiss-like roof and an overhang giving a sheltered veranda.

'The McBain house. You know, from *Once Upon a Time in the West*.'

'Of course! Must be in the bit I haven't seen yet.'

'Next to the railway track and station – although that's closed for renovation. Of course, in the film, Jill has quite a long horse-and-cart ride from the station to the McBain house – they must have done a big loop round the set and arrived the other side.'

'Only to find her new husband and his kids had been killed by Henry Fonda.'

'Yes. I can't bear that bit. But at least she gets the house and makes a life for herself in the end.'

'True.'

The girl looked at the clock on the wall. 'You should go now. At five they play "Jill's Theme" there.'

'Oh my God, just like they used to when they were actually filming, apparently. Brilliant, thanks!'

There wasn't time to get her phone, so she followed the girl's directions and after a sweaty crossing of the baking town square she made her way along the strip of shade from the Bank and a series of smaller town buildings and turned down a short alley to an opening with another well and… there it was. The McBain house. It was much quieter here, with just a few pensive couples stepping respectfully onto its veranda, or coming out with a wry smile.

Then the music started. Simple at first, leading you in, but then the orchestra and wordless soprano took you soaring up and up, until your heart felt like it would burst… Juliana imagined Claudia Cardinale acting with this in the background, perhaps Mama looking on, her 'angel' too, shortly never to see each other again. Then it came to her that somewhere in this park was the last place she and Mama were together… The house blurred.

A gravelly Spanish question came from behind her. It was the horse-and-cart man, trying to persuade her to have a ride away from the house back to (and presumably round) the town – the reverse journey to that of Claudia Cardinale's Jill. She wiped a tissue over her forehead and then eyes, making out she was just overheated rather than overcome. She was going to leave the horse and cart until tomorrow, but she *was* overheated, and starting to like the idea of being able to just sit there and, when it was over, get dropped off near her cabin. He was now mumbling an exorbitant price.

Taking her hesitation as a likely yes, he leapt down like a cat and offered to take her hand to help her up into the cart.

'S'okay, I've got it,' she said, getting up and settling onto the thinly cushioned seat.

He stared at her a moment. It was hard to tell, with his wide-brimmed hat, but he could have been the creased-face cowboy at the entrance. 'Ingleesh?'

Oddly, she'd forgotten to speak Spanish. 'Yes.' She decided not to mention the half-Spanish thing for once; she didn't feel like talking about Mama now, and coping with his rough, consonant-light Andalusian.

His English was even less intelligible. As they trotted around the village, there followed, as far as she could gather, an autopilot rattling-off of the famous films that had been made there, and who had used which buildings for what. It had been a visitor attraction since the Eighties, but was still used for filming – a *Doctor Who* episode, something for *Game of Thrones*… All of this she already knew. She considered asking him to just keep quiet and let her take in the ambience, particularly now they were on the outer road next to miles of desert. In between his chatter, you could hear nothing, not even a single bird. Something resembling a discarded rope wiggled away to take cover behind a rock, but he didn't comment, just pointed out a clutch of wigwams she'd given a miss earlier. He might have been saying that he'd played an American Indian a few times – not surprisingly, given his wide face and black hair. If it had been the friendly old barman who was doubling as the horse-and-cart man, she might have replied that she'd played a few herself.

'Could you leave me near the log cabins?'

She pointed to herself and the cabins, as he didn't seem to understand; his English was clearly a one-way, one-topic affair.

Back in the cabin, she bed-flopped and drank again, then looked over at her phone charging on the table. The late-afternoon light would give her some gorgeously golden pictures, and she could cool off and relax by the pool knowing she'd done everything. After an early breakfast in the Saloon tomorrow, she could go home and get on with the decorating.

She started with the happily posing old barman, then worked her way round the buildings. She snapped everything, even the row of small buildings she hadn't got around to on the way to the McBain house. One of these, the Milliner's, turned out to be the place where people hired costumes, something her blog fans might like. She went in, explained to the woman there that she was just looking…

There were three girls' Native American outfits on hangers. She held up the one for five-to-seven-year-olds. Her arm began to shake. She looked around the dark, cramped shop, remembered the cloying smell of make-up, the stench of old clothes. *This* is where she'd been. This was the last place she saw Mama. She'd left her here, dressed as a little Native American girl. Mama had had to go somewhere. Quickly, not feeling well. Juliana wasn't to move. She hadn't. Until the woman in the shop had taken her to an office. She'd been given a drink and a nasty meat sandwich. Uncle Arturo, whom she barely knew, collected her and took her to a flat somewhere – until Dad arrived. Mama was a little poorly, they'd said.

She made herself continue to Jill's house, took pictures and then went in and sat down at Jill's kitchen table as if asking her for advice. What happened here, to make Mama suddenly decide to desert her? Having just that morning bought her a flamenco party dress for her grandmother's birthday party? Her only other memories of the day were a pretty white horse, a metal lizard on a belt, and Mama telling someone she was seven and a half. Arturo must know something. Was it a coincidence that he happened to be down from Madrid? Here to help? She looked around, imagined Jill putting the coffee on for her. If Arturo wasn't ready to tell her more, he wouldn't have insisted on her coming here. She'd call him tomorrow.

She went back to the cabin, took a swim in the pool, enjoyed a sunset sandwich on her little veranda. Then she went indoors and set up her laptop. Feeling tired but wired, she decided to tackle all her Spanish photos, sorting them into several albums. It was taking hours, but calming her. Eventually she was back on Day 2, with all those frowned-upon photos in the cemetery. She laughed at the wilting wild flowers she'd put on Mama's plaque; what was she thinking of?

Then she gasped. Her heart thudded. She leant forward, prised the photo larger.

ANTOÑITA FERNÁNDEZ GARCÍA
+ EL 5 DE JUNIO 1996
A LOS 46 AÑOS

Ninety-*six*. Why in hell hadn't she noticed? She died in ninety-*six*. When Juliana was seven and a half. Unless the cemetery had made a mistake, with both the year and Mama's age, *Dad had taken two years to tell her that Mama had died*. Mama probably died right here, the day she last saw her. She hadn't deserted her at all.

TEN

DAY 29

She woke early, much too early to call Arturo. She was tempted to call anyway, but it wasn't going to be easy; he too should have told her the truth about Mama's death.

Dad was probably going to lie and improvise like a pro; there was no point in talking to him until she knew the facts. But tomorrow was Thursday, when he always called. Regularly, dutifully, around five – as if she'd been slotted into his work and golf schedule, even though – or maybe *because* – she could never talk for more than a few minutes because she had to leave for the band rehearsal. Tomorrow, maybe she'd leave *before* he called.

It was also too early for breakfast. She showered and packed, then took a stroll around the empty Wild West town, ending up in front of the costume hire place. Mama was often unwell with asthma; this she knew to be true. Dad had said she'd decided to stay on in Spain because it was better for her asthma; that was clearly a lie. Mama had left her in the costume place because she felt unwell – at least, that's what she *thought* she remembered. Perhaps she'd looked for the First Aid room, near the Saloon…

The Saloon door was open. She went over to it and found the old barman there.

'Good morning,' he said with a smile. 'You can come in early if you're hungry, I'm just setting up.'

She thanked him, helped herself to toast and jam while he made her a mug of tea, and sat down at the table nearest the bar. It seemed that the other cabin residents were still coping with children or hangovers; she and 'Paco' – she read from his badge – were alone, except for a lady singing to herself as she filled the cutlery tray.

'Can I ask you something?'

'Of course. Try me.'

'Can you remember a youngish woman collapsing and dying here, back in the summer of 1996?'

His eyebrows went up. 'My God. No. Who was this? Not your mother, I hope.'

She hesitated. 'Yes, I'm afraid. She died that summer, but I don't know exactly where.'

'I'm sorry…' He shook his head. 'A woman got in the way of one of the horses once…'

Juliana's heart thudded.

'But no, I was in the show then, so that must have been the Eighties.'

'Ah. I think my mother died of an asthma attack.'

'You must have been very young… how awful.' He looked down, then up again, holding out a finger. 'I tell you who you should ask, got a memory like an elephant: Fran.'

'Fran?' She looked over at the lady, who smiled back.

'Francisco. Didn't I see you in the cart yesterday? Ask Fran.'

She nodded, but wondered how on earth she was going to communicate with the man.

'He'll be at the gate from nine – good time to ask, not many people arrive then.'

'Thanks.'

She finished her breakfast and went back to the cabin. There was no reply from Arturo; she'd try again later from the car. She dropped off her key and pulled her bag along to the car park.

The reception cabin was closed. She tried Arturo again – still no answer. Maybe there was something wrong with his phone. Was it worth waiting for 'Fran'? She was desperate to get to Arturo's. Her uncle collected her that day, wanted her to come to this place, and would surely now tell her every-thing that had happened; she didn't need the unreliable recounting of a consonant-light cowboy. She turned on the engine and was about to drive off when a battered tin-coloured car whizzed in and screeched to a halt in a cloud of dust.

Fran got out. He was a small, wiry monkey of a man with a slight limp in his cowboy swagger. He'd probably been one of those short little boys who were good at gymnastics and grown up and trained as a stunt man – only to come a cropper at some point and end up being kept on for whatever needed doing for the tourists. She switched off the engine, got out and went over to him as he unlocked the cabin.

He said good morning and then stared at her, as if unsure whether he recognised her or not. Eventually he seemed to ask her where she wanted to go, thinking she wanted directions.

'I've got a question. The barman said you were the person who might know.'

He thought for a moment. 'No, no, I no speak ingleesh *bien. Momentito…*' Once inside, he opened the shutter and offered her a fifteen-euro book about the studios.

'Oh… No thank you. Paco said I should ask you. You might remember… something in the Nineties,' she said in Spanish.

It was like she'd dropped a coin in a slot. He asked her what she wanted to know.

'Can you remember a woman collapsing and dying here in June 1996?'

He looked at her, eyes squinting in the sun. Then over at a car winding its way round the hill. He came back to her. 'You're English?'

'Yes.'

'And this woman was… English?'

'No, Spanish. Antoñita Fernández.' She didn't want to go into this any further. 'I'm asking for a friend.'

He nodded slowly, glanced at the approaching car. 'I will… ask some people. If I learn something, I will call you, okay?'

'Okay, thanks.' She turned to go back to the car.

'Your telephone number?' He was holding out a pad and a Fort Tabernas Studios biro. She wrote it down. 'And name?' She wrote that down too.

She drove off and pulled over halfway up the hill to try Arturo again. Still no reply. She tapped his address into the satnav.

———

She parked facing the beach with its gently tumbling waves, breathed out heavily several times. *Don't Drink and Drive* and

Tiredness Can Kill they say, but they should add *Anger Causes Accidents*; it was a miracle she'd arrived and hadn't killed anyone. She must somehow calm down before she got back into the car again.

Just minutes after she'd joined the dual carriageway, a cascade of memories of Dad's lies in those two years had come flooding over her: the birthday and Christmas presents apparently 'all the way from Spain'; the typed letters from Mama saying how sorry she was to hear about Tabs getting run over, how happy she was to hear about Juliana's grade three ballet and getting Dorothy in the school's *Wizard of Oz*... Never a photo or a phone call. Never going on those promised visits. Never-ending nights she spent lying awake wondering... Also, there was never any news of what *Mama* was doing – because what she was actually doing during those two years was lying in the wall behind the plaque in the cemetery.

'*Fucking hell!*' she exclaimed, and imagined for the umpteenth time what she was going to say to her dad. On the other hand, maybe she wouldn't say anything; she could just refuse to take his calls. Block his number. He'd know why. He must have known she'd go to the cemetery and see the date. She'd wait and see when and if he came up with an adequate explanation for lying to her for not just two but twenty-three years.

Arturo also had some explaining to do, but just for once she was going to control herself; he'd obviously had some kind of plan for how he was going to get her to ask the question, and she had to trust him. She transferred her laptop to her bag and made her way down the seafront to his apartment building.

'Hooliana, what a surprise!' María José said on opening

the door, and kissed her. 'He's just got back from the hospital, so a bit tired.'

'Hooliana!' Arturo called out croakily from the living room.

She went through to him. He was dressed in the usual crisp polo shirt and linen trousers, but looked pale and small in his favourite peacock-blue armchair.

'What happened? Are you okay?' she asked in Spanish.

'Yes, yes... just a bit of old man troubles, nothing to worry about. How lovely to see you – and in your *green* dress from the *mercadillo* this time. Come and sit down. Earl Grey?'

'That would be nice.'

He nodded at María José. 'We even have some Scottish shortbread a friend of mine brought me back from London.' He looked at her carefully. 'And how are you, my dear? How was Tabernas?'

'I loved it.'

He seemed to be waiting for her to go on. 'But you have something to ask me.'

'Yes.'

She thanked María José for the tea and biscuits and waited until she'd left the room. Looked down at the Níjar-design rug in blue stripes, and wondered if it had been there when she came here that first time. 'Did Mama die in 1996?'

'Yes,' he said immediately, then heaved himself up and sat next to her on the sofa. He took her hand. 'I thought you'd *never* ask.'

'I was looking through my photos and suddenly noticed the year on Mama's plaque.'

'Your father made me promise not to say anything. You've no idea how much I've wanted to tell you, and how I've hated this lie feeling like a barrier between us. Finally, we can tear it down.'

'But *why* didn't Dad tell me?' Then it came to her. 'Oh God, was it not an asthma attack, but something…'

'No, no. It was the asthma. Poor Antoñita. She was so strong, so full of life, but she always thought it would take her before her time. It was often an emotional upset that set her off. Do you remember anything bad happening at Tabernas that day?'

'No! We were enjoying ourselves. Why would she be upset?'

'Maybe it was the dust. But at least her last day was a happy one with you.'

'So… what happened?'

'She collapsed. By the well, I think it was. They called an ambulance but… it would have taken time to get there… They found her passport in her bag and called your father. Then he called and asked us to collect you. It was such a shock.' He shook his head. 'Rosita and I were still in Madrid working then, but just happened to be down here in Almería for a few days, thank heavens.'

'Miguel made me some hot milk.'

'Did he? Must have been fourteen at the time. I remember him insisting on popping out with Rosita to buy you some clothes – you were still dressed as an Indian.'

'Oh God…'

'Your father arrived on the next day's flight, and repeated to all three of us that you were only to be told that your mama had been taken ill. Rosita looked after you while we went to Antoñita's funeral. He said you were a fragile child and wouldn't be able to take it. I assumed he'd tell you when you got back to England.'

'But he never did, so…'

'I was in London on business several months later, and asked to meet him. I couldn't believe you still didn't know. He was angry and told me he knew best, that if I was going to go on about it he couldn't invite me to come to the house and see you. So that was it. Of course, once he met Olivia, a couple of years later—'

'When he wanted to marry again, he *had* to tell me Mama was dead.'

'Yes. Or maybe he talked to Olivia about it and decided it was time you knew.'

They sipped their tea.

'I don't remember you coming to the house much when I was a child.'

'Well, once he remarried it was a bit awkward. It's not like we were ever friends. I wanted to keep in touch with you though.'

'You've never forgotten my birthday, not once.'

'I wish we'd seen more of each other, over the years.'

'Well, I'm here now.'

He smiled, but he looked tired.

'I should let you rest. I'm sorry to come barging in like this.'

'I'm glad you did. Finish your tea and have one of these gorgeous biscuits before you go.'

'Okay.'

'Of course, you *will* have to talk to your father about this. Did you tell him you'd been to the cemetery?'

'I can't remember. Probably.'

'Then he'll be bracing himself.'

'He can brace all he likes; I don't want to talk to him.'

'Leave it a few days.'

'I don't want to talk to him ever again.'

'Hooliana. He'll have had a reason, even if we can't think what it could possibly be. He may even have terrible regrets about it. Take your time, but at some point you do need to hear what he has to say.'

She nodded slowly.

He squeezed her hand. 'What's important is that you now know that your mama didn't desert you.'

ELEVEN

DAY 30

Dad rang when she was having breakfast on the terrace. He said he needed to call early today, something to do with her stepsisters having their first night in the chorus of *Phantom* somewhere.

'Julie?'

How hard that 'j' sounded, after being 'Hooliana' here. When the twins used to taunt her with 'Julia Julia is most peculiar' she used to make herself remember Mama calling her 'Hooli' – a name sounding like hoopla, hula hoops and fun things...

'Are you there?' he asked.

'I can't talk now... I've got to go out.'

'Well *really*, I'm sure the beach can wait.'

'I'm not always on the beach. There's no signal where I'm going today... and I'm leaving now.'

'Where are you... Is something the matter?'

'I've leaving now, sorry.' She hung up and struggled to finish her toast.

He rang back. 'Just tell me what this is about,' he almost whispered.

Her head throbbed with anger. 'You *know* what it's about!' She hung up again, put the phone on silent and sat there with her heart pumping. Then got up from the table and somehow knocked her plate to the ground.

'Everything okay over there?' Josemi's concerned face appeared over the wall.

She hadn't realised he was outside. 'Yes.' She picked up the knife and miraculously unbroken plate. 'Tough, these Níjar plates, aren't they?'

'But are *you* okay?'

'My dad. There might be a few more conversations like that, I'm afraid.'

'Oh.' He looked like he was about to ask if she wanted to talk about it.

'Anyway, I'm off out. Somewhere with no coverage. I told him I couldn't be reached.'

'You could of course just switch it off.'

'I know, but somehow that's not enough.'

He chuckled. 'I tell you what. I've got to drop off a load of paintings in San José. Would you like to help me? We could take a swim afterwards.'

'Oh – so the water's warm enough now?'

'Only for little boys, English visitors or… locals who just can't wait.'

'Oh, okay!' Her phone buzzed. It was Toby asking about Tabernas, but she put it back in her pocket.

'Get your things and come to my front door.'

A morning with Josemi; what a perfect distraction. She put a flappy pink market dress over a bikini and got her things together as quickly as possible – as if he might change his mind. Then she went upstairs and knocked on his near-identical front door.

His living room was similar to Arturo's, but there was that slight oil paint aroma she'd come to associate with Josemi, and Kim had told her his room doubled as a gallery during the summer months. There were semi-impressionist seascapes using what looked like his trademark turquoise, but also some equally magical but more intricate paintings of the Alhambra in Granada, and an elegant high street that could be Madrid…

'Hooli! Help me put these wrapped-up ones in the van; I'll be late for the client.'

'Okay, but how much is this one?' People rinsing sand off their feet under the taps at the lifeguard station near Arturo's apartment building. She found the price tag. 'Oh my *God*!' She put a hand over her mouth. 'Sorry. Not that it isn't worth it…'

He laughed. 'Come on, grab those two by the chair. Oh, but is your hand okay now?'

'Hand's fine, thanks. Right.' She picked up the paintings carefully. She couldn't bear to drop his beautiful work, any more than she could have watched Chica drown.

They soon had about twenty paintings in the back of his van and were driving off – watched, she noticed, by his mother from the window across the road.

They took the road up to the blind summit and the dizzying view of the rocky coast beneath them, then drove along the side of the mountain. There were steep drops to the sea far below, but he was a steady driver and she felt safe.

She asked him about his art and learnt that he'd studied in Madrid, staying with his musician uncle Pepe.

'And when you left art college… was it difficult?'

'Well… not at first. I got picked up by an agent. In *every* sense… She got me exhibitions, galleries… until after a couple of years another artist caught her eye and… everything stopped.'

'Oh!'

'Suddenly I'd lost my heart, home and work; not a good time! But I asked for it really – always moaning about the crowds and the cold winters, always wanting to escape to Almería and feeling bad about my mother. I love Madrid, but only to visit. How do you cope with London?'

'I don't. I've been trying to think how I can move out and yet still get enough work.' Move out of the *country*, in fact. 'So, what happened after Madrid?'

'I was in Almería for a few years. Lifeguarding, playing the harmonica in a band for extra money… and then things started to happen with my art – there, and in Madrid again, after a competition. A few years later I bought the place in San Rafael and persuaded my mother and some of her friends to come back too.'

'Come *back*?'

'I grew up in San Rafael.'

'Oh!'

A San Rafael boy who'd come home: how lovely. And how lovely he looked today: shiny hair in a ponytail, a pale blue shirt showing a hint of the manly chest she might see more of at the beach, black shorts revealing lovely lifeguard-worthy legs that she was trying not to be caught looking at.

They were on the flat now, the mountains a backdrop to the fuzzy, rounded hills that made you want to stop the car and run up and down them. Then coming around a hill, San José and its sandy bay was before them – a seaside village several times larger than San Rafael, with swanky villas perched on the hills either side of it.

'Have you been here?' he asked.

'Just briefly, stopping off at Kim's house. I keep promising I'll go to the weekly expat group in a bar here, but somehow never do.'

'Ha! Like me with the Rafaelarte Art Club bar meetings. Now somewhere with good coffee and cake like Café Nido, that's another matter.'

'Quite.' She wondered whether they'd go there again after tonight's rehearsal.

They were coming into San José, with the usual series of little roundabouts trying to outdo each other with their large shrubs and wacky seaside sculptures. He turned off onto a road going up the hill, soon giving them a view over the village, beach and little marina.

'Wow, I had no idea! My exploring started the other side of San Rafael, and I've only got as far as Los Escullos.'

'But you've got so many – and all the best – beaches still to visit!' He turned into a steep road of large white houses. 'We're doing the client first. Won't take long.' They pulled up at a house near the top of the hill. 'What d'you think?'

'Well, great view, but a horribly overlooked terrace, a break-neck climb up from the beach, and where the hell d'you buy bread?'

'Exactly. No way we'd swap our little houses.'

Our houses. She wondered for a moment if Arturo had told him about the conditions – but he wouldn't do that; it was a secret.

She helped him carry in a large painting and two smaller ones, then heard him decline a drink for 'you and your wife' before they got back into the car.

'The rest are for the new gallery. It's great – I desperately need more space for my paintings. Gabi and Oscar only just bought it. I've been helping her decide which artists to include, and no doubt we're going to upset some of the Rafaelarte group.'

Juliana tried to figure out whether he said Gabi *and Oscar*, or just that Gabi *deserved* an Oscar for creating a new gallery. How common was the name Oscar in Spain?

He glanced over at her before starting the car. 'Am I talking too fast again?'

'Well…'

'Or, wait… You thought Gabi and I were partners? Romantically? Not for many years. We're friends and *business* partners these days. They live in Granada but spend as much time as possible down here in the summer. He's an architect, great chap.'

She smiled. 'I suppose I did wonder.'

They were down in the main village now. He looked over as if expecting her to say more. 'Have you got a partner, back in England?'

'No. Not of either type.'

'Ah, I thought maybe that chap who comments on your Spanish house blog…'

She'd forgotten that she'd told him about the blog when she asked him to take a picture of her painting the blue squares round the windows at the front.

'Can you understand it?'

'Well, half. It's funny. You laugh at my country but also love it. This chap loves it too, I think.'

'Toby and I also stopped being partners many years ago. He's just a friend – whom I seldom see.'

He nodded. 'Here we are.' They parked in front of a smart gallery freshly painted in white and turquoise.

Gabi opened the door. 'Ah, hello, Hooliana, I hope he's taking you to lunch for your help.' She tilted her head towards Josemi and winked at her.

'Better than that – he's taking me to the beach!' Juliana said.

'Okay, but get something savoury from the baker on your way past; there'll be nothing but biscuits and a flask of coffee in his rucksack, you can be sure.'

Josemi grinned and shrugged. 'If she doesn't start shifting paintings, she won't be fed at all. Are you two going to help?'

They unloaded the car and started unwrapping the paintings while Gabi fetched them some sparkling homemade lemonade.

'Mm, this is delicious,' Juliana said. 'I'm going to start making this, rather than pickling my insides with Coke.'

Josemi was still pulling off tape and paper.

Gabi tapped his arm. 'I'll do that. Go and enjoy yourselves before you both do your bit for the Níjar musical community tonight. Where are you taking her?'

'It's got to be Mónsul.'

Playa de Mónsul. Mónsul beach. Perhaps it was that volcanic place with the mountainous sand dune that she blurrily remembered from her last trip here with Mama. Once back in the car, she looked it up on her phone.

'Your dad?' he asked.

'No, I'm looking up Mónsul. I thought it sounded familiar; I think I went there with my mama when I was little. Oh, and it says they filmed a bit of *Indiana Jones and the Last Crusade* there.'

They stopped off and bought some *empanadillas*, then carried on up the hill, passing between two peaks to a caldera valley of red and ochre hues like the one San Rafael sat in. But this one had nothing but *palmitos* and agaves, with just an ancient windmill and a couple of shepherd huts as far as you could see.

'Oh! What an amazing place!'

As they rumbled down the unmade road, he pointed out a long bay of golden sand. '*Playa de los Genoveses*. The first of the wild beaches. All protected by the national park status. And they never get too busy, because once their little car parks fill up, they put a barrier on the road.'

'God, it's like paradise.'

They passed the turning to Genoveses and carried on for some while, passing another windmill and pastures of grass. 'Amazing, these patches of green after the rain,' she said.

'You should see it in the winter.'

'I'd love to.' Kim had told her that daytime winter temperatures here were like a sunny English September but with spring wildflowers; perfect for hilly exploring.

They parked in a post-and-railed area with a couple of other cars and started walking down the hill.

Juliana looked at the sandy cove with its giant volcanic rock in the middle and the dune hill of soft sand to the side. 'I can't believe how well I remember this – I was only seven.'

'And how many beaches would still be exactly the same? It's all thanks to Doña Paquita, an incredible lady who owned all this land and fought to make it a protected reserve after she died. But come on, let's get down there!'

They were soon camped on a blue elephant-design Níjar sheet in the shade of the volcanic rock, but Josemi looked restless and stood up with a cloth bag he'd taken from his rucksack. 'I'm sorry, I have to… scavenge first.'

'At least you do something with your treasures; mine just go in bowls and doorstop buckets.'

He laughed as she stood up to join him with a similar bag, and they wandered along the sand together, bending to examine anything that caught their eyes – mostly pebbles and shells for Juliana, but Josemi's collection included pieces of wood, rope and a couple of wooden ice cream spoons. 'I wish I could resist, but I've made seaside debris pictures since I was a child and I can't stop. As if I haven't enough to do! I should be back finishing a painting right now.'

'Well, we don't have to stay long—'

He touched her arm. 'No, no. It's wonderful to… be able to show you this.'

Her arm tingled where he'd touched her. She couldn't think what to say. They were standing in the gentle waves, the water not seeming so cold anymore. She bent down to feel the water with her sandy hands, and got her dress soaked on one side.

'Here, give me your dress and bag; I can see you want to go in.' He beckoned with his hand, his big eyes so gentle it would be hard to say no to anything he asked.

He felt the light weight of her treasures. 'It's very sandy here; I could show you a beach where the pebbles would make your heart flip.'

She couldn't answer that either. He beckoned again, for the dress. She took hold of the hem and lifted it up – forgetting the couple of buttons at the neck.

'Hooli! Wait!' He chuckled. She could only see pink, but could feel his hands dealing with the buttons, his hands touching her neck. Then she was free of the dress, and stunned by his closeness, stepped back and nearly lost balance.

An arm came around her waist. 'Careful! It's best to go in gradually.'

She could hardly breathe, her body melting despite a cool wave patting her thighs. He looked down at her, said something about the turquoise blue of her bikini, looked back into her eyes… Then turned back to their little camp, her dress over his arm, unbuttoning his shirt.

This side of the volcanic rock, the beach was totally

theirs; even the other side, there was just one couple, right the other end. They could climb the warm, deep sand of the dune, laugh and have lunch together – totally alone. The place was so secluded, so private, that if she were a different kind of girl – and they weren't neighbours – they could also have sex, right there on the blue Níjar cotton. But she sensed she wasn't the only one holding back.

He'd taken his shirt off and was walking back into the sea. She couldn't watch, so she turned and faced the horizon, padded along the soft sand until she was up to her thighs, and dived in. She came up shrieking and laughing, but was soon back in again, swimming on her back and watching him come towards her.

'Hooli! How is it?'

'Cold! But now gorgeous... although maybe only for five minutes.'

He laughed and dived in too, with a grace that made her heart ache. Then he popped up beside her like a sea lion, hair sleeked back. 'Better than last time we were in the water together.'

They swam around for a bit, paddled round the rock pools and then went back to their camp, pulling it over into the sun and soon drying off and warming up again. Josemi produced a flask of over-strong coffee.

'Don't you need a photo of the beach for your blog?' he asked.

'Oh yes.' She took out her phone. 'Uh... A *voicemail* from my dad. Don't you hate voicemails? People too lazy to type.'

He groaned. 'It's a parent thing.'

There was also a message from a Spanish number. 'Oh!'

'What?'

'This chap at Tabernas Studios said he'd contact me if he

found out anything about my mother. I told him I think that's where she died.'

He looked serious. 'Who is he?' he asked quietly.

'Oh… someone who's worked there for years. Used to be an actor I think, now does the horse-and-cart and whatever else needs doing.'

He looked down at the sand, smoothed it with his hand as if wiping out a picture. 'What does he say?'

'He's inviting me to lunch at his home in Tabernas, with his wife… Oh, but he's not sure when, because he's got to do some extra days at work; somebody's off sick, blah, blah… He'll let me know.' She looked up. 'Maybe it won't happen.'

His hand had stopped. She waited for him to say it wasn't a good idea, she didn't know this man, he could be a weirdo – like her father would have done. But he nodded solemnly. 'You should go. Maybe take Kim with you, but go.'

TWELVE
DAY 31

She could see Josemi clattering around on his terrace, pulling the awning out so he could paint outside. She was planning on taking her muesli and tea downstairs, but having decided not to shower until she'd rubbed down and put a first coat on the iron front gate, she had last night's scruffy plait and was wearing her shapeless decorating clothes. As Nanny Martin would have said, she looked quite a sketch. Not that Nanny Martin – or any member of Dad's family – had ever looked a sketch in their lives. She herself was all for comfy, convenient and occasionally cute, but... *Josemi*. This was one of the problems of having a thing for your neighbour; it seriously cramped your lack of style.

She had a word with herself and took her breakfast downstairs anyway. Sitting under the sunshade sipping her tea, she wondered if she and Josemi would go to a beach together again soon. They hadn't gone to the rehearsal together because he'd had to drive there from a meeting with a client, and hadn't been to Café Nido because he'd been asked to stay on and fill in for a singer who couldn't make the rehearsal. Good God, did he *sing* as well?

Her phone buzzed again; she was already getting a lot of comments on the Mónsul beach post. It had been a mistake to use Josemi's picture of her there, even if her bikini was covered up; Toby had called her a beach babe and said how much he wanted to join her there.

Now he'd sent a WhatsApp. *'Who took the photo? We all want to know! Were you on a secret beach with a Spanish hunk?'*

She could have said *yes*, surprise him for once, although she hated the word 'hunk' at the best of times, let alone applied to a quality human like Josemi. She decided to treat it as just another Toby-style rhetorical question.

She put the phone down and moved into the sun for a few minutes, closing her eyes. She really needed to get on with the decorating; she might have two more months, but after about eleven it was just too hot to do it for long, and once the rehearsal schedule – and the heat – stepped up further, there would be very little time. She still had the whole of the lower floor to do. Unsure as to what the added value of this condition was supposed to be, she'd been more than usually meticulous about her preparations, and was becoming intimately acquainted with every corner, nick and bump in the house. If the idea was to make her love the house more, that wasn't possible – but she certainly now couldn't bear the thought of renting it out to people who didn't care about it like she did.

Her phone rang. She'd thought it was on silent, but she must have turned it on again by mistake. *Toby*.

'Hi! How are you?' she asked.

'Good, good.'

When wasn't he? Other than his parents divorcing when he was fifteen, his life had been all good, all golden.

'You didn't answer my question – you've got me all worried,' he added with a chuckle.

Even a few days ago that might have got her heart tapping, but now it was just an unfunny joke. 'I went with my neighbour,' she said, even though Josemi might hear her. 'It helps to have a local guide. My God, you wouldn't believe it – really the most perfect, wild beach in the world, I swear.'

'Ah.'

There was an awkward silence in which she tried to find the words to ask him for the point of this call.

'You know, the more I read about Almería – and your blog of course – the more I think it has much more appeal than the Costa de La Luz.'

'I wouldn't know, I haven't—'

'For my Spanish adventure. I've been looking at a *cortijo* not far from Sorbas. D'you know it?'

Sorbas: on the map, a couple of inches inland from Mojácar. There was even a very wiggly long mountain road to it from Níjar. On the dual carriageway, it might be less than an hour away. 'No, I don't.'

'And there's another near Vera.'

Vera: nearer the sea, on a bit from Mojácar.

'Any chance of you having a look at them for me?'

'What, the towns, or the actual houses?'

'Both!'

'Oh… I don't know, I'm really busy, and how would I know what to look for? It's a very personal thing, a house.'

She could hear Josemi go inside to answer his doorbell.

'I'm confident you'd know what I like. Quiet, genuine. A challenge, but a house that could be done up in three months. Ninety days, like yours.'

'But…'

'I'd trust your judgement even more than my own.'

'Oh.'

'In fact, that pretty much sums up our friendship, doesn't it? You've always understood me better than anyone else I know.'

There were times when his saying this – given the impossibility of being in a relationship with him again – would have been the very best she could hope for. A validation of a unique, special importance in his life.

'Jules?'

'That's—'

'Hooliana!' An urgent-sounding Josemi had appeared at the wall.

'I'm sorry, gotta go, talk to you later,' she said to Toby.

She went over to Josemi.

'I think your dad's here! He came to my front door by mistake.'

'What?'

Her doorbell rang.

'Tall, fair. Like the actor in *Day of the Jackal.*'

'Oh God.'

He squeezed her arm. 'Good luck!'

The doorbell had already rung again; never a patient man, Dad. She went in and upstairs to the front door.

'Juliana…' He came in, kissed her cheek and put his hands on her shoulders. 'I had to come, darling. We need to talk.'

She glanced down: no flight bag, so he wasn't expecting to spend the night in the house.

'We're here for just one night. In San José. Olivia dropped me and has gone to check us in.'

She offered him a drink and, although he was flushed and sweaty in his smart long-sleeved shirt, he wanted tea. 'Toast with it?'

'Please.'

He used the bathroom while she made him breakfast. She couldn't believe he'd flown all the way here to explain himself, not even having a mini-break while he was about it. Not that she wanted him hanging around.

They sat down at the table and he started to eat, seemed more himself. He looked around. 'So, this is the room you've decorated?'

'Yes. And I've done all the front. Except the gate – which I was about to do when you turned up.' She watched him spread jam and listened to him go on about how the Spanish grow oranges but don't understand what marmalade is about. 'Why *have* you turned up?'

'As I said, we need to talk. You haven't been answering my—'

'*You* need to talk. Why did it take you two years to tell me Mama had died?'

He swallowed and took a gulp of tea. 'Let me finish this and we'll… sit on the sofa.'

She couldn't watch him. She went over to the kitchen area and wiped a surface, changed a drying-up towel. Drank a glass of sparkling water. She wondered what she'd do if he'd just come here to repeat the same old nonsense.

When she saw him go over to the sofa, she went through and sat on the one opposite him. 'Well?'

He looked down at the floor, put his hands together as if in prayer, and started up about her having been such a fragile child, and so young.

'Oh no-no-no. That's what you told Arturo, and no doubt what you told yourself. Come on. A delay of a few days, while you were in shock yourself. Maybe until we were back home. But *two years*?'

'But you were—'

'Fragile? You thought me tough enough to be put through all those West End *Annie* auditions, for heaven's sake! If you're not going to tell me the real reason, you may as well go now.'

He looked up. For once looking rabbit-in-the-headlights. Scriptless.

'Dad, I need the truth now. Whatever it is. It can't be worse than you caring so little about what I'd feel, and what Mama would have wanted, that you said *nothing at all*.'

'It wasn't that I didn't care! I did everything I could to reassure you, made presents and letters from her, telling you she loved you, which I know she—'

'Yes. But nothing could take away the fact – the *lie* – that she'd left me. When *were* you going to tell me? If Olivia hadn't come along—'

'Olivia made me... stronger.'

This wasn't going anywhere. She breathed out heavily and shook her head. 'And that's what you've flown all the way here to tell me? Really?' She started to get up. 'This isn't—'

'Okay.' He sat forward, put a hand to his head. 'Maybe... This is going to sound dreadful... It *was* dreadful, but... I think I was angry at Antoñita. The way she went off every year back to Spain, never saying what she was doing, irritated if I—'

'She was going back to see her parents and brother! What's wrong with that?'

'Nothing, of course. But she'd started wanting to go over for a winter visit too.'

'Because of her *asthma*, you told me.'

'Maybe that too, but really... The truth is, she was gradually leaving me. And...' He put a hand to his mouth. 'If I'm really honest, I think I wanted you to see this... betrayal. Feel what I was feeling. You so adored her, couldn't be bothered with me! It was terribly wrong, I know. It was *me* who was fragile and unbalanced. Only when Olivia came along and I had someone I—'

'Wanted to marry.'

'Someone I could really talk to, and who made me see that I had to put things right. And yes, I did want to marry her – not only for myself, but for you. Give you a new mum – even though you always refused to call her that.'

'So you're saying… you took out your hurt feelings on your own daughter.'

'It's… complicated. But yes. If you want the awful truth.' He looked up at her, with tears in his eyes. 'I'm so, so sorry.'

'And afterwards? You were never going to tell me that Mum died rather than leaving me?'

'I *thought* about it, but… as time passed, and we had our new family, I didn't want to… risk something coming between us.'

It occurred to her that, instinctively, she'd always felt something had come between them. Something about the way he'd never seemed to want to talk about Mama.

'I never realised how much damage I'd done.' He got out a handkerchief and wiped his eyes, then got up and came and sat next to her on the sofa.

She didn't know how she could be sitting there dry-eyed. 'And I'm sorry that… it's going to take some time to get used to all this. At least you've told me; I'm grateful for that.'

He put a hand on hers and smiled. 'You're not fragile at all. You've come out here and got stuck in with the decorating, started a new blog, and agreed to be in a show. Brilliant. And… I'm sure you'll be rewarded.'

'Rewarded?'

'Well, Arturo's obviously thinking of leaving the house to you in his will, isn't he? Just imagine, your own little holiday home. Renting it out for most of the summer. You could afford to be choosier about the work you take. Or find a better place in Ealing. Good for you, darling!'

'Oh, I don't know about that – he has his son Miguel to leave it to. But hopefully he'll let me come and stay here again.'

'The village has certainly come up in the world.'

'I suppose you haven't been here since Mama's funeral.'

'No.' He looked at her, then lowered his voice. 'Maybe we could go and say hello to her, in the cemetery.'

Her eyes finally pricked with tears. 'I'd like that.' And *she*'d like that. 'Then afterwards… would you like to go to the beach?'

'Yes! Olivia's probably already there; the hotel's right on it. She's looking forward to seeing you. Then maybe I could drop you back while us oldies have a siesta, and come and pick you up later for dinner.'

After dinner, or maybe before, he'd be in no state to drive; he'd end up sticking in her in a taxi. 'Oh no, I'll drive over, it's easier.'

'Of course! I'd forgotten Arturo lent you a car too. Spanish house, Spanish car, you're really getting into it, aren't you—'

The phone pealed in her pocket. It was an unnamed Spanish number, but the code looked familiar.

'*Hola?*'

Some slow but rough Spanish came back down the phone at her. Francisco. Fran. She asked him to repeat what he said, but he went into English.

'I have day. Tuesday, the eight-teen June. Is far, sorry, but okay?'

'Er… yes.'

'Three-clock. Is good, kitchen and ve-gables? I no' know food ingleesh.'

'I think you mean – *quieres decir* – chicken and vegetables.' She tried not to laugh.

'Yes, yes, *this*,' he said. Then said in Spanish that he and his wife would tell her what she wanted to know, and were looking forward to talking about old times.

She thanked him and ended the call.

'Who was that?' Dad asked. 'Are you going on a dinner date?'

'No! It's this… couple I met at Fort Tabernas Studios. They've invited me to lunch. They've got lots of photos of the old days; he's worked there for years. Should be—'

His face had gone deadly serious. 'Don't go, Juliana. I know you wanted to see where Mama worked, but don't go back. The place never did Antoñita any good, and you don't know these people. Keep away.'

'But it's quite safe. Uncle Arturo—'

'Don't listen to Arturo on this; he likes to play games. Promise me you won't go back there.'

THIRTEEN
DAY 38

'If it wasn't for *croquetas*, we'd probably never have met!' Kim said, as the waiter brought a plate of spinach-and-cheese ones, with chips on the side and a heaped plate of mixed salad for them to share.

They were sitting on a late-sun terrace overlooking Níjar's small main square – a place of elegant cast-iron benches surrounded by trees with pale bark and neatly trimmed pom-pom heads, old shuttered houses and an ancient church.

'Wasn't it *pisto*?' Juliana said with a laugh. 'Anyway, here I am just over a month later and you've got me considering a total life change.'

Kim swallowed her mouthful of chips and shook her head. 'You were already thinking of it. Almost as soon as you got here, I reckon! Anyway, what did you think?'

She'd just spent three hours at Kim's English school, which was set in a converted old one-storey house just off the main street, within walking distance of both the drama centre and the cactus garden.

'Well...' She was a bit overwhelmed: tired after her

efforts to take it all in, excited about the possibilities. She grinned at Kim, breathed out heavily.

'You were *brilliant*. God, and what a treat to have an assistant. Maybe before you were ready to have your own class in the next-door room, I could increase the class size if you were with me.'

Juliana couldn't stop smiling. She looked over at the little boys playing in the square. 'I thought I might find the kids hard-going, but they were such fun. Hm… apart from that naughty little…'

'Ah, he's new, I'll soon get him sorted out!'

'And you think I'd be able to earn enough to…'

'To rent a little flat in San José? Yes. Especially with a few private adult students too – and your blog, when it starts earning for you. San Rafael's more expensive, now it's become this art hub – but wouldn't your uncle let you stay on for a low rent?'

Hopefully, she'd be there rent-free in her own home, but she mustn't rely on that. 'I don't know. But either way it looks possible – if I can get the money together to do the course in Granada.'

'Maybe your dad would help out. You said he was very encouraging on his whirlwind trip.'

She hadn't wanted to darken the day with telling Kim the real reason for her dad's visit. 'True.' She took another mouthful of croquette. 'Mm, and I'd be working in the town with the most gorgeous *croquetas* – and pancakes – ever!'

'Oh yes, speaking of pancakes and gorgeousness – how's it going with Josemi? Why didn't you go to Café Nido with him again last night? In fact, how come you never drive to the rehearsals together?'

'One of us is always coming from somewhere else. Yesterday it was me, going to that big *ferretería* in Campohermoso for more black metal paint; that terrace gate is going to take *gallons*, and it's the only shop that…'

'What?' Kim raised her eyes to the heavens. 'Honestly, you two workaholics and your painting materials. Maybe you could combine *those* trips. Have you really not seen each other since your romantic beach day?'

'Kim! Beach *morning*, and it was lovely… but not romantic.' Well, not for him anyway. 'Of course I've seen him – he's the other side of my wall. Oh, and we had a coffee and orange *bizcocho* celebration – and a peach for Chica – for the wooden rail he's put up on the bank. You know, next to the little path I made between our houses, to stop any more accidents.'

'Jesus *wept*!' Kim's big blue eyes glanced skywards again, then she wiped her mouth, put down the napkin and wagged a finger. 'Look, tell him you're planning to try living here, so you stop looking like those two English girlfriends who both buggered off back to Blighty, and just see how quickly he jumps your bones!'

Juliana winced. 'Kim! *Please*. It's not like that.'

Kim laughed. 'Okay, okay…'

'Sooner or later I'll tell him about it, but I've still got to think things through. Maybe I should watch the adult classes too, see how I feel about dealing with stressy exam candidates.'

'Yes, you should.' She looked at her watch then back at Juliana. 'I know, how about this for a plan: leave your car here, come to the San José expat bar with me, stay the night at mine, and then come back here tomorrow morning for the adult classes?'

'Oh! Well…' She looked in her bag. 'Yup! Got some contact lenses. Thanks, we're on.'

They were soon on the half-hour drive to San José, the low

sun throwing a golden hue over the reddish earth, shadows setting the rounded hills and the craggy mountains behind them into dramatic relief. Like one of Josemi's paintings, Juliana realised, but she wasn't going to mention that now she'd finally managed to steer the conversation away from him and back to the six levels of language proficiency and the Cambridge exams.

'Wow.'

'Stunning, isn't it,' Kim said. 'But not everyone's cup of tea – thank God!'

'And then there's the beaches... The whole of Cabo de Gata is one huge, heavenly secret.'

'I know. I was like you when I came out... what, six years ago now... Couldn't think of a reason to go back. Well, my mum of course, but two years later, when I bought the school, I persuaded her to come and join me.'

'How *is* your mum? Not well again, poor thing.'

'Oh, it's nothing really. This always happens around now. Gets too hot for her, and she doesn't drink enough water. She goes back to England for July and August, and I join her for a few weeks. England's wonderful again when it becomes a place to visit rather than live in.'

'I can imagine. Never mind the folks, I'd have to go back every now and then for a fix of Thai food – the Spanish don't seem to have—'

'Ah, but they've *started* to. I'll happily show you two great restaurants. Carlito's not keen, so I'm always looking for someone to go with. Okay, they're both about an hour's drive, but—'

'Well, that clinches it, doesn't it?' Juliana said with a laugh.

They were driving through a tiny village not far from San José.

'Pozo de Los Frailes. The monks' well. Expats who want a garden or are a bit strapped rent or buy here. Great value for money – if you don't mind driving to the beach. Mind, you probably have to do that in San Rafael.'

'No, I walk. It's about twenty minutes, but flat. I'm thinking of renting a bike; Josemi whizzes there and back in no time on his.'

'Oh yes, likes his morning swim, I remember Beth saying.'

'Beth?'

'His last English girlfriend. She was always moaning that he had no time for her, with his swimming, painting and music. But she was a bit… needy, having a long holiday at her sister's basically, didn't have a life here. Not like you, with your decorating, blogging, kids' play, show, flute, beachcombing… and plans to change career.'

Resisting the temptation to ask more about Beth, Juliana concentrated on the glimpses of sunset beach between the houses on the narrow road they were going down. 'Ooh!' She pointed to a little church on the other side. 'Is that the one you were telling me about? Where you and Carlito will get married?'

'Yes! And then we'll all just cross the road to the restaurant overlooking the beach.'

'How lovely.'

Kim parked near a bar with a blue octopus painted on the front. They got out of the car into a warm, salty dusk with a light breeze. 'Don't worry, there's an even more beautiful church for you in San Rafael.'

'Kim!' She laughed but put up a stop-sign hand. 'Please. Josemi and I may well end up being just really good mates. And… it's important for me to completely separate my feelings about him from my excitement about the idea of living here.'

Kim put both thumbs up. 'Too right, girl. Absolutely. Sorry I've got carried away. But… before I shut up, I've got to say one thing: that's exactly the kind of independent spirit that Josemi needs in a woman.' She did a zip motion over her mouth and gave Juliana a quick hug. 'Right. Let's see who's here tonight.'

Apparently, there were only about ten English people living in the area, and only some of those ever turned up on any given Friday; it wasn't going to be the packed Irish pub Juliana had imagined. That night, among the Spanish locals, there was a friendly couple in their fifties who had a holiday rental business; a retired gentleman who lived in the next village and his quiet daughter who'd come out to visit for a few weeks; and a pretty girl about her age called 'Minty' – short for Araminta – who ran an organic tea room with her partner. From the old boy she learnt about a lovely outdoor municipal pool in Níjar, the rental business couple knew of a good stationery shop for printer stuff, and Minty told her how *mosto* comes with *tapas* because, although it's non-alcoholic, it's made of grapes. She shared the newly increased opening hours of the San Rafael botanical garden.

'So you're here for three months, doing up your uncle's house in San Rafael?' Minty asked. Kim had admitted to telling people here about her.

'Yes. It's hard work, but I'm having an amazing time.'

'I love San Rafael. Whereabouts is the house?' Minty had a make-up free, arty-hippy air about her; Juliana could just imagine her there.

'Calle del Campo, shortly before it turns into a goat paddock.'

'Oh, you must know Josemi.'

'He's my neighbour.'

The rental agency woman leaned over with a grin. 'And saviour. Didn't he scoop you out of the raging *rambla*?'

'Okay yes.' She looked over at her friend. 'Kim!'

Kim put a hand to her face. 'I'm sorry. Come on, I *had* to tell that story.'

'What a hero!' Minty said. 'He's a good guy. Just not an ideal boyfriend.'

Juliana's heart skipped a beat. Could Minty be one of the English ex-girlfriends? But minutes later everyone was saying hello to a cropped-haired equally pretty girl who was linking arms with Minty; it was soon apparent that the partner Minty had spoken about was a girl.

Kim took her arm and whispered to her. 'She's Beth's sister. Beth was spending the summer here before starting a new interior design job in London. Needy. Really nothing more to say.'

Minty came back to Juliana, with a puzzled look on her face. 'Hang on, your uncle's place... isn't he selling it to Josemi?'

'What? No!' she said rather too quickly. 'Well, not that I know of.'

'Because it would be weird to do it up when he and Gabi were planning to slice it in half. The idea was to expand Josemi's studio on the top level and convert your lower floor to a holiday apartment they could rent out.'

'When was this?' Juliana managed. Why on earth hadn't Josemi ever mentioned this?

'Last summer. I think they were quite serious about it. My sister Beth had a fling with Josemi, but you can imagine, what with his painting and everything else, as well as all the meetings about buying the house...'

'Well they've got the gallery here in San José now, haven't they,' Kim said.

'No, that was already changing hands. Ah well, I suppose your uncle must have changed his mind.'

Juliana took out her buzzing phone. 'Talk of the devil! Setting up our next lunch.'

'Juliana my dear, I hope all is well and that you've recovered from the shock visit from your father. I'm so relieved that you managed to make some kind of peace.

'I'm afraid I need to move our lunch, I'm going away for a bit. Could you do the following week, Tuesday the 18th?'

Juliana put down her drink and tapped out a reply.

'Hello, I'm fine, thanks. I'm sorry, I can't do the 18th – I'm having lunch with one of the cowboys (and his wife) from Tabernas! He has worked there for years and has old photos to show me.'

'What is his name?'

She found Fran's first message, then went back to Arturo's WhatsApp. *'Francisco Montoya.'*

A minute passed. *'Why didn't you tell me this before?'*

'I asked him if anyone remembered a woman dying at the studios back in 1996. I didn't for a minute think he'd get back to me. There's not much point in me going, now I know the truth, but—'

The phone rang in her hand. Arturo. She made a sign to Kim that she was taking the call outside, and went out onto the road and crossed over to where a little gap between the houses let her see the moon and the village lights quivering in the dark water below.

'Sorry, I was in the bar with Kim's expat group. I couldn't hear.'

'Wonderful. How lucky that you've found such a lovely English friend here.'

'Well, not just a friend; some time in the autumn, she's probably going to be my boss! She'd like to take me on as a teacher in her English school, if I do the month's course in Granada.'

'Hooliana! Oh…' There was sigh, a little cough. 'That's fantastic! I did wonder if that would occur to you. I want to hear all about it. But listen, I get back on the 16th. Let's have lunch on the 17th.'

'Let me just check, I've got a feeling…' She flicked to her diary and came back to him. 'I've got to be in Níjar at four o'clock for a rehearsal on the Monday. How about—'

'We'll just have to have English-time lunch then. Anyway, I was going to suggest coming to the house, so that will save you time.'

'Okay!'

'I don't want you to cook. I know you're busy – and not very good! I'll come at about eleven. See if you can book somewhere for one o'clock.'

'Most of them seem to close on Mondays. How about Wednesday?'

'No.' He cleared his throat. 'It's important I see you before… your visit to Fran.'

'Oh. Should I not go? I could think of a reason to—'

'*No.*'

Was that, no she shouldn't go, or no she shouldn't cancel? 'Dad said I shouldn't go, but he always sees Tabernas as some awful place that never did Mama any good.'

Arturo gave a chuckle. Dad's talk about Arturo playing games came to mind.

'Hooliana, you have nothing to fear. You absolutely *must* visit Fran and hear more about those times. I will see you on the 17th. Now you go back and enjoy yourself with your new friends, and don't worry.'

FOURTEEN

DAY 43

Juliana looked out from the restaurant's terrace over the shockingly green undulations of the Vera golf course, and took another mouthful of *panang* curry. She couldn't shake the feeling of having sold out, cheated, like some *I'm a Celebrity, Get Me Out of Here!* contestant sneaking off the set for a burger in a glitzy hotel.

'Everything okay?' the smiley English waitress asked.

'Oh… *really* lovely, thanks.' She ordered another *mosto*, without fear of it coming with *tapas* here.

Another phone buzz from Toby.

'*Wait*,' she typed. '*Sorting out the photos.*'

She'd already sent him a video of each house, along with her basic impressions of Sorbas ('*stunning, but houses hanging off cliffs not my thing*') and Vera ('*appealing and useful old town of yellow-ochre – like the earth round* here'). She'd also reminded him this was ridiculous, she was no surveyor, and anyway she was probably biased by Vera's proximity to the sea and Thai food.

He buzzed some more, but sod him, she thought, he could wait. She finished the *panang*, ordered a coconut sorbet and went back to the honey-gold photos of old Vera town and the snaps of the Vera farmhouse she'd taken during the agent's tour. It was perfect for Toby here: he could blog about doing up his crumbly Spanish house in its own valley – but somebody had already done the roof and sorted out the services; he could make out he was brutally rural, with whatever 90,000 square metres was of orange trees and hillside – but continue to have someone else farm it and be within fifteen minutes of fine dining.

'*I've just offered the asking price,*' floated over her screen.

'*What?! I haven't even sent all the photos yet!*' He was crazy. But then, he probably had the entire amount just sitting in his bank account. '*This is going to cost you a few Thai lunches, btw.*'

'*Absolutely! Calling you.*'

'*NO,*' she quickly sent. '*Not cool, only two couples in the restaurant here with me.*'

'*Aw, okay. Thanks SO much Jules. This is going to be great. We're going to have so much fun xxxxxxxx.*'

We? By the time he got out here – August at the earliest – she would either be in England waiting the ninety days before she can come back into the country, or in Granada with a student visa.

———

'Hi, Mama, I saw these in Vera.' Juliana put some yellow plastic flowers in each of Mama's plaque-vases, mixing them with last week's red ones. 'Oh Gawd, you're looking rather loudly patriotic…' She looked down the row to see if any of the others had such a bright display – and noticed Dolores in front of her family plaque. She turned back to Mama. 'Jose-mi's mother,' she whispered. 'Come to think of it, probably only a few years behind you at the school here. Well, assuming *she* grew up in San Rafael, as well as her son. Wish me luck, I'm going to offer her a lift.'

She got into the oven-like car, started the engine and put on the air con. Waited a while. It was going to look odd if she sat there for too long, but then Dolores came out and started slowly walking up the hill. She drove over to her and put the window down.

'Hello, would you like a…' What the hell was a 'lift' in Spanish? 'To come with me?'

Dolores's black eyes widened.

'To your home?' Juliana added.

'I can walk.'

'I know. But maybe your new little dog would like to see you sooner.' Josemi had recently taken her to the dog rescue centre.

A nod, possibly a slight smile, and Dolores went over to the passenger's side and opened the door. Juliana moved her bag to the back, the printouts to the front shelf.

'Thank you,' Dolores said, sitting down next to her with her hands together.

They drove off. Juliana tried to form a dog question, but something about this woman made her Spanish evaporate.

Dolores, meanwhile, must have been eyeballing the papers in front of her. 'You are moving to Vera?' You'd think she'd be delighted to get rid of the *inglesa*, but she looked oddly insulted; there was no pleasing the Miserable Bag.

'No, no. I was looking on behalf of an English friend.'

'*She* wants to move there?'

'He wants a project. To renovate a house.'

'He is your boyfriend?'

Aha, keeping her occupied and away from her son. Afraid not, m'dear. 'A friend. We were at school together.' Well, Saturday morning Stageclub, but she didn't need to get into that.

'He will come before you go?'

'I don't know. But anyway, I'll be coming back. I love it here.'

Dolores fixed her with those big fiery eyes. Surprisingly, there was definitely a little smile this time. 'I'm sure your mother is pleased.'

'Yes, I think she probably is,' Juliana replied, taken aback. 'Here we are.' She pulled up outside Dolores's house. 'What are you calling your little dog?'

'Checho.'

'Oh. Isn't that going to be a bit confusing, with *Chica*?'

'That's what Josemi says, but... I don't care,' she said with a defiant smile. She opened the door and turned to her. 'Thank you, Hooliana.'

Josemi came out of his front door, crossed the road to exchange some words with his mother, and then came to her window. 'That was a long time at the *ferretería*.'

She'd forgotten she'd asked him if he wanted anything from there before she set off – only to get a reply from the estate agent and suddenly change her plans. 'I've been exploring.'

'Come over to mine when you're ready; I've got a favour to ask.'

'What flavour will the favour-asking come with?' she asked. Josemi had recently bought a smoothie maker.

'Er... banana and kiwi? And more besides.'

'Okay, give me five minutes.'

She parked the car, went in at the terrace level and washed her face. Brushed her ponytail and considered releasing it – but why would anyone do that in this heat? Sprayed a tiny bit of perfume. He probably just wanted her to do his terrace gate with her leftover metal paint – something she'd been going to offer to do anyway, to thank him for the wooden rail on the bank.

'Hi,' she said as he opened the door. She felt a little silly to have turned up at the front entrance for some reason, like a date. But then she looked around in amazement: the room had turned into a fully stocked gallery, complete with board partitions maximising hanging area and dividing the room into little corridors. All set off by some relaxing Latin music. 'Oh my God!' She started looking round, but he put a hand on her back.

'Not now, you'll have plenty of time…' he said, and directed her to the partly folded dining table pushed back against the window, where two smoothies waited for them next to a notebook and a laptop.

She sat down, her knees bumping his warm bare leg, the imprint of his hand still tingling her back. She gulped down some of the smoothie. 'Mm. So, what can I do for you?'

'I've got to go to Madrid. Isabel, my ex, has asked me to exhibit somewhere at the last moment. I think the other artist let her down. Or probably she let *him* down, and he's decided to leave her in a mess. Anyway, like an idiot I've agreed to fill in, even though I'm unlikely to get a lot out of this.' He shrugged.

Juliana chuckled. 'Probably more than I'll get out of having spent the day checking out two farmhouses for Toby, *my* ex!' She picked up her drink and clinked glasses. 'Here's to the put-upon nice guys.'

He laughed. 'Toby wants to buy a house? *Here*?'

'Near Vera. He's already put in an offer. But it's just a project to him: do it up, write about it – who knows, maybe a TV programme – then sell it on or visit a couple of times a year and pay someone to look after it. It's not a real thing like *my* hou—'

He looked up. Maybe he was about to ask the inheritance question, like Toby and Dad had done.

'Well, it *feels* like my house… because I'm sure I'll come back.'

'Of *course* you will,' he said with a broad smile that melted her heart.

Tell him you're planning to live here, and just see how quickly he… jumps your bones. Yes, Kim, but supposing he didn't, just listened to her plans with neighbourly interest? She wasn't ready for that. Nor was she quite ready for anything to happen – especially with him about to spend time with his ex in Madrid. 'So, what's the favour I can do you?'

'I'm supposed to be opening the gallery this Saturday. It's on the Rafaelarte group posters everywhere, on my website… My artist friends are all busy, and Rodri, my assistant, has a wedding.'

'So your only choice is your neighbour, a person who knows absolutely nothing about art?'

'You have *feeling* for it – that's all you need. Along with a few things I'll show you. Honestly, you'll be great. Saturday ten until two, then five until nine. Eight hours, plus maybe another hour after closing… I'll make it a hundred euros, plus ten per cent commission on paintings sold.'

'Hang on, hang on, that's probably too much – and I haven't said yes yet!'

He patted her arm. 'If you're worried about your decorating, I'll throw in a couple of hours' help with that next week, if you need it.' He pointed to her glass. 'Another?'

How could she ever say no to him? Especially today: a warmth in those eyes, hair all shiny mahogany with those gold sunned-on bits, his defined and curly-haired limbs just inches away. 'Yes... No. First show me what I have to do.'

He grinned and got up. 'Come.'

He took her to the first of the paintings by the door and pointed to a white card with bold black handwriting giving a title, the technique, size and price. 'Everything they need to know is there,' he said in slow Spanish, making sure she understood everything. 'I'll have finished all the cards before I leave tomorrow evening. They get ten per cent discount if they buy two or more paintings. You'll be busy, so try and get them to just reserve, collecting and paying after I get back on Monday night – there are red stickers to put on cards of sold paintings. Don't forget, do it right then, or they'll kill you later. If they insist on taking the paintings away...' He showed her where the wrapping material and cash box were, and went over the card machine and his house alarm an embarrassing number of times.

'Just call me if you're not sure about anything. Ah yes, I realised today that we should have each other's numbers.' They got out their phones and exchanged them, like a couple meeting at a party. The Latin salsa diva was singing about a kiss.

'Who's this?' Juliana asked.

'Gloria Estefan, from my mother's playlist – keeps her happy when she's helping out round the house. Cheesy, but I seem to have let it roll.'

'I like it. Now let me wander round, see if I think of anything I need to ask.' Beaches – translucent or densely gloomy, some she recognised, some she was still to discover.

The local mountains in glorious late-afternoon sun. The Alcazaba and other ancient buildings in Almería. More beaches, but in watercolours. A series on the square in Níjar where she and Kim had discussed him… And a little corner, near the front door, of five 'mixed media' pictures using rope, netting, splinters of wood, buttons, shells… to make fantastical boats. A gorgeous one, with the wooden spoons she saw him collect, already had a red sticker. 'Someone's got good taste.'

'She has indeed,' he said. 'Let me show you how to note who buys what. See these numbers on the cards?'

He beckoned her back to the table. 'It'll be easier for you to just write down the sales and I'll transfer to the spreadsheet later.' He opened the book and showed her the columns.

'She hasn't paid?' Juliana asked, looking at the entry matching the boat picture with the red spot.

'No, and she isn't going to. Or at least she *will*, but by…'

'Oh my God – it says "Juliana". Thank you! I love it!' With anybody else, she'd have done the Spanish two-kiss thank you, immediately, but she stood back instead; you'd think he was surrounded by some kind of worryingly unpredictable magnetic field. All she could do was grin uncontrollably. 'I'm going to put it up in my bedroom… so I can see from the bed…' she blabbered. 'I'm sure Arturo won't mind. Actually, he's coming over for lunch on Monday.'

'Ah. That's a shame. If it was Tuesday I'd be back and could say hello.'

Gloria was singing about how it hurts to lose her chap, a sad but irresistibly lilting song that seemed familiar… 'Oh, I *know* this one. They used to play it in my beginner's salsa class.'

'Ha, yes! Maybe in mine too.'

'You did salsa?'

'When I was about fifteen. My friend and I thought we'd have a good choice of girls, but...' He shrugged.

'It's all a bit weird, isn't it? Lovely music, but why would I want to spend the evening being pushed and pulled around like a train carriage?'

He laughed. 'And yet there was that step called *tell him no*. What was that all about?'

'I've *no* idea!'

'I mean...' He stood up and took her hand to pull her up with him. 'You start off just going backwards and forwards...'

'Can you remember it?'

'Er...' He drew her towards him and put his other hand on her back, between her shoulders. As usual, he smelled of paint and something like that rosemary bush on the bank. 'Think I had to push your hand to make you step back while I...' They stepped back and forth in time to the music, with Gloria singing about the madness when she felt her chap was near. 'And then the girl turns...'

'Yay!' she said, giving a twirl.

'And now you *tell me no*.'

'Coming up, if I can.'

'Don't we each go off to one side or something?' he asked, continuing the basic step.

'Okay, let's try, five, six, seven...' They both moved with ludicrous conviction and collided, Juliana almost falling over onto the table. 'Oops!'

Having been pulled away from harm with more of a *rambla*-saving than a salsa-lead, Juliana found herself bumped against his warm chest and held there.

'Ah, Hooli, Hooli...' he said into her hair as he hugged her tighter. Rocked her from side to side to the music, sending her into a daze as she put her arms round his warm, T-shirted body. He moved even closer, his whole body against her... His hand came to her face. He looked into her eyes, down at her lips... Then sighed and hugged her again, but more loosely, kissing the top of head: a hug of *apology*. From a friendly neighbour. Who would be mad enough to have a thing with a neighbour?

'My all-time favourite neighbour,' he said, as if reading her mind.

She pulled away, adrift and hurt, but trying to smile. 'Chica would be mortified if she heard that,' she said. For something to do, she handed him her empty glass.

He put it back on the table and took her hands in his. 'It's not an easy time for you. There are things you... have to work through.'

'What d'you mean?'

'I couldn't help it, and I've been waiting for a moment to tell you... I overheard some of the argument with your dad. Enough to know he lied to you about when your mother died.'

'Oh. I did wonder. Sorry. Lot of shouting.'

'And that he doesn't want you to go to Tabernas and learn... more about her life. Are you still going? Did the horse-and-cart man there confirm a meeting?'

'Yes. I'm having lunch with him and his wife on Tuesday.'

He nodded. 'This is good.'

'Right. But it's okay, my father and I have sort of made peace.'

'Yes, so you told me.'

'I'm okay, really I am.' He smiled and kissed her hands. Opened his mouth to say something, but changed his mind.

'Hooli... I'm not going anywhere, okay?'

She bit her lip. There was something odd about this she couldn't put her finger on.

'Okay?' he asked again.

Gloria had stopped singing about how much it would hurt to lose her man. If there was some reason he felt they had to wait, better that than lose each other. She smiled and nodded.

FIFTEEN

DAY 48

'And you're sure you don't mind the sky blue in the bathroom?' Juliana asked.

'Of course not!' Arturo said. 'Same colour as your dress.' He plucked at the shoulder of it. 'Not from the market this time.'

'No. From the boutique on the corner. Thought I'd have a couple that didn't have to be hand-washed.'

He nodded, always glad to have his advice taken, the broad grin pushing his cheeks into little folds. How come he looked so much older than Dad, despite the healthier living? Maybe it was the sun. But he tired more easily too; a tour of the house and terrace had left him breathless and needing the support of a dining room chair.

'The house was never meant to stay the same,' he said. 'I love Josemi's boat in the bedroom, all your extra Níjar rugs and cushions – and pebbles everywhere. And as for your decorating… you're a fine workman. Work*woman*. I can see it's been a labour of love for you.' He looked around the room again. 'I can't tell you how happy it makes me to see all this.'

'Good!' After hours of anxiously whizzing round the house before his arrival, she was happy and relieved. 'The bedrooms won't be difficult, but I was going to ask you about the stairs: would it go against the conditions if Josemi did the ceiling and top of the walls for me? With his height and this long roller thing he's got, he says—'

'No, let him do that. After all, it's part payment for your splendid efforts in his gallery on Saturday!'

She refilled his glass with sparkling water. 'And how are you, Uncle? No more "old man's troubles", or whatever you called them?'

'No, no. I'm fine.' He took an olive from the little Níjar bowl. 'All's well.'

'Did Miguel and Susana come down for the weekend?' His son was so busy with his fashion business and golf that he often cancelled at the last moment.

'They did. We had a lovely swim, and then when we were having lunch they told me they're finally having a baby!'

'Oh! That's wonderful!' She got up and kissed him, gave his bony shoulders a hug. 'You'll be a fabulous grandpa.'

He smiled and nodded. Rather sadly, she thought; Madrid was a long way away.

Then he looked at his watch, even though they still had about two hours before their lunch reservation down the road. 'So, Hooliana. Let's go through the conditions. Do you still have that printout?'

'Oh... yes.' She took it out of a drawer in the dresser, put it on the table in front of them and moved her chair nearer.

He produced a fountain pen out of the pressed linen jacket he'd declined to take off.

Number one, about the decorating and household things,

was awarded only half a tick – but also a cartoon jug, boat, rug and smiley face that made her giggle.

At the next point, about the neighbours, his pen hovered and spotted like a teacher marking homework. 'How's it going with Dolores?'

'Terrific!' she said with a grin, but raising her eyes to the heavens. He wasn't amused. They were back in Raf tomato territory; it was okay for him to be light-hearted about the conditions, but she was supposed to take them deadly seriously. 'Well, *better*. I gave her a lift from the cemetery and managed to hold a conversation. Oh, and I introduced myself to her little new dog. I'm trying.'

'What did you talk about in the car?'

'Um… The dog, the house I'd seen for Toby…'

'He's buying a house here?' He was frowning; he'd always been critical about how much time and heartache she'd wasted on Toby.

'Near Vera. It's just a three-month project, really.'

He still seemed perturbed; Toby was not in the plan. He looked down at the page of conditions, as if he was about to add one, but then put the top back on his fountain pen and fixed her with his serious, downturned eyes. 'Hooliana, you do remember that the conditions list for your having this house is our secret, don't you?'

She took a breath. 'Of course.'

'Good,' he said, but seemed to be waiting for her to go on.

She refilled her juice glass with some sparkling water and drank it. Put down the glass. Smiled at him, and then looked down at the conditions sheet, as if willing him to continue.

'But you told Toby.'

'No!' she said, meeting his eyes for a moment.

He raised his eyebrows.

She looked down at the table again. It was unbearable to have a lie between them – and anyway, she had a feeling he somehow already knew. '*Yes.*'

He breathed out heavily, with a little growl. Turned his head away.

'I didn't show him the list, just said that I had some things to do for the house and a few things that were good for me... for it to be mine. I didn't *mean* to tell him, it was... He promised never to mention it again.'

He sighed. 'I'm very disappointed, Hooliana.'

'I'm so, so sorry, Uncle. The minute I said it, I hated myself for it...' she said, her voice catching.

He put his hand over hers. 'Okay, okay. I don't want tears over this. And I appreciate that you've now told me the truth. But listen, about this Toby. Have you asked yourself why he's so interested? I take it he pressed it out of you.'

She shrugged.

'Maybe you should look at how Toby is towards you these days, and work out why he so... needs to know where you're going to be.'

'Well, by the time he's in Vera, I'll be in England sorting myself out – and then should be studying in Granada for four weeks to get my English teacher qualification.'

'And you're definitely going to work for your friend Kim?'

'As long as I pass the course, yes.'

He clapped his hands down on the table. 'This is *splendid*. Of *course* you'll pass it, a bright girl like you. Have you booked it already?'

She thought she'd have enough for the accommodation, but she'd been working up to asking Dad to loan her the course fees. 'Er... *about* to.'

'*Please*, let me pay for this. Email me the details of the course – because I'd also love to see where you'll be. What a fine place to study! I'll put the money in your account so you can book this.'

She was overcome and started thanking him profusely, but he put up a stop hand. 'My pleasure. Really. But now let's get back to this, since it's now even more important that the house becomes yours.'

He put half a tick by the getting-on-with-neighbours condition and then a series of ticks down the page until number nine. 'Beaches?'

'There are a lot, aren't there? I think I've got nine more to do.'

'Only those that are *easily* accessible; no scrambling down steep hills.'

'Like Playa del Barronal?'

'You did that?'

'With Kim.'

'Hooliana. We don't want any broken legs. Especially at the moment.'

'Okay.'

His pen went down to the last condition, the one about photos and diaries. 'Make sure you keep a record of everything. Even the weekly visits to the cemetery, a friendly message from Dolores...'

What? He trusted her, didn't he? Not for the first time, she was struck by the lunacy of all this. And as for that last one... She imagined kidnapping the yappy little dog until Dolores agreed to message her a super-friendly invitation to lunch – and had to put a hand over her mouth.

'I'm serious, my dear. I want you to fulfil all these conditions; I want you to have the house.'

'I'm... sure I can.' She still had six weeks to go, for heaven's sake. 'I *will*. I feel at home here.'

'I'm sure your mama is pleased.'

'That's exactly what Dolores said.'

'Really? She said that?'

'She did. Would they have known each other, Mama and Dolores?'

He took a sip of water. 'Yes, at school.'

'But they weren't ever friends.'

'No. Dolores was three or four years younger.'

Exhausted after the appraisal – especially the bit about Toby – she was in need of a cup of sugared tea and went off to make one. The 'meeting' part of the visit was done; they could just enjoy each other's company now. They'd have a nice lunch at El Minero, and then she'd insist on driving him back to Almería rather than let him get another taxi.

'What would you like to do now? Sit in the shade of the terrace? Josemi's away but I could show you his gall—'

He was still poring over the sheet. She thought they'd been through everything, but his pen was at number four – unmarked, she now noticed. Tabernas.

She sat down with her tea. 'Well, we could have a tick for that one,' she said. 'All done and documented. In fact, now I know what happened to Mama there, I don't really *need* to have lunch with Fran. I've—'

He looked up, eyes wide. 'Yes, you do.' He'd done a half tick next to it – no cartoon cowboy hat or anything.

'I suppose it would be rude, ungrateful… But it's not as if he himself would have known Mama; he's not old enough.'

'Ha! Haven't you heard about ageless cowboys? He's definitely old enough.'

'You *know* him?'

'I was there with Antoñita for the first month of the filming, remember. Everybody knew the stuntmen. Especially the ladies.'

'Oh…'

'Not that Fran was a Don Juan. More of a *horses'* man.'

'Are you trying to tell me that... he was Mama's "angel"?'

He looked at her steadily. 'Possibly. I do remember them striking up a rapport, right from the start. You're finding that difficult to believe, aren't you. Just because he couldn't speak English well, and was spouting the place's history as instructed, you thought he was a bit of a... *monkey.*'

Oh dear. That was *exactly* what she'd thought, helped by the simian agility – despite the limp – with which he'd leapt off and onto the front of the cart. 'I was tired, still at the stage where all-day Spanish was wearing me out...' She thought for a moment. 'But if he *was* her "angel", why didn't he say he knew the woman who died?'

'Because he probably suspected you were her daughter, and needed time to decide whether to talk to you or not.'

'I don't see why; I mean, their relationship was before she met Dad. And it's not like he did anything wrong; from that letter, it sounds like she didn't have the courage to make a go of it after all, and left him.'

'Yes. But... there's one more letter. I wanted you to have it before you see Fran. I think your mama would want you to read it, now you're ready.'

Her heart started to tap, even though she didn't know what she was afraid of. From his pocket, he produced a faded blue airmail letter as thin as a petal. She looked at the address box.

'To Teresa again. Didn't she write to *you*?'

'Of course. But to my lasting regret, she never shared anything about this love affair with me. Probably because I sided with my parents about her first boyfriend. I hope I'm making amends by helping her daughter understand what she thought *I* wouldn't understand. Read it, my dear.'

Flat 2, 43 Eden Road,
Ealing,
London W5.
Sunday, 29th September 1968

My dear Teresita,

I'm sorry to take so long to write to you. I hope you and Bernardo are well and enjoying preparations for the wedding – which I'm so sad to have to miss. At least my friend Ana María is planning to drive back down next summer, so I'll come and see you in your new home then. It's a shame we couldn't see each other before I left, but it all happened very quickly, and I was in a terrible state. As you will have guessed, I lost my angel.

*By July, he and I had come become inseparable, meeting at the studios but also the apartment, once I had it to myself. We had to keep our affair secret – or **tried** to – but I really believed we'd be together properly one day, and thought he did too. Then there was the accident.*

I was working in the costume room, humming along to 'Jill's Theme', when there was an odd commotion outside. I went over to the main square to see what was going on. They could have been filming a circling crowd, the music soared on – but nobody was manning the cameras. I got through and saw a man, motionless on his back. The doctor was giving an injection, so I knew he was alive. Then I saw his hat on the sand… My heart stopped. A woman was wailing, holding his hand to her lips. Beautiful, as he'd told me. Beautiful, and not a bad woman – just not the wife for him. But their parents had thought otherwise.

Then there was muttering in the crowd, and people parted to let me through. Even though I couldn't move. Hearing them, the woman looked up – her flamenco dancer's fiery gaze landing on me. As if I'd done this to him. She could be right; maybe he'd lost his concentration, after our tearful meeting earlier. It was my fault.

I started having a bad attack, but didn't care. I just wanted to be *with him. My angel. But **not** my angel. Ana María must have fetched my inhaler, or I wouldn't be writing this. She took me back to the apartment and called a doctor. I got better. But I never went back to the studios.*

I couldn't send a message to him and risk hurting that woman more, so I waited to hear from him. Days. Weeks. Whether he couldn't, or his silence was the message, I'll never know. All I do know is, when Ana María managed to find out that they thought he'd walk again, it was both a relief and a reprieve. Time to do the right thing. To get a passport, pack my things, move away to start a new life.

It's nearly two months now, and still not a day goes past without me thinking of him. But life here – apart from the weather – has been so kind to me. I share a house with Ana María and two lovely English girls who laugh at our English but also help us with it. I'm already getting plenty of work – not just as an extra, but as a dressmaker. And the handsome drama student son of the boss of Bowen Martin Casting has just asked me out on a second cinema date. He's called Edward, like the littlest English prince. I think he suspects I'm heartbroken, but he's kind and tactful enough not to ask. A real gentleman.

I look forward to hearing all about the wedding, and your life in Almería. Until next summer!

With much love,
Antoñita

Juliana put the letter down. 'So… they never saw each other again? Although hopefully she soon fell as much in love with Dad.'

'We can't be sure. Of either of those things.'

'There were no more letters?'

'There were, but these were the only two Bernardo found.'

'And Teresa didn't talk to him about any of this?'

'No. But…' He paused, sipped some water.

'What?'

'He did tell me one thing. Antoñita would visit them most summers. On one occasion, the two friends went off to stay in San José for a few days, but Teresa came back early, saying she missed her son. Bernardo said there was something odd about it; he thought Teresa and Antoñita had had an argument.' He wiped a handkerchief over his forehead. 'I asked him to see if he could work out when that was, and he got back to me a few days later. It was when Fran could have been involved in the Tabernas Studios filming at Mónsul beach for *Indiana Jones and the Last Crusade*. San José was so tiny then, Antoñita and Fran could easily have come across each other. Or maybe… they even planned it. But Hooliana, this is the thing: it was May, 1988.' He looked at her carefully.

'So… *twenty* years later? Or d'you think they'd kept in touch, and saw each other every year she went to Spain? Oh dear, poor Dad.'

'We may never know the answer to that. Maybe I'm wrong, and they never saw each other again at all. But *May* 1988, Hooliana. If they did meet up in San José…'

Juliana's heart thudded, leaving her giddy. 'Oh God, you mean…'

'Yes. We can't discount the possibility that Fran is your biological father.'

She shook her head. 'No! I can't believe Mama would do that.'

'She loved her "angel",' Arturo said. 'And probably thought there was no risk, believing herself to be infertile.'

'What? Dad's always said they left it very late to have children, so only had me. He never said… Is that what Mama told you?'

'Yes. She was… irregular in her cycle, so they always assumed it was her problem. I suggested having tests, but I don't think they ever did.'

'And then, she comes back from Spain, and eight months later I arrive… But no! He can't be my father, he just *can't*!' She got up from the table and went over to the window, crossed her arms over her thumping heart, looked out over the mountain – towards San José, she realised. Where – *maybe* – she was conceived. Fathered by this funny little cowboy man she could barely understand. Wouldn't she have felt some connection with him when they met? She'd felt the complete opposite.

Arturo stood up and put his hands on her shoulders. 'I'm sorry, my dear, I know it's a lot to take in. And of course, I could be wrong…'

She turned to him. The downturned eyes looked at her steadily. She sensed he didn't for a moment believe he could be wrong.

'Does *he* know, d'you think?' she asked.

'Fran? Maybe. Your dad? He may well have *wondered*… and you said he told you he felt Antoñita was "gradually leaving him".'

'Uh… What do I do? Fran doesn't… *feel* like my father.'

'Of course not. Your *dad* is still your father, in all the important ways. And you don't *have* to do anything. But I couldn't let you go to lunch with Fran and not let you know as much as I know.'

She nodded, starting to feel rather wobbly.

He put his arms round her and kissed the top of her head. 'Talking of lunch, I think you need some. Apart from everything else, you need strength for *Annie* later.'

They walked over to El Minero and took the shady table she'd reserved in the corner of the terrace. She couldn't seem to focus on the menu, so Arturo took over and ordered lots of little things for them to *picar* at.

She was trying to remember how Fran had been with her – but he'd treated her like any other tourist, even once she was asking about the woman who died there. Either he had no idea he had a daughter, was a better actor than she imagined, or simply didn't care. No, he must care, or he wouldn't have invited her...

Arturo patted her hand. 'Remember he's your mama's "angel"; he can't be that bad.'

'True.'

'Maybe take your mind off it for a moment, or you'll never get any food down.' He jerked his head at something across the road. 'Like, check out the full awfulness of those two paintings over there.'

Juliana looked over at the posters on the houses the other side of the road. It was more of those ghastly phallic-obsessed beach paintings. 'Oh I know... God, she's taking over the whole village with them. Call that art?'

'I call that the work of a woman who's either never seen the full male anatomy, or has a fantasy about three-legged men.'

Juliana spluttered in her drink. 'Oh God! Either way, she's up for a massive disappointment. And honestly, how long does it take to do that? Half an hour? Josemi seems to take *days* to do a painting – probably for the same money.'

'Ah, Josemi. Now *there*'s an artist. And how are you two getting along?'

'Well, I haven't seen his third leg, if that's what you mean.'

It was Arturo's turned to splutter his drink. 'Juliana! Is this suitable uncle–niece conversation? I think not!' he said, but laughed and patted her hand again. 'Give it time. I was friends with Rosita for about a year before she was my girl-friend, working together, having a laugh… never thought she'd take me seriously.'

'Oh. Well maybe there's hope then.'

Their little dishes arrived. Along with the beautiful salad featuring the Raf tomato and a little plate of finely cut chips, there were *croquetas*, crispy aubergine fritters with honey, triangles of semi-cured goat's cheese, the *chipirones* she surprised herself by liking last time, and some sardines on a bed of lettuce that she suspected she was going to have to try. They went round the dishes, each assigning them marks out of ten for enjoyment.

He put a little bit of boneless sardine on her plate.

She took a mouthful. 'Oh my God… Salty sea delicious-ness. That's a ten!'

'One step at a time, we'll have you eating all Spanish food,' Arturo said, smiling.

'Now I'm all Spanish. Well… *maybe*.' The news came back to her with a bump, along with the jittery realisation that this time tomorrow she'd be at Fran's.

He took her hand and squeezed it. 'Listen, Juliana. Even if both of these fathers score a five, one thing is for certain: the two of them together have created a ten, okay?'

She leant over and kissed his cheek. Neither of them would ever be the father he was to her.

SIXTEEN

DAY 49

Fran, her father. *Papá*. Maybe. No, almost certainly. The straight dark hair, the wide face – that had had both of them cast as Native Americans. Why hadn't she seen it? You'd think the genes in every cell of her body would have buzzed at the proximity of his. Try as she might, she couldn't – and never had been able to, she realised – find any characteristics linking her to Dad. Maybe he felt the same, and yes, Mama's pregnancy after twenty years must have made him wonder… Poor Dad. At least he ended up happily remarried, with two more girls who might just as well have been his and were everything he could have hoped for.

How would Fran feel about *her*? Perhaps he and his wife already had a houseful of offspring, and this was a reluctant duty for them. She wasn't sure she'd *want* him to feel anything about her. She didn't need another father – that would always be Dad, for better or worse. Recently, better. But if Fran *was* her biological father, she felt she must, for Mama's sake, make some connection with him.

Two more hours until she had to leave. She started to feel

jittery and impossibly in need of another pee – otherwise known as feeling nervous. She hadn't had much sleep, but she'd managed to eat, been for a swim, put out a spotted dress and decided it was too on-the-nose 'I'm now half *gitana*' – as the Spanish Romani are called. Instead she laid out one of the market ones with some small horses on it. She smiled to herself; it was impossible not to see the funny side, as she often tended to, when she was nervy – much to Arturo's irritation, bless him. Kim had called last night, and at the end of a long chat they'd started listing the benefits of having Fran's genes – the gift of eternal youth, discounted Fort Tabernas tickets, and *The Importance of Being Spanish* for gaining amorous confidence from her twice-English-bitten neighbour.

She decided to cool down and relax with a bit of watering. First her own, and then down the bank and up to Josemi's terrace, where he'd had Juan Luis's brother take away some of the low wall and put in a gate.

As soon as she banged the gate shut there was bleating from the other side of the fence. She opened the hinged plank and there was Chica, pushing her head through into Juliana's hand for a scratch.

'Aw, you're missing Josemi, aren't you? But you won't like it over here today, I'm about to do the watering.' In the corner of the field, she could see the rest of the goats going over to Diego. 'Looks like you're off for a walk and a munch anyway. Have fun!'

She patted her and closed the fence, went over to the tap – and jumped. 'Oh! Didn't see you there!'

Dolores was standing at the terrace door with a tub full of wet sheets. She seemed to come over once a week to help with Josemi's housework; Kim had warned her about Spanish mums spoiling their sons.

'I can do that,' Dolores said, pointing to the hose.

'I really don't mind.' The little dog came up to her. She didn't know anything about dogs, but he was quite cute with his brown-and-white calf colours. 'Hello, Chicho!'

'Checho,' she was corrected.

'Is he…' She couldn't think of a word for settled. 'Calm now?' When he wasn't yapping, that was.

'Yes.'

Jesus, there certainly wasn't going to be a diary-worthy friendship photo this morning. She hurried through the pots and prepared a smile with which to turn around and say goodbye, but was surprised to see Dolores sitting on a chair, her solid form for once rather slumped.

'Are you all right? Can I get you some water?'

'My blood pressure measured low this morning. This happens sometimes. I just need water and coffee and biscuits.' She started to heave herself up.

'No, no. Let me.'

She sat down again, heavily. 'Black, two sugars.'

Juliana came back with them as quickly as she could; she didn't want Josemi's mother conking out on her. Dolores was definitely peaky, but *Dios mío* could she tuck away five biscuits in a hurry. 'You went to the doctor this morning?'

'No. I measure it myself, with a little machine,' she said, tapping her arm, then added cold water to the coffee and downed it.

'Does he… need to know?'

'Sometimes it's high and I take the tablet, sometimes low and I do this. I know my heart better than any doctor.' She pushed the bowl with the last biscuit towards Juliana.

'Good for you. My dad's so bad about his high blood pressure. He complains about the tablets and won't always take them, refuses to use the monitor his wife bought him, and then had to go to casualty because he was feeling poorly when it went really high.'

Dolores shook her head. 'Very bad. He is covering the sun with a finger.'

'Ha! I like that. In English we say "burying your head in the sand", like a... er... that huge black bird in Africa that doesn't fly?'

Dolores gave her the Spanish word for ostrich. 'This is a good expression!'

Juliana looked at her watch. 'Oh, I should be going... Are you sure you're—'

'Dressed like *that*?' Dolores pointed up and down at Juliana's T-shirt and loose cotton shorts.

How did she know where she was going? Her clothes would be fine for an appointment with a dentist or hair-dresser. 'No, I'll change.'

'You need a nice colourful dress. Go! I don't want to make you late with my silly heart.'

Juliana stood up, feeling a little light-headed herself.

'And Hooliana... thank you, dear.'

Back in her house, Juliana was pleased she'd made a little step forward in neighbourliness for the condition, but she also really wanted to get on better with Josemi's much-loved mother. *Josemi*. She wondered for the umpteenth time what he'd meant by saying he 'wasn't going anywhere'. Was he waiting for her to get used to the facts about her mother's death and meet Fran to talk about it more? Or did he mean he'd be there to pick up the pieces as a good friend, and was wisely avoiding having an affair with a now possibly long-term neighbour?

She put the second dress on; did her hair up, down, and then somewhere in between. In the car, she switched between laid-back blues and energising reggae. Luckily there was only one route. It turned out that meeting your biological father – or *possibly* biological father – felt like it was all about worrying indecision. Was he or not, would they like each other, and did she even want to be doing this? Certainly Dad hadn't wanted her to. But his covering-the-sun-with-a-finger head-in-the-sand way of doing things wasn't hers – well, maybe it *had* been, but not anymore.

———

It was a small apartment building not far from the main square, with wooden balconies that wouldn't have looked too out of place at Fort Tabernas. She parked up next to what looked like Fran's battered silver car. Inside, it was surprisingly neat, with a cute cactus air freshener, a leather CD box, and a Fort Tabernas magnet sticking what looked like an order for a cake to the dashboard.

She was a quarter of an hour early. The sun was bearing down and – contrary to her cinema-gleaned knowledge of deserts – there was hardly a breath of wind. She opened her car door, thinking she'd try and calm her nerves with a stroll around in the shade for ten minutes, but a woman called from above. 'Hooliana?'

God. She looked up.

'I thought it was you!' she shouted down, waving at her from a pink-and-red-flowered second-floor balcony. 'Come up, don't wait down there in the heat.'

At the top of two flights of worn wooden stairs, the woman was waiting for her at the door to the apartment. She'd imagined Fran's wife as the usual, square-bodied *señora* who, once grey enough, turned herself blonde, but was greeted by an attractive sixty-something in a fitted sleeveless dress over her trim figure. 'Welcome! I'm Josefa, Fran's wife.'

She kissed Juliana firmly on each cheek. 'So, you found us all right?' she asked in nicely deliberate Spanish. 'Come through. I've made some lemonade. Would you like that? Or you could have, let's see…'

'Lemonade would be great.' She followed her through a small but tidily cluttered living room on to the shaded balcony.

'Fran's just getting changed; he agreed to go in to work to cover for someone, but told them they'd have to manage without him between two and five.'

'Ah!' Juliana started to feel a little more relaxed; bubbly Josefa would clearly be filling in the gaps if conversation faltered between her and Fran.

The table was laid for three, complete with a little vase of flowers clipped from the multitude of pots. The balcony looked over towards the ancient church and the hill with its old yellow-brick fortress. 'This is lovely. Can I just use your loo?'

'Of course.' She showed her where it was, although it wasn't difficult to work out.

It was the smallest of rooms ever, but spotlessly clean and horse-themed with china ornaments under the mirror and framed photos all over the walls. Including, she noticed with a mixture of excitement and concern, some with a sweet-faced riding boy at various ages. A half-brother?

Back on the balcony, Josefa poured lemonade into a glass for her. 'If you need more sugar, help yourself.'

'I see you like horses,' Juliana said, pointing to some rather cheesy cushions.

'Yes! How did you know to wear that dress?' Josefa asked with a laugh.

'I don't know!'

'It's how Fran and I met. I had to sell a horse after struggling for years after my first husband died. Fran turned up to buy him, and seeing how upset my little Joaquín was – he was about eleven at the time – said we were welcome to visit as often as we liked. So we visited the horse – and his kind, handsome owner!'

'Oh, that's wonderful.' A *step*brother, and Fran had taken him on and been a father to him.

'And here we are, nineteen years on!' She tilted her head towards the corner of the room.

Fran was there. He'd been letting Josefa finish her story, or maybe watching Juliana. He was smiling. Even changed out of work clothes, he was still a cowboy – tight jeans and a short-sleeved check shirt – but gone was the hat covering his high-cheekboned face; his long dark hair was dustless and wet from a shower; and his eyes – almond-shaped like Juliana's – didn't have to squint in the sun. It wasn't difficult to imagine how both Josefa and her mama might have been taken with him as a younger man.

'Hooliana.' He came over, and she stood up so he could – after a funny little hesitation – do the Spanish two-kiss. He was *chiquito*, as Arturo would say – only a little taller than her – and smelt of dark wood and, despite the shower, horse. 'I'm so glad you could come.'

They sat down. 'Are you here with your family?' Josefa asked.

'Er… well I don't have my *own* family… My father, stepmother and stepsisters are in England. The only family here is my uncle Arturo, my mother's brother. I'm here for another six weeks painting his summer house in San Rafael.'

Fran and Josefa exchanged a possibly slightly concerned look.

'I'm afraid I lied at the studios, Fran; the woman who died there was my mother, Antoñita.'

He nodded. 'And I lied too. You took me by surprise… I knew her. In fact, she was my first real love,' he said, speaking much more slowly than she remembered, and looking a lot less sure of himself.

Juliana gasped. 'So you were her "angel"?'

They look puzzled.

'Sorry… she called you that when she wrote about you to her friend; seems like she didn't want to give your name.'

He shook his head. 'That's nice, but I *wasn't* an angel. I should explain…' He sipped some lemonade. 'I was married, very young – our *gitano* families wanted to bring rival riding schools together. María Carmen danced flamenco, but when we moved here it was harder for her to get work. Then she was caught driving when drunk, lost her driving licence – and stopped working at all. She wanted babies, but they didn't come. I tried to interest her in working for the studios, but she didn't want to be one of a group of dancers or barmaids. She started lying around reading magazines and drinking with friends during the day, picking arguments when I came home – but didn't want to divorce. Then along came happy little film-mad horse-loving Antoñita…'

Josefa put a hand over his and looked at Juliana. 'It's easy to forget how young they were. Twenty-two and your mother only eighteen…' She picked up an old photo album with an envelope marking a page. 'We got these out to show you. Look, here she is… and here…'

Mama, looking happy and not much more than a child, with other laughing girls and women in Wild West clothes. Another group shot, including a smiling Claudia Cardinale, in which Mama and a handsome young Fran were caught exchanging a little look. 'Oh! These are lovely.'

'We'll make you some copies,' Fran said.

'Thank you.' She took some pistachios and tried to think

how to phrase her next question. 'So… she just turned up at the studios after twenty-eight years? She… didn't realise you were still working there?' she put to Fran.

Fran scratched his forehead. 'It was quite a surprise, I can tell you.'

'And… you were still married to María Carmen?'

'Yes. She'd calmed down a bit, was helping out at a new dance school. But somebody must have told her they saw Antoñita at the studios and after that…' He shook his head, and Josefa looked down at the table. 'But you mustn't blame your mother; she had every right to show her daughter where she once worked.'

'My only memories of the place – before she disappeared – are a pretty white horse, a lizard on a belt, and Mama telling somebody I was seven and a half. And then we went to the dressing-up place and she started feeling ill…'

He shook his head, the smile fading. 'You must be very close to your dad, being left together like that.'

'Well… we're very different.'

'Oh?' He leant forward with interest – like you might expect, if he were her biological father – but with a surprisingly sinking heart that it seemed less likely now.

'He co-owns a casting agency, used to be an actor himself. He's all about the *show*. He finds my reluctance to get up on a stage very trying.'

'So what work do you do in England?'

'Well, I've been a film and TV extra since I was a child… but I prefer writing blogs.' It looked like they might not know what those were. 'And I'm now going to study to teach English here.'

They both broke out in smiles and congratulations, and over the promised chicken and vegetables lunch they talked about where she might live, how different the villages were to what her mother would have known.

Afterwards, Josefa waved her out of the kitchen. 'No, no. Let Fran drive you over to see Tito – the horse that brought us together. When you come back, the cake will be ready.'

Fran had already picked up his keys; this seemed to have been planned.

In the car, she learnt that Josefa ran a small cake-making business, and that Joaquín had inherited her talents and was a chef in a good hotel in Granada. Meanwhile, Juliana looked at his hands on the steering wheel and wondered if she'd inherited his hypermobile thumb. Maybe she'd ask him outright at the field. There was a glimmer of hope when he offered to lend her the Ketama CD in the car, suggesting he wanted them to meet again.

Watching him petting and talking fondly to gentle mahogany-brown Tito reminded her of Josemi and Chica – the sweetness, the laughable jealousy of an animal. She'd swung round to being suddenly sure this kind, simian cowboy *was* her father, and wanted with all her heart for him to admit it.

He turned to her, eyes squinting in the sun and impossible to read. He'd been talking about Tito, but she hadn't been able to listen. He muttered something to himself and laughed. 'This is ridiculous.'

It was indeed, and she'd gone so speechless that she couldn't even ask what he meant.

'Do you have something you want to ask me?'

Apart from the obvious, something else was playing on her mind. 'What happened with María Carmen after she found out my mother had seen you at the studios that day? You said she… changed.'

He looked surprised, then put a hand on her arm. 'Don't

think badly of your mother. María Carmen… was a very, very difficult person – for herself and others.'

'*Was*?'

'She went to live with her sister's family in Almería… and a year later she was dead. After a house fire she caused when she'd been drinking, taking two more souls with her.'

'Oh no, how *awful*… I'm so sorry.'

'It was terrible. But I don't want you to dwell on that now. It's not the time. And… I think you have something else you want to ask.'

'Er…' She put a hand to her mouth. It was that stupid nervy laughing thing. But he was no better, looking down and grinning, kicking a weed with his cowboy boot.

'Are you?' she asked quietly.

He looked up. 'Can't you tell?' He took her hand. 'We even have the same thumb!'

'I know!'

'Can I… finally give my daughter a hug? Last time you just wanted to pick the lizards off my belt.'

'Oh… yes!'

He flung his arms round her and squeezed, very different to the restrained fatherly hug she was used to. 'I never thought… I had no way of finding you, just hoped one day you'd…' he said into her hair, and then held her by the shoulders and looked into her eyes. 'I can't believe this!'

'Well, we've got my Uncle Arturo to thank; you didn't give *anything* away at the studios.'

'What? Couldn't you see I nearly passed out when you said June 1996?'

'No!'

They stared at each other in tearful smiling amazement until it was too much and they had to have another hug.

'We have to go back and tell Josefa,' he said, letting go. 'We were worried that you might not want to believe that...'

'I was worried *you* wouldn't!'

They got back into the car and drove back – and seeing Josefa on the balcony waiting for their return, Fran made a series of jolly beeps with the car horn. Fran and Josefa were exchanging *olé*s for a moment, and then Fran took Juliana's hand and they run up the stairs to yet more hugs and tears all round.

The flat was filled with a warm scent of lemon, and harmonious flamenco-pop Ketama was playing softly in the background.

'So... cake I think!' Josefa said, drying her eyes. 'You two sit down and I'll bring it through. I bought English tea to go with it, and Fran, you promised you'd give it another try.'

'How can I not – with an English daughter.'

They sat down and held hands, laughing at the similarity of them. Juliana's favourite track 'Problema' came on, sounding soothing rather than sad today.

'I understand how you are English even though Spanish. Edward has raised a fine daughter and will always be your *Papá*. I don't want to make problems for you. Does he have any idea?'

'I don't know. I'll have to tell him, of course but...' It wasn't the time to explain to Fran why she and her dad weren't ready for another upset in their relationship at the moment. 'I'll tell him when I go back to England.'

'*When* do you go back?' Josefa asked with concern, bringing in a large tray.

'End of July, not for another six weeks or so. Then I'm back in October to start work.'

'Ah *good*!' they both said.

'Ooh, this looks gorgeous,' Juliana said, looking at the beautifully lemon-and-almond decorated slice on her plate.

'We want to start catching up,' Fran said. 'Although when you have time, of course…'

They talked about further visits, a first riding lesson for Juliana on patient old Tito, meeting their son Joaquín when he next came down, a swim in the Tabernas Studios' pool… All they had to do now was find a time when Fran wasn't working and Juliana wasn't rehearsing the show.

'And… maybe we can come to that?' Fran asked. 'Only if it's not a problem.'

'Why would it be a problem? Of course you can come!'

SEVENTEEN

DAY 50

She turned over in bed and reached for her phone. It was amazing: this time yesterday, she'd felt both nervous and irritated at the prospect of seeing Fran; but now she was smiling at last night's text from his wife saying that the little hole of sadness in Fran's heart after being introduced to his seven-year-old daughter that day had finally been filled. Josefa had gone on to thank her for something else: Fran had finally agreed to ask to go part-time at the studios, to give himself more time for the family... which now included Juliana. Then there was the happy response from Arturo, using nearly as many emojis – now she'd shown him how to use them – as Kim did in her messages.

She padded to the bathroom and then upstairs, where she decided that another piece of Josefa's divinely tangy lemon cake would be perfect for breakfast. Next to her on the table was the Ketama CD Fran had insisted on lending her; she'd decided to leave explaining the wonders of Spotify – along with the concept of blogs – for another day. Which would hopefully be soon.

Washing up her plate and mug, she looked over at Mama's plastic flower collection. She'd wanted to go to the cemetery as soon as she got back, but had noticed Dolores setting off in that direction. Out of the kitchen window she could now see Dolores on her way to the supermarket with her shopping trolley bag, but stopping to chat with one of her friends; now was the moment.

She took a lightning shower, grabbed some plastic flowers and a notepad, and decided to take the car to save time.

There was just one old man inside, as far as she could see, and he was several rows along. She approached Dolores's family plaque, heart beating hard. Her parents, her brother... and *María Carmen*. Just as she'd remembered. The night before, a website had showed María Carmen was the most popular Spanish baby girl's name in the 1940s; it could be a coincidence. But yes... Dolores's sister María Carmen had died just a year after Mama, as Fran's María Carmen had – and with two others: Dolores's husband, Manuel, and twelve-year-old daughter, Cristina. What had Juan Luis the boiler man said? The only house fire in the area that he could remember was caused by a drunk woman smoking in bed. That woman was María Carmen: Fran's estranged wife. Dolores's sister. And Josemi's aunt.

It turned out that the mere fact that María Carmen's old rival Antoñita had turned up – and *hadn't* ended up childless, as she had – was enough to set her on a downhill path to tragedy. Heaven knows what María Carmen would have done if she'd found out that the stranded half-English girl was in fact Fran's; she was so unstable, he hadn't dared admit it.

Juliana didn't need that notebook; there was nothing on this plaque that she could forget, nothing further she had to confirm – other than how much this could affect her friendship, let alone any possible romantic relationship, with Josemi.

She moved along to Mama. 'I don't blame you, and nobody should,' she said, remembering how Fran had insisted on this. 'Apparently, you didn't even know he'd still be there.'

Arranging the flowers – all romantic red – she turned her mind back to Fran and Josefa and smiled. 'I've met your angel. I feel monstrous for discounting him at the studios. His English is awful, his technology stuck in the 1980s, but he's funny and kind and… has such an understanding of how others are feeling. Seems you don't always need lots of education to be wise. And Josefa is adorable, and lovely about you.'

She put a finger to Mama's photo. After a lifetime of being told she was just like her mother, she now had a reason for her flatter hair, her broader face… maybe her gymnastic ability at school, as the daughter of an ex-stuntman. Josefa had said they had the same cheeky grin.

A memory came to her of Dad polishing the glass over the photo with his handkerchief. 'Obviously I'll tell Dad – but I'll leave it until I'm back in England. My only problem is Josemi. Shall I talk to him about it? Or d'you think he and Dolores have already guessed Fran is my father, from how I look? It certainly explains the way they were both so odd when they first met me, questioning my Englishness.'

Juliana saw Arturo's downturned eyes in Mama's. 'Yes, I'll talk to Arturo about it.' One of the roses had flopped over, so she straightened it to be proud and tall. 'Don't worry, I'll get myself together.'

She went back to the car, and remembered going back to it the day before, with Fran saying 'a little at a time, okay? Much to talk about! Much to *think* about – but not now, okay, because you must drive carefully. And then rest; this is wonderful, but tiring!'

He was right. Even after a long night's sleep, she was somehow still exhausted. She decided to take the day off – from both decorating and Josemi – and made a plan: a swim at the café-backed beach of Agua Amarga that Josemi didn't like; a leisurely lunch there with her book; come back for a siesta and then take a stroll round the botanical garden.

Her phone buzzed. A WhatsApp from Josemi. '*The couple who bought the four Mónsul paintings just came to collect them and told me how brilliant you were. Thank you again!!! I could come and paint that stairwell at about six tonight, if you like.*'

'*Thank you, but I'm busy today*,' she sent off before she knew it – and with a tell-tale lack of emojis. What was the matter with her?

He stayed *online*, as if pondering how to take this, and then disappeared.

Coming up their road, she saw him in front of his house chatting with Elise and introducing her to Gabi. She changed her plan and swerved into a side road, making for the botanical gardens.

The entrance was through an elegant terracotta-coloured building that used to be something important in the village's mining days, but now had rooms of geological, fauna and flora displays; a central courtyard where – along with the amphitheatre across the road – summer concerts were soon due to start; and the best loos in town.

Reception was unmanned, you just had to grab a guide from under a stone if you wanted one. Everybody she knew loved it – even if the labelling was sometimes confusing, and you could see many of the plants just growing wild on the hill the other side of the pumped stream border. It went on and on, so you could wander aimlessly along the network of smooth-stone paths, taking in the scents of thyme, rosemary and scorched earth, not caring too much about the names of anything, hardly seeing anybody else.

Except, possibly, Ben. The English gardener. Nobody would have looked twice at him back in horticultural college in soggy Sussex, but here he'd become a golden, wiry charm of a chap, and – according to Elise – was being passed around the village girls like a bag of sweets. He'd invited Juliana out for a drink, but she'd declined; he was just the kind of three-monther (if you were lucky) that she was determined to avoid these days. Besides, his appeal paled – literally – compared to Josemi's. But he was fun to exchange a few English words with, and there was nothing wrong with appreciating, from one of the many shaded benches, the shapely brown legs coming out of his Noddy-like shorts.

'Juliana. How are you doing? Finished that decorating and up for some socialising yet?'

'Uh, it's never-ending, and now my show rehearsals are stepping up.'

He leant on a spade, Noddy legs artfully displayed. 'Oh yes, I must come and see you in that. Who are you in it?'

'A flute! I'm just in the orchestra. But yes, do – it's in a good cause – money goes towards subsidising music, dance and drama lessons for people in the area who can't afford them.' She pointed to the newly tidied up area with the giant cacti and started walking towards it. 'Looks good. *You* did this?' They had a joke that he tended to make out *he'd* done everything, although he was actually one of five gardeners.

'Well of course!'

She walked through the huge Mickey-Mouse-eared cacti, aloes like bunches of swords and agaves with serrated tongues, then sat down on a new bench under the Washingtonia to enjoy the view over the gardens and down to the sea.

Ben came over again.

'Can you take a photo of me for my blog?' she asked him. She was going to need something to say, and it was good to promote the gardens. She handed him the phone, but one of the other gardeners came over and took it from him, and the next moment Ben was next to her, his damp arm round her shoulders.

'It's purring!' the Spanish gardener said, handing it back to her.

'Ah, thanks.' It was Arturo. She got up and walked through the shade of the palmed area to be on her own.

'Hooliana! How are you doing?' he said. 'You must still be in shock!'

'Yes! But oh, he and his wife Josefa were *so* lovely.'

'Ah... I told you the "angel" couldn't be too bad. Had he and Antoñita kept in contact?'

'No. The meeting in San José *was* by chance, and he said he didn't hear from her again until she turned up at Tabernas that day with me.'

'Or so he says.'

'Well, he seems a very... open person, so I believe him. And if he's not telling quite everything, it's his and Mama's secret and that's okay too.'

'Ha – yes, exactly. I'm so glad, my dear. I was so worried he'd deny it – but then, who wouldn't want to have you as a daughter?'

'And... I also know about María Carmen.'

'Ah.'

Was that all he could say? 'And the fire. Josemi's father and—'

'Yes.'

'I suppose Josemi and Dolores have guessed I'm Fran's daughter.'

'From the moment they saw you, I imagine.'

'Then...' Then why didn't he tell her? Why was she always the last to bloody know everything? In that wobble of a day, she was tempted to snap her phone shut rather than hear the usual stuff about being ready for things, but she'd told Mama she'd ask for his advice.

'So what do I do about Josemi?'

'You... ride it out. If I didn't think you could cope, I would never have set you this challenge. But I suggest you don't talk about it with Josemi or Dolores until you've had time to absorb things.'

'That's what I'm doing. I'm relaxing – hiding – in the botanical gardens.'

'That place has restorative powers.'

'I wish you could join me here some time. I could take you for lunch at this new place that's opened up near the bridge.'

'I'd love that but... I've got to go away again.'

'Oh?'

'Business stuff, helping Miguel... But we should get together soon. I want to hear all about your day with the "angel".'

'Okay. Speak soon.'

After another hour of absorbing things, she went back to the house, crept around getting changed and putting her bag together, opened the front door – and found Josemi there, hand forward as if about to ring the bell.

'Just checking you're okay.'

'I'm fine,' she said, forcing a smile.

He looked at her bag with the octopus towel in it. 'Off to the beach?'

'Just for a bit. Agua Amarga.'

'That's a long way for a bit.'

'I'm… doing a blog on it. Well, not *on* it, but…'

He put his head on one side and studied her. 'Are you sure you're okay? You seem a bit… flustered. How did it go at Tabernas?'

Beyond him, she could see Dolores looking over. She invited him in and closed the door. 'Fine. D'you want a drink?'

She fixed him a Coke, although that might not have been what he asked for.

'*That* looks nice,' he said, spotting the rest of Josefa's lemon cake slices in the fridge.

She considered offering him a bit and then seeing if he'd still eat it when he knew it had come from Fran's.

'So what happened? Did he know your mother?' he asked.

'Yes. They both worked on *Once Upon a Time in the West*. He had some amazing photos of a whole group of them on the set.'

He nodded. He was in paint-splattered work mode, but looked appealing nonetheless. It was odd to simultaneously want to be in his arms again, and yet feel angry with him about the way he was going to let María Carmen be a problem for them. It wasn't *her* having to get used to her 'heritage', or whatever he'd called it, but *him*. 'Fran's wife made the lemon cake. It's divine. Would you like some?'

'Oh, she'd probably want *you* to have it.'

'Rather than his ex-wife's nephew, you mean.' Her heart thudded. Where did that come from? She filled a thermos with lemon tea and took it over to the beach bag as if she hadn't said anything. Or better, as if Josemi wasn't there. So much for waiting until she'd absorbed things.

'So you know,' he said.

'I'm Fran's daughter, yes.'

He hung his head and nodded slowly before looking up again. 'And how d'you feel about that?'

'You ask as if I've just received appalling news. He didn't make your aunt happy, but that doesn't make him a bad person. He's quite the opposite, in fact.'

'Well, it's early days; you hardly know him. Or even if he's speaking the truth.'

She stood for a moment trying to take this in. Her heart began to pound. 'So, you think my mother might have shagged some other Spaniard and lied to Fran?'

'No! I mean—'

'Just *leave*. Please.'

'Hooliana!' He put gentle hands on her arms. 'I think we need to wipe this conversation and restart another time. When you're—'

'I don't see why this has to have anything to do with... *us*.'

'But *of course* it does; we can't just pretend it never happened.'

'But... we're still the same people as we were a week ago. And you said...' He'd said he wasn't going anywhere.

He let go of her. 'You're right. Nothing has changed. My mother and I wondered if you were Fran's daughter when we met you – and when I saw your English dad, it was obvious. We've known for a while now. Nothing has changed.'

And nothing *will* change, she realised with sudden clarity. The time on the beach when he nearly kissed her, the time when he held her so close against him that she could feel his hardness – they were just mistakes. Maybe there would be more of them. Maybe, sooner or later, they'd even have sex – although good God would *that* be a bad idea. Because nothing would change. They were *friends* – a miracle in itself, given their family histories.

'Hooli? I said, could I have the spare key?'

'You want the key to your house back.'

'Don't say it like that! You should have it, I'll bring it back. You can give me yours, if you like. But I need mine to lend to a friend of Gabi's for the gallery on Saturday.'

She stared at him blankly.

'When we're at the rehearsal, remember? We were going together, weren't we? And recovering from "There's No Business Like Show Business" with pancakes afterwards.'

She smiled weakly. They were both getting so sick of that song.

He pointed to her beach bag. 'And don't drive all the way to Amarga today. Go to the village beach. You don't have to avoid me – I'm not going anywhere today.'

'Okay,' she said, and fetched his key. There was a kiss on her cheek, a neighbourly hug, and he was gone.

She made a new plan: go to the beach, sob in the sea as long as needed – which could be a while – then come back and… relax. Eat. Listen to music. Re-ravel. Carry on. *Ride it out*, as Arturo said – and he was always, eventually, right.

EIGHTEEN

DAY 53

'So you're *Spanish*, that's fantastic! Somehow, I always knew it,' Toby said down the phone.

You'd think the fatherhood issue – given the extreme difference between Dad and Fran – would be the first thing to comment on, but Toby's life was all about roles and characteristics.

'How does that make you feel?'

Juliana lay back in her new hammock. It was kind of him to call, and perfectly timed with her painting break. 'Confused. I've spent my whole life looking and feeling oddly un-English, and now I know I haven't a drop of English blood I realise how English I am.'

'And you're not just Spanish, you're a *gitana*!'

'*Half* gitana, yes.'

'Does he like flamenco?'

'Well of course!'

'And could he get you supporting artiste work at the studios?'

'Yes, but he understands I don't want to do that anymore.'

'Oh yes. And anyway, how much will you need to work once you...' he lowered his voice '...well, might not be paying rent? You could just earn from your blog; probably wouldn't have to bother with the little teaching job.'

'No, I *want* to teach. I'm not that keen on monetising the blog – trying to control annoying adverts, having to write pieces to please sponsors.'

'Rather than lazing around in the botanical gardens with the local talent and posting that.'

'Uh...'

'So are you and he...'

'No! It was just a great picture for the blog.'

'True. And that blog is amazing, Jules. Which brings me to why I've called you. I'm going to ask my agent if she could talk to some publishers about a book describing my Spanish adventure. Maybe nothing'll come of it, but I'd like to show her your blog and put you forward as a ghost writer.'

'You... don't want to write it *yourself?*'

'Well yes, I'll pour it all into a diary, but I'm no writer. You'd be brilliant, and I can't imagine putting myself in anybody else's hands. I don't know how much you'll get, but I'll insist on you getting a good rate. And it *will* be you; I'll say I can't work with anyone else! Besides, think of all the fun and Thai meals we'd have when you visit. Come on, what d'you say?'

'Well... may as well see what she thinks.'

———

'Why would they suddenly ask us to come in and start the rehearsal two hours early?' Juliana asked, as Josemi pulled on to the road out of the village.

'No idea. I nearly just texted back a *no*.'

'I bet half the orchestra doesn't see the message; *that* would be annoying,' she said.

'Yes.'

They drove over the blind summit, the rocky, mountainous coast laid out beneath them. 'Oh... I don't think this view will ever stop stunning me. And look at that sea – I should be *in* that now.' Rather than sitting here with a grumpy, overworked artist, however appealing he might look in his denim shorts and red T-shirt.

'I swim first thing in the morning, to energise me for work,' he said.

Well, bully for him. And she already knew that; it was probably one of the reasons that further beach trips together hadn't happened. 'I *work* first thing in the morning, and swim afterwards,' she said.

'No, you don't. I wouldn't say you keep to any routine at all. Not that there's anything wrong with—'

'I wasn't aware you were tracking my movements.'

'Your way of doing things seems to be getting obsessed with one thing then moving on.'

'What? Example, please.'

He concentrated on turning right onto the Níjar road, even though there was only one car in sight. 'Well, it was all Níjar, Níjar, Níjar for a while, day after day.'

'I was trying to—'

'Now, you *live* in the botanical garden.'

'I've done a blog there.'

'*Two* blogs. In three days? I'm sure you missed a swim or two for that. But I suppose the second one featuring the

English gardener will appeal to your English fans. Wonderful pictures.'

'Well, it's true I've promised myself a few beach days next week to make up for it. I'm soon to launch an obsession with the Cabo de Gata beaches.' He'd told her about the pebbles there. 'I'll be sure to take my bucket.' Not even a smile. 'I can't wait to discover Puddle Beach, with that big oasis-like lake next to it. Have you been there?'

'Beautiful place. Will you be taking Ben with you to identify the flora round it?' Straight-faced, but maybe a twitch of his mouth.

'Now you mention it, that sounds like an *excellent* idea.'

He glanced over at her and caught her cheeky grin and eyes raised to the heavens. Honestly, first Toby and now him; amazing how men can come over all jealous even though they don't want you themselves.

'Ben is trouble for ladies, Hooli. You can ask Nerea's daughter.'

'Nerea?'

'You know, from the Rafaelarte group. I'm just telling you.'

So now he was big brother as well as friend and neighbour. 'He's not trouble if you just chat over a cactus and drinks-machine Coke once in a while. *Jesus*.'

He frowned. 'What d'you mean, "Jesus"?'

'It's an expression, like *Dios mío*.'

'We don't say this, in Spanish.'

'Yes, well I'm English.'

They drove on in silence.

'The ceiling of the stairwell looks great. Thank you *so* much,' she remembered to say. 'I just feel bad I wasn't there to help.'

'It's better that you were out.'

She turned her head to look at him. Had he deliberately been only available when he knew she'd be out meeting Kim and the expat group?

'I mean, because you wouldn't have been able to go up and down the stairs. *Jesús!*'

She laughed. 'No, no, you've got to give it the English emphasis. *Jee*zus.'

'*Joder.*'

'That's very rude, in English.'

'Yes, well I'm Spanish.'

But it would be nice if he occasionally spoke her language. 'Do I have to fall into the *rambla* again, before you'll speak a bit of English?'

'Hooli! I'm driving the car!'

'How much d'you understand the English song lyrics in the play?'

'Some. Like…' He cleared his throat and started to sing. 'There's no bees-ness like show bees-ness, there's no bees-ness at all!'

Even larking around, his voice was rich and tuneful – and made her want to put a hand on his chest to feel the vibrations, the warmth of the sound and his skin… Luckily, she could laugh instead. 'You sound like you're singing about bees' nests!'

He laughed and carried on singing. 'Ever-thin' about it is app-allin'.'

Juliana guffawed. 'No! App*ea*ling! Although *appalling* is spot on.'

'*Dios mío* what *tonterías* this song!' he said in half-English. 'And we left… *nos queda?*'

'We have four weeks left! Not sure I can bear "Anything You Can Do" that long either.'

'No, I like that one.' He started the argumentative duet

and she joined in, but couldn't get further than the first line. 'God, how do Sandra and Sergio remember all that?'

'Oh,' she said. They'd pulled into the arts centre – and seen there were just two cars and a motorbike. 'Did we both get this wrong?'

Josemi put a hand to his face. 'This happened once before,' he said, back in Spanish.

'What did?'

'Come.' He got out of the car and strode off so fast she had to trot to keep up with him.

Pedro the accompanist, friendly musical director Enrique and the less approachable young head of drama were waiting in the doorway of the music block.

'Josemi, Juliana... thanks for getting in early,' Enrique said with a big smile, as he and the drama guy stubbed out their cigarettes. 'Do come in.'

They went through to the room where Juliana had sung Annie to help the kids learn 'Doing What Comes Naturally', but they all sat down and nobody went to the piano. They were offered Cokes and Fantas, but Josemi waved them away and asked what was going on.

Enrique put his hands together as if in prayer and started to explain how Sandra and Sergio were up in Valladolid, with Sergio's father. It sounded like she and Josemi would have to fill in for them today. But Josemi had started putting forward names.

'Oh, I'm sure we can do it,' she said, and got a huge beam from Pedro and Enrique.

But Josemi stared at her then got out his phone and showed her the translation for *stroke* on WordRef. 'You don't understand. Sandra and Sergio won't be coming back for some while. They're asking us to take on the Annie and Frank roles. Not just for today's rehearsal, but for the *show*.'

Juliana went cold all over. She couldn't do it. Annie, the star of the show. Even in an amateur production in a remote corner of Spain. It was the kind of thing she still had nightmares about — even though she hadn't been star of a show since primary school. And how on earth could she learn it all in time?

'Hooliana, I've heard you sing, and you've had training as an actress.' Pedro turned to Josemi. 'We'll never forget what a cracking Marius you put in for *Les Misérables*, when we asked you stand in then. And of course, the two of you are neighbours, so you can easily practise together. We'll help you all we can, with plenty of extra rehearsals.'

Enrique put up a finger. 'And I've cut out verses to some of the songs, to make it easier.'

'Nobody would blame you if you went on with scripts,' the young director said. 'In fact, Enrique tells me that when that happened some years ago for a chap covering *Phantom*, the audience gave the biggest donations ever. We want to put on a great show — which we will — but let's not forget the cause.'

Juliana didn't see how they could say no, but Josemi was putting a hand through his hair and had a face like thunder. While she was waiting for him to say something, she ran through Annie's songs: 'I've Got the Sun in the Morning' — easy; 'You Can't get a Man with a Gun' — a lot of words, a lot of movement, but easy to relate to; the 'Anything You Can Do' argument duet with Josemi — it wouldn't be hard to get into the spirit for that. But not the swoony 'They Say It's Wonderful'. Falling in love, that was. Making her sing that to Josemi was just… *cruel*. But he'd just said yes.

As soon as she nodded, there were grins from the three men, and the Spanish two-kiss thing from each of them — although oddly, not between her and Josemi. Then — with the slick urgency of surgeons preparing for an operation – they produced two heavy scripts, the score and a rehearsal schedule before Pedro took Josemi to the piano and Enrique wheeled her off to another music room further along the corridor.

An hour later, they were given forty-five minutes to go for a break before coming back for more. They asked each other how it went, shrugged, and walked in silence to Café Nido. Pancakes were ordered, and Josemi looked at his watch. He was still angry, behaving as if it was somehow *her* fault they were in this situation.

'If Enrique had told me one more time what a great thing I was doing for the community of Níjar, I'd have thumped him with the score,' Juliana said. 'I mean, why didn't they sort out...' What was the word for understudies? 'Spare people, from the start?'

'They never do. Nobody wants to learn all the stuff and not perform it. Uh, how am I going to find time to learn all this, coming into my busiest time of the year? It's all right for *you*.'

'Why?'

'Well... you've just got two little rooms to paint, a blog to do when you want, and to see Fran again before you go. Will he be coming to the show?'

She frowned. 'I *have* got a lot on too, I'm not "going", and if Fran coming to the show would be a problem for you and Dolores, I'm sure he'll understand.'

It was his turn to look confused. 'What d'you mean, you're not going?'

'I told you I'd be back, I'm sure I did.'

'Well yes. Oh, you mean to visit.'

'No, to live here. I'll be back in the autumn after I've done a four-week course in Granada. I'm going to work for

Kim.' She also might be working with Toby, but it was never a good idea to share Toby's rash suggestions with anyone. Besides, Josemi was looking surprised enough.

'That's… *wonderful*, Hooli.' But he wasn't smiling. 'When did you decide this? After meeting Fran?'

She struggled to say thank you for the pancakes arriving between them. Was he going to keep bringing Fran up? It was none of his bees' nest.

'I started thinking about ditching my grey, background-person English life not long after I arrived. I made up my mind after sitting in on Kim's classes and talking to her about life here.'

He looked up, still seeming confused for some reason.

'And stop mentioning Fran all the time. It's annoying.'

'Okay, sorry.' His mouth twitched into a smile, and he put his hands up as if protecting himself. 'But, Annie, *you can't get a man with a gun!* You don't need to be so… angry.'

'You don't need to be so… grumpy.'

'Ha! You can talk!' Then he put up a finger. 'Wait,' he said in English, and started mouthing something. Then he leant forward and sang quietly. 'Any grump you can do, *I* can do better.'

'I can do any grump *better* than you,' she sang back.

He laughed and patted her hand. 'That's more like it,' he said, back in Spanish. 'Now let's eat. We're going to need energy for this, my sharpshooter friend!'

NINETEEN
DAY 56

They hadn't gone back and done the duets; it was thought Josemi needed more time to get his tongue round the English. Instead, the rather intense young drama guy had gone through their lines and blocking for Act One – in front of a very understanding entire cast.

Now she was on her third day of learning her words, and horrified by how much harder it was in Spanish – as she would be explaining to Josemi later, when they went through the script in her living room.

They were both multi-tasking today: she was getting her script covered in sun cream and squashed ants while logging up Cabo de Gata beaches, and he'd apparently recorded the whole thing and was listening to it while he worked. In fact, for somebody who'd moaned so much about how he wasn't going to cope, Josemi was sounding quite cocky; she'd just rolled over on the towel, reached for the pinging phone in her bag and let the breeze flip pages over – just to read his message: '*Any lines you can learn, I can learn faster.*' She'd replied: '*I can learn any lines faster than you,*' and knowing this was unlikely to be true, added a perplexed emoji.

When it all got too much, she went into the sea – which was nowadays a perfect non-shock cool. She was used to beaches here being quiet, but on the Cabo de Gata ones – or rather *one*, because they were just different sections of the same long, long narrow stretch of sand and gorgeous pebbles – it was easy to isolate herself enough so that nobody intruded into her Wild West world.

Other than by phone. Despite being surrounded by flamingo-filled salt marshes, a mountain and the sea, the internet signal was as good as ever. So far today, she'd heard from Dad, with a photo of her thirteen-year-old self playing Sitting Bull in *Annie Get Your Gun* at Stageclub; both her step-sisters, asking how the lines were going; Minty from the expat group offering to lend her some dungarees; and Kim, bless her, offering times she could come over and help with the lines.

But every time she'd heard a ring or a pop, her heart had sunk when it wasn't Arturo. She'd been sure he'd be so happy to hear that she and Josemi were now playing Annie and Frank, but all she'd had so far was congratulations from María José and a promise she'd pass the news on. She was beginning to wonder if something was wrong.

Finally, it was his name on the screen.

'Arturo! How are you?'

'Fine, fine, I'm sorry... just a silly little illness.' As if to emphasise this, he'd got his beloved Bee Gees singing 'Stayin' Alive' on in the background.

'What little illness?'

'Bit of a chest infection. Now getting better. But Hooliana! What news! Although I feel a bit bad to have got you into this; I know how you have a bit of a horror of acting after your bad experience at college. I never for a moment thought you'd have to do more than play your flute.'

'Oh... don't worry, it's different here. I've only had one rehearsal so far, but it was fun and no pressure – well, except for learning a lot of lines in a hurry! Nobody's expecting me to be a star, or the daughter of Bowen Martin Casting. You might have done me favour!'

'Well that makes me feel better! And of course, you're with your Josemi.'

Her Josemi? But it was the way they talked about good friends here.

'I can hear waves. Are you learning your lines on the beach?'

'Yes! Cabo de Gata. Pebble collecting after each scene. Swimming after each act.'

'Ha! I'll let you get on. Send me your rehearsal schedule and I'll see when we might have lunch.'

'Okay! I'll do that when I get back. Meanwhile, look after yourself please; no more little illnesses!'

'I promise.'

———

Josemi sighed with delight as he sat down on the sofa, spreading his arms wide as if feeling the space. 'Great to be in a living room that's not an art gallery!'

She put a homemade lemonade down on the table in front of him.

'Ooh, *that* looks good.'

Trying not to say how she'd learnt to make it at Fran's house, she said something else she'd decided not to mention. 'Apparently, you and Gabi wanted to buy this house, so you could extend your gallery.'

'We thought about it,' he said casually. 'The idea was to divide the house and rent the lower part out. But Arturo didn't take long to come back with a firm *no*.'

'So you *would* have done it?'

'Hooli! I don't know. What does it matter? I promise I won't slice your home in half, okay?' he said with a laugh.

She sighed and sat down on the opposite sofa. 'It *feels* like my home, now I've painted nearly every tiny bit of it.'

'Just the bedrooms to go?'

'One.'

'You'll you get it done in time?'

She put down her drink. *Your home. Get it done in time.* She was alarmed for a moment that he somehow knew about the conditions – but of course, he just meant finishing the decorating before the three months here were over.

'Yes.'

'And you'll… rent it from Arturo when you come back, or live somewhere else?'

'I'm… plucking up the courage to ask that,' she said, even though it didn't sound very plausible that she and Arturo wouldn't have sorted that out by now.

He nodded and smiled, seemingly pleased by her answer. 'So, let's get started. Shall we stand up and try the blocking we were shown, or just sit here and go through it?'

He was in shorts and a black singlet; any acting of the they-say-falling-in-love-is-wonderful duet was going to be a very tingly, skin-on-skin affair. 'Let's just test each other on the words for now. Shall we leave out the songs?'

'Yes. Except the ones with just the two of us.'

'Oh. Okay.'

Josemi was on first, and Juliana was shocked out how easily he became cocky Frank the sharpshooter – and irritated at how quickly Annie becomes besotted with him.

'I mean, she's in love with him even before he's opened his mouth, even before she can see what he can do with his...' She searched the text for the Spanish word for rifle.

'But his reputation goes before him,' he said with a wink.

She blushed, groaned and shook her head.

'I don't think any of this takes too much analysis,' he said. 'Especially if we want to get to the end.'

'Okay, okay.'

At the shooting scene, Josemi gave himself a double thumbs-up for remembering all the words.

'Uh, you're turning into Frank! This is a nightmare.'

'And you're turning into Annie, shooting at everything!' He mimed rifle shooting into every corner of the room.

'Maybe we need a break. It's much harder in another language, you know.' She got up and went towards the kitchen.

Josemi followed, and patted her shoulder. 'It must be. You're doing really well. Wait until you hear me messing up the English song lyrics.'

She got out some asparagus *tortilla*, finely chopped salad and orange *bizcocho* cake, all picked up from Elise's. 'I'm getting worse and worse at making my own food; she's just too good.'

'I know. Shall I make some coffee?'

'Please.'

'Ooh, new machine?'

'Yes... Arturo told me to replace anything that was faulty.'

'Ah.' They sat down. 'And which beach did you go to today?'

'The Cabo de Gata ones.' What was wrong with her? That sounded so silly. Why would anybody do a crawl of four different sections of beach in one day? 'I still haven't been to

Puddle Beach, though.' Then he did look puzzled. 'You know – the one with the lake next to it.'

'Yes, I know it.'

'Maybe you and I could go there together sometime.'

He looked at her and smiled – in that way that made her melt all over. 'After the show. We'll deserve a treat then.'

After the show, she'd have just seven days left. Then she'd be back in England until she started her course in Granada; she probably wouldn't see him for two or three months.

They got back to it, both making more mistakes as they went on.

'I think we should stop here and do the rest another evening,' Juliana suggested.

'Yes. But let's just try the two songs. At my place. I've got a better sound system.'

'Does it matter, for now?'

'Yes! They're beautiful songs.'

She followed him out through her front door and into his, then through to the only accessible sofa in the gallery.

'You can't sit down – we need to act these out.'

'But we haven't done these with—'

'I think we should have a go on our own, not just wait to be told what to do or not do. Don't you? Let's start with "Anything You Can Do".'

As the jaunty music began, they stood looking at each other with a disapproval that seemed to come all too naturally, and were soon making each other laugh with their miming and pointing of fingers as the competitive boasting went on. But even with the cuts, there were a lot of verses, and it was getting late.

'Er… any line you can fluff, I can fluff better!' Juliana sang-laughed, and waited for his return phrase.

'I can fuck any-who better than you!' he sang back.

'What?' Juliana shouted above the music, laughing. 'I said *fluff* – make a mistake – not... And what the hell does *fuck any-who* mean?'

He grinned. 'Maybe I mean, any*how*... or any*where*!' he shouted back in English. 'It's better, no?'

'Oh God!' She blushed and put a hand to her face as they both shook with laughter. 'Uh, I can't handle any more of this.'

'Hand-el?'

'Cope. *Manejar?*'

'No, no. We have to do the other.' He went to the CD player, turned it off and came back to her. 'Is like this.' He stood next to her with his arm round her waist, like they were both looking out at something. He'd obviously been watching the film, where Frank and Annie are between carriages on a train. 'And later—'

'After he's told her he's known love "once or twice before". I mean, can't he remember? Is it once, or is it twice?'

'Hooli! Please give the boy a chance! Maybe with the music...'

After her opening verse, he stopped the music. 'That was lovely. Really. But why are you acting so... sad?'

'That's what *she* does. I thought you'd seen the film? She doesn't think she has a chance.'

'Yes, she does. She's not sad, she's just... dreaming.'

He restarted it, and Juliana went for dreamy-sad. He squeezed her arm in encouragement. Then he stood back and did his 'I've been there' bit, but toned down compared to the film; maybe he'd been there once or twice with those heartless English girls. Then he held her close and sang the last bit so beautifully that her little 'so they say' response came out as breathless as Betty Hutton's.

The music stopped. 'Surely after that they...' he started.

'No, they have all sorts of problems to get through before...'

He pulled her towards him, holding her tightly... Then his hand came to her face, and his lips were on hers – gently at first, then more insistent.

The music player clicked. She thought. But Josemi let go and turned around.

Dolores was standing there, the door closed behind her. Just visible through the paintings – as they would have been to her. Juliana blushed, but good God, couldn't she have knocked?

Dolores looked cross, but was also apologising – as Josemi said something in rapid Spanish about calling at the door and keys. His mother mentioned a hospital appointment the next day, picked up an empty dish from the kitchen, and left.

Josemi turned back to Juliana, hugged her and kissed the top of her head; they were back to neighbourly affection, it seemed, after a timely reminder from his mother. Now he too was apologising, saying something about being careful with this.

Careful with this scene? This mutual attraction? His mother's feelings? *I don't understand*, she wanted to say, but felt so shaky, nothing would come out.

'It's complicated, Hooli. I'm sorry, give it time,' he said, and stood back. She waited for him to say more, but he didn't; it was her cue to leave.

Back home, she washed up their glasses and plates, remembering their earlier laughter. *Bawdy* laughter, as if their attraction for each other had to come up for air once in a while. While they waited. *Giving it time*. How long would it be like this? Until after the play? Puddle Beach? October? Forever? After all, why choose *her*, when there must be a woman out there for him who wasn't a neighbour and whose mother wasn't someone you were brought up to hate.

She made a fruit tea and tried to settle on the sofa with her book – but the room was full of Josemi's presence; there was no escaping it. So she took the tea down onto the terrace with its softly glowing new solar lights adding to the gleam from the full moon. A kindly, warm breeze started to dry her idiotic tears. What the hell was she upset about? *He'd kissed her.* She just had to keep *riding it out,* as Arturo said.

She lay down on the sunbed with her phone and headset, and pressed Spotify, looking for a song to match her mood – or bring her out of it. As she'd done as a heartbroken nine-teen-year-old. What had it been then? She listened to Cold-play's 'Viva La Vida', and The Killers' 'Human' that she and Toby had had on in the car; probably *not* them, with their lyrics as incomprehensible as the break-up with the soulmate she thought she'd had in Toby. What were they doing on her 'Liked' list? She removed them, and added Fran's favourite, 'Problema' – which pretty much summed up her relation-ships with all the male people in her life – other than Arturo.

As if disputing this, the phone buzzed in her hand. A WhatsApp from Toby.

'*The agent loved the proposal! We're going to tweak it and then put it out to publishers. I'm flying over tomorrow and will be with you by about eleven to see your house, then take you off to mine, a Thai meal, and my hotel pool for brainstorming. And don't worry, bring your script along, Annie, and I'll be your Frank as long as you need xx*'

TWENTY
DAY 57

Juliana was sitting in the armchair with a view of Dolores's house. In the spirit of telling herself it was just an ordinary day – rather than one she was going to spend with Toby, having not seen him for at least a year – she'd got up early and painted the ceiling and two walls of her bedroom, and was now exhausted. In the same spirit, she was un-made-up and casual in her thin turquoise *mercadillo* frock, and – other than taking down underwear hanging on the line on the side terrace – hadn't fussed with the house. She had, however, already packed swimming things and her script into her bag, and done everything she needed to do an hour before Toby's arrival – except for seeing Josemi take Dolores off for her hospital appointment.

She thought Dolores had said half past ten, but maybe she'd said they were *leaving* at half past ten. It was always the same; any stress seemed to trip her Spanish switch off. But either way – unless she'd got it completely wrong – they should be out of San Rafael, thank the Lord, by the time Toby turned up.

Keeping her contact with Toby a secret was a time-hewn habit; Dad blamed the break-up with him for her failure at drama college; friends blamed him for failures with subsequent boyfriends; and others, if learning about her continued (if unbalanced and unsatisfactory) connection with him, would pester to be introduced. Keeping Toby's visit a secret from Josemi was just about not wanting to give him any more reasons to feel that getting together with her was a bad idea.

Finally, Dolores came out, and Josemi crossed over to her. While Juliana was pleased to see their happy and jokey greeting, suggesting the hospital appointment was just routine, she was also a bit galled to see that Josemi's anger at Dolores walking in on them yesterday evening had already totally evaporated. She got up and stepped back from the window, and soon heard them getting into his van and driving off.

Not ten minutes later, the doorbell went. Surely it couldn't be Toby already? She had an image of the immigration queue parting to let golden King Arthur through. Irritated at her annoyingly familiar palpitations – another time-hewn habit – she opened the door. She'd forgotten that the tousle-haired, stubbly Toby was even more attractive than his clean-shaven King Arthur persona. He was in pale trousers and a light blue T-shirt the exact colour of his eyes – and smiling radiantly.

'Jules!' He hugged her so tightly she yelped and he laughed. Then he stood back and held her by the shoulders. 'Well look at *you*! So dark and gorgeous and… Spanish! One hundred per cent!' He patted her hip. 'And I swear you've lost a stone.'

'I don't know, could have done!' She'd also forgotten how loud he was, projecting like a stage actor. She quickly closed the door behind him. 'What d'you want to drink?'

'What d'you think?'

He followed her through to the kitchen, looking around him. 'This is lovely. Simple. Spanish. Cosy. Did you just have to do a fresh coat of white?'

'Bit of filling here and there, replaced a few tiles on the skirting... Nothing compared to what you're going to have to do!' Or rather, *get done*.

While she was making his tea – still white-no-sugar, she assumed – he touched cushions and jugs, pointed at rugs, ran his hand down the dark wood window frame. He picked up the pebble with Chica painted on it. 'You did this?'

'No!' she said, wanting him to put it down, and hoping he'd assume it came from the gift shop. After he'd admired the view over the valley to the mountains, she took him downstairs to show him the two bedrooms and then the terrace.

'Wow – you'll have to advise me on cacti... Ah, and this is the river you got fished out of when it was flooded? Seems hard to imagine.'

'I know, but it was up to that wooden handrail, and monstrous.'

He looked over at the path on the bank, and she immediately wished she hadn't pointed it out.

'Why's there a path going round to your neighbour's house?'

'It's not. It's just so we can both garden the bank, make it pretty.'

He looked up and down the *rambla*, over again at the mountains, and then at the back of the house. 'Lovely. And you could probably make another terrace on the roof. Fabulous views, and good for escaping the neighbours. Are they all right?'

'Very nice, on both sides. But yes, a roof terrace would be lovely in the winter.'

He sat down on the bench, his arm along the back of it. He patted the bench next to him, and once she'd sat down, the arm came around her. 'You've done a fantastic job on this perfect little house. I can't believe your uncle won't—'

'Shh…'

'Okay,' he whispered, like it was a game. 'What else is on this list? You said there were things you had to do that he thought would be good for you.'

Once again, she cursed herself for having been such a blabbermouth. So many of the conditions made Arturo sound like a complete crackpot; maybe he *was* one, but a crackpot she loved, trusted and had started to understand. 'Oh… just some cultural things… and of course the show, so I contribute to the community.'

'Nothing about *people*? Shagging or not shagging the local Spanish talent?' he said with a smirk.

'No! Now let's go and see *your* house, come on,' she said, getting up.

———

They pulled over at the top of the hill and looked down at Cortijo de la Naranjera in its own valley of orange trees, *palmitos* and ochre terrain. Toby looked dumbfounded.

'You said you wanted quiet, no neighbours… Just hope I haven't over—'

'It's *perfect*.'

'Hm, not close up, it isn't! Let's go down and get you in there. *Gawd*.' She bit her lip.

He patted her thigh. 'Don't worry! I've studied every frame of the video.'

They wandered through the house, Toby exclaiming with delight at the traditional tiling, the dark wooden beams and window shutters, adorable arches everywhere, the old paved courtyard whose beauty he could envisage despite it being covered in vicious weeds and debris. All things that Juliana had appreciated too, on her first visit, but this time she was also struck by the extraordinary quantity of furnishings and clutter left by the previous ancient inhabitant, the cracked and flaky walls, the appalling bathrooms and kitchen. There was a hell of a lot of work to do here, before he should make plans – as he was doing at that moment – for the two dilapidated outbuildings and a small pool.

'I hope you've got an army of volunteering friends – hopefully including a builder or two – coming out to help. You know, like those Brits in *Escape to the Chateau*. Ha – I've already guessed the name of the TV programme: *Escape to the Cortijo, with Toby Campbell-West!*'

He turned from admiring the ornate old stable partitions that he was determined to reuse. His hurt face – all big blue eyes and open, perfect mouth – would have melted the hearts of his Arthur fans into a country-wide lake.

'No. Not at all,' he said, more quietly than usual. 'For one thing, I don't have that many friends these days. Not real ones. Anyway, that's not what this is about. I'm going to do everything I can, myself – I've already been watching YouTube and learning a few things. What I can't do, will be work for local builders, who I'll work alongside.'

'Oh! That sounds… brilliant. Just a shame you've picked such hot months to do it in!'

Over the Thai meal, he explained more. 'I'll have three months before filming of *Northanger Abbey*, and then there'll be the next series of *Arthur*… If I don't start in August, it would be well into next year – and getting hot again. As it is, I've turned down an ITV drama – in which I'd have been playing another historical hunk.' He skewered another olive and sipped his sparkling water. 'I want to create a Spanish getaway for myself – while letting people have a laugh at posh pretty boy getting his hands dirty and being sweaty and grubby for a change. Let them see another side. Good for me, good for my career.'

'Well, as I say, this is great. But… what is your *other side*?'

'The grafter: people don't realise how hard I work. And the dickhead who's messed up his relationships and ended up on his own.'

'Toby! You can't "end up on your own" at thirty-one! If you can't find a girlfriend it probably just means you can't commit to anyone at the moment. Nothing wrong with that.' She took another spoonful of panang and, despite being very impressed by his new intentions, was acutely aware of two things: she was surprisingly un-intrigued by his single status, and the buzzings of her phone had had a Josemi-like feel to them.

'That's not true, Jules. Who wants to be alone? Do you? Or are you in a relationship now?'

'Not at the moment, but… I've got some good friends here and that's okay for now.'

'Ah.'

When he went off to the loo, she looked at her phone.

'*Any cake you can buy, I can buy larger,*' Josemi had typed, under a photo of an entire bizcocho. Unwilling to wait any longer for the answer, he'd added: '*I can buy any cake larger than you.*'

She found and sent an image of Mary Berry using a shovel to move a slice of cake larger than herself. '*Sure about that?*'

Josemi is typing, her phone said. He seemed to be taking a while. Maybe he wanted help with the cake and the song words, and was asking when she'd be back. But no. '*I'm sorry about last night, Juli. It was my fault,*' arrived like a blow to the tummy. He then went into the schedule of tomorrow's rehearsal in Níjar, and what time they should set off.

'*Okay x,*' was all she could think of for a reply – and anyway, there was no time to write anything else.

'Everything okay?' Toby asked, sitting down again.

'Just looking at the rehearsal schedule.'

He declined desserts for them; he might be about to be seen tousled and grubby, but he wasn't going to let that perfect gym-toned body go. Perhaps she should have told him that other men eat cake without any obvious ill effects.

They drove back to Vera and checked in to his boutique hotel. He'd booked her in too, he explained, so they wouldn't question her using the pool. There was something odd about that, and the smiley smitten girl on reception didn't look like she'd be up to interrogating him on anything, but Juliana went along with it and followed Toby up to the room.

Toby started unbuttoning his shirt.

'I'll change in here,' Juliana said, going into the bathroom. He was right, she must have lost weight; the bulge round the black bikini top had gone, and the tummy control was no longer having to strong-arm her into shape. But she was still happy she'd remembered her pink cover-up.

Toby was happy to stand there in his pants. No, they were swim trunks, but short and orange. The sort a guy has to be very confident to pull off. He looked her up and down and seemed about to say something, so she went to her bag and got out her towel and script. 'You sure you want to help me with this?'

He laughed and nodded.

It was quiet down at the pool, just a couple sunbathing and a chap with his laptop in the shade. The water was like a bath, but still heavenly after the heat and dust of the *cortijo*.

'So what d'you think?' he asked, swimming up to her. 'Could you be my ghost writer, if it comes off? We could see what you should include from my diary later, depending on how things work out.'

'How what things work out?' she asked, treading water.

'Well, obviously there'll be a narrative – the house, the people I meet…'

If he were anyone else, Juliana would have told him to consider that there might not *be* a narrative; he might not connect with anyone at all, or at least not in a publishable, narrative-worthy way. But this was Toby, the people magnet.

'It'll be a heart-warming story about love of the land-scape, the *cortijo*…' he continued, 'and love of a Spanish lady, of course.'

'Ah.' Where did he plan on sourcing her then? He was quite picky and it didn't sound like he'd have the time or energy for driving off to lots of bars.

She must have looked puzzled, because he was laughing at her. He took her forearms and pulled her closer. He was standing, but she was still out of her depth. She found the side of the pool and studied his smiling but slightly anxious face. *Surely* he couldn't mean…

'Jules. My *casa* will be your *casa*, as they say. Which also means my *cama*.'

His bed. 'It's up to you. Do what you like with me!' he said with a chuckle.

'For ninety days.' Jesus, Toby offering to be the ultimate three-monther; no thank you.

'Yes, but this isn't a *role*. You know I love you. It's just that for a long time I've been too stupid to see it.'

He loved her. But love is an easy word to throw around when you want something, and there's love and *love*.

He was smiling more confidently now, and stroking her arm. 'We could of course start a prologue.'

For a moment, she felt dazed and receptive; it had been a long time, and he'd be patient and tender as he'd always been. But it would just be difficult-later friend-sex with gorgeous golden Toby, when she'd rather be making love with dark and bear-like Josemi – a chap who could be grumpy, but make him smile or laugh and life took on a whole new meaning.

'I can't do that, Toby.'

He looked down and sighed. 'I knew you'd say that, and if you don't change your mind, I deserve it. I've taken you for granted for *years*.'

'What you're planning to do is impressive. But I can't stay in your house, and it won't work if you keep... making suggestions.'

He looked at her a moment. 'You're in love with someone, aren't you.'

'Yes.'

'The guy who saved you from the river? The guy on the beach? Oh, or the Frank in *Annie*?'

'Maybe one of those... but it's complicated. If I'm going to do this ghost writing, you have to be really careful what you say on social media, okay? Promise?'

'Of course.'

'I mean it, Toby.'

He smiled. 'Don't worry. I promise.'

TWENTY-ONE

DAY 64

'Thought we'd go for pure white for a change, Mama.' Juliana stood back and admired the thick bunches of white plastic roses against the black plaque.

'I saw Fran again yesterday. Just a short visit. He was in a lot of pain with broken toes – after all those years with the horse and cart, he let the wheel roll back over his foot! So annoyed with himself, and hating being inactive. By the time he's back at work, he'll be on his new part-time contract.

'We talked more about you. And about... María Carmen. Apparently, Dolores really didn't want her sister living with them, rang Fran several times, begging him to help his wife find somewhere else to live. It was as if she knew something awful was going to happen, he said. He tried to persuade María Carmen to come home, didn't think it right for Dolores's children to witness all her drinking. How sad it all is.'

She arranged the white flowers more. 'Anyway, it wasn't *your* fault. The woman was ill. And Fran thinks Dolores might see it that way, and *wouldn't* have brought Josemi up to hate you. He couldn't believe it when I told him Dolores and Josemi had moved back to San Rafael and were my neighbours! And when I admitted I was smitten with Josemi, he found a photo of him as a little boy in a family picture, all big-eyed and mop-haired. He says Josemi was a quietly cheeky chap, very sweet, always with a piece of wood in his hands that he was chiselling into an animal. His dad was a carpenter, apparently.'

She sighed. 'Oh, Mama, what am I going to do about Josemi? He's barely said a word to me for a week – unless it's in the script. Uh, that lovely song in the show, "My Defences are Down…" *Defences are **Up***, more like. It's *killing* me.' She looked around her. 'Perhaps that's not a good word to use here. Sorry, people. I know, I'm young, healthy, and this is a non-problem.' She put a hand on Mama's photo. 'But I think you know what I mean.'

She walked back towards the village. How much hotter it was, how much paler the land – and warmer the sea – than when she'd arrived two months ago. It was now the third of July. The month – and her feelings – would keep burning on, until she had to get on that plane, in three and a bit weeks' time. It would whizz by, with all the rehearsals for the show in – God – just sixteen days.

She settled herself on the terrace under the parasol with her script, trying to ignore Josemi next door, clattering around in his studio while singing his part of 'Anything I Can Do'. A week ago, she would have shouted over the wall and offered to sing Annie, but he seemed to be in a holed-up high-productivity mode.

She looked down again at the script and put her hand over Annie's response on hearing that Frank had gone off to shoot for a rival show – but Josemi's word-perfect tuneful singing was putting her off.

'*Sounds good*,' she tapped on WhatsApp to him. '*Practise later?*' There was a big run-through rehearsal tomorrow; surely he'd want to.

'*I've got to finish a painting*,' he wrote, and went offline. Then he came back. '*How's* your *painting?*'

'*I've finished!!!*'

'*Really? Fantastic!*' He disappeared offline again. This was ridiculous – he must be about five metres away. '*Let's celebrate in El Minero. Give me an hour.*'

'*Okay!*'

She had a shower, even though she'd later be getting salty and sandy at the beach. There was really no reason to get excited; it was just a neighbourly lunch, not a date. To remind herself of this, she went over to his place using the leg-scratching bank path.

He came out onto the terrace. 'Hooliana Martin, the master painter. Congratulations!' He kissed her on both cheeks. 'Let's go.'

El Minero was just five minutes' walk away, but although she and Josemi had discussed the merits of the chef's orange *flan de casa* – a sort of lighter but eggier crème brûlée – she'd only ever been there with Arturo or Kim. They took a table by the side of the road, right opposite an enormous poster advertising the Rafaelarte group's works and gallery opening times.

'You've done it? Everything your uncle wanted you to do?' he asked.

She hesitated, then reminded herself he was asking about the house repairs, not all the conditions. He couldn't possibly know about those. 'Yes, and thank heavens; it's much too hot for it now.'

'I warned you.'

'You did.'

'And August is even hotter. But you'll be back in England then.'

'Yes.'

'And Granada in September, for the teaching course?'

'Yes, then back here in October. Here or San José, I'm not sure yet.'

He slowly nodded.

Why was he asking? He knew all this. They'd never had to *make* conversation like this before. But she was just as bad; she couldn't think what to say next. What she'd *like* to say was: *Why aren't we a couple?* But even if she dared, she had a complete mental block about how you said that in Spanish. *Un par?* But that was just a pair, like a pair of socks. Or idiots.

They looked at the menu. She told him she'd started eating seafood, and he thought that was great. He bemoaned the way chips came with every dish in Spain, and she agreed. Then an artist friend came past, and he stood up to do that man-back-slapping thing.

'Hooli? This is Kiko, who did that surreal picture of the cacti in the poster by the—'

'Oh! I love that!'

The balding jolly Kiko was soon giving her a kiss on each cheek, while Josemi was introducing her as his lovely neighbour over from England.

'Ah – and the wonderful co-star of the show, I believe?' Kiko asked.

'She is!' Josemi said, patting her arm and leaving a tingly imprint.

Kiki apologised to Juliana and sat down at their table to talk to Josemi about something to do with the art group.

During their earnest, rapid and incomprehensible discussion, Juliana remembered what fun she'd had here with

Arturo – laughing about the three-legged men paintings, showing him how to use emojis on his phone…

Kiko had gone and Josemi was giving their orders to the waitress. Then he turned to Juliana with a closed smile.

'So, it's been a good week then?'

'Yes.'

'Working hard. Except when you had that day off with Kim.'

She was going to have to tell Kim about her white lie, just in case. Josemi had been on his terrace when she got back from Vera and, stupidly, it hadn't occurred to her that – like any neighbour – he might ask what she'd been up to that day.

'Yes.'

'Any news from home?' he asked.

'How d'you mean?'

'Well, family – maybe friends – coming to the show?'

'No. Dad and Olivia are going to be at an old friend's wedding.'

'Your friends don't fancy a mini-break? The teacher friend you wrote the play for? Toby, with his love of Spain?'

She began to feel a little queasy. 'No, they're busy.' Another lie; Toby had said he wouldn't miss it for the world, despite a hectic schedule. Sooner or later she'd have to explain about working with Toby on his book, but she told herself there wasn't any point saying anything until they'd heard from a publisher.

Their fishy meals arrived, along with the shared salad, and she began to wish she'd just gone for the comforting tomatoey *salmorejo* soup.

Another of Josemi's artist friends came by and had a quick word – a pretty red-headed girl called something like 'Pili', who would surely make a well-matched and uncomplicated girlfriend for him. When she'd gone, he told Juliana she was the very successful artist who did the rather abstract bathing figures. *The phallic-obsessed artist, you mean?* she wanted to say. *Arturo and I nearly choked with laughter.* Josemi went on to tell her the poor girl was equally *un*successful in love, as if considering how to put that right for her.

Then there was a couple waving from across the road who called out that they were loving the paintings they'd bought from him.

'Wave, Hooli – *you* sold them!'

She did as she was told, even though she didn't remember the couple. The day in his gallery, and the one before that when she'd danced salsa with him there and ended up pressed against his body, felt like ages ago. Perhaps that's what he wanted her to feel; he'd brought her here to show her how she was one of many friends – some of whom may also have been pressed up against him.

'You're not eating. D'you want to order something different?' he asked.

'No, I… I'm just a bit tired.'

'Not drinking enough,' he said, and ordered her non-diet Coke, presumably to perk her up. She certainly hadn't been much company – but then, nor had he.

Yet another artist turned up. But she recognised this lady – Nerea, with the daughter who'd apparently had her heart broken by Ben from the botanical garden.

Nerea tapped Josemi's shoulder and tipped her head at Juliana. 'So,' she said with a little laugh, 'did you unravel the mystery of what young Ben was doing driving a top-of-the-range Jeep last week?'

Josemi looked over at Juliana, as if she'd know.

She shrugged. 'No idea.'

Nerea looked puzzled and laughed some more. 'But *surely*… I mean, where did you go, off-roading?'

Jeep. Her heart thudded with dizzying force. That's what Toby hired. Nerea must have thought she saw her in the Jeep with *Ben*; round here, one chap with a mop of fair hair probably looked much the same as another. She had to make a lightning decision as to whether it wasn't Ben, or wasn't *her*. 'Ah, no… that wasn't Ben.' That didn't seem to be enough for her. 'It was an old friend of mine from England.'

Pili, who'd been chatting to a girlfriend on the next table, came over with a big grin. 'My God, Hooli, your friend in the Jeep stopped and asked me if he was in the right road. I said yes – *far* too enthusiastically! Never seen such a beautiful man. Like an angel, he was. *Is* he an angel?'

'I wouldn't know… He's an old school friend.'

'Really? Wow,' Pili said, and like many a girl before her, seemed like she wanted an introduction.

'Well anyway, that explains it…' Nerea said, looking embarrassed. 'I'll leave you two to your lunch.' She walked off. Maybe the nosy cow thought she and Josemi were a thing, and she'd dropped Juliana in it. Had the woman turned around and seen Josemi's troubled face, she would have been convinced of it.

They ate in silence.

'I didn't see Ben,' she found herself saying, knowing full well that wasn't the issue.

'Nor did you see Kim. And…' He put down his knife and fork, and leant forward, his fiery eyes fixing hers. 'I don't understand why you lied to me. It's been a week, and I'm still waiting for you to tell me about… you and Toby.'

'There *is* no—'

'I don't want to talk about this here,' he said, and asked for the bill. She got out her purse but he waved it away. Her

Coke finally arrived, and they waited uneasily while she drank it.

A part of her wanted to say that it wasn't any of his business. She was single; Josemi kissed her and left her confused. That was it. She could go off in a Jeep with anybody she liked, without having to tell him. But it seemed he was more committed to them waiting to be together than she thought – or at least, up until the moment he'd discovered that she'd lied to him.

'I can explain,' she said quietly, feeling shaky.

But he stood up and went over to the bar to hurry up the paying of the bill. She sipped her drink while she watched him exchanging smiles with the staff, saying he had to be somewhere. Maybe he *did* have to be somewhere, and they'd walk back to their houses and he'd drive off. Oh, *why* hadn't she just told him the truth?

When they were back in their road, he stopped outside her house. They went in, still wordless, and he sat down on the sofa. She sat down on the other end of it.

'Toby wants me to help him with a book about doing up his old Spanish *cortijo*. His agent is discussing it with publishers and, having read my blog about being here, she's putting me forward as his... ghost writer.'

She wasn't sure how ghost writer would translate. Not well, by the look of the frown on his face.

'His *what*? Ah, I know. You write it for him, but don't get credited, just paid.'

'Basically I'll read his diary, we talk about it, and then I'll turn it into a book.'

'I see. So he came over to talk to you about this.'

'And to see the house.'

'And to see how much... *involvement* you wanted.' He stopped gazing at the floor, and looked directly at her. She swiftly took up the surveillance of the floor. 'Hooli... I've no right to... I just want you to be honest with me. You must know how I feel. But if you—'

'It's *his* adventure, and I'm not part of that. And... I wouldn't *want* to be.'

He nodded slowly. 'But... doesn't it bother you that it would be like being a supporting artiste again? Uncredited, in the background? Taking direction? I thought you wanted to put all that behind you.'

'It's crossed my mind, but I like what he's trying to do, and think it would be good for my writing, and my blog.'

He seemed to weigh this up for a moment. 'Yes. But there's the question of how much you trust Toby, and whether you both see things the same way.'

She looked up. 'What d'you mean?'

'Balance is everything in a relationship – and especially in an *ex*-relationship. For example, with Isabel and me, there's mild mutual dislike tempered by the occasional need to respect each other's talents; easy. Gabi and I had a relationship that is forgettable compared to how much we enjoy being business partners; no problem. But I sense there hasn't been balance between you and Toby.'

True, but – unbelievably – the balance appeared to have tipped a little bit in the opposite direction. She was hoping it would tip back again, like some crazy child's seesaw, to become balanced before she started on the project. Josemi didn't need to know about that, but he definitely needed putting straight on *her* feelings.

'I'm no longer in love with Toby. In fact, I told him that...' God, how should she put it? Maybe he wasn't ready to hear that she was in love with *him*. Totally besotted, in fact. He was, after all, still sitting the other end of the sofa.

'You *told* him you weren't in love with him anymore?' he asked.

'I didn't need to. I told him… there was someone else.'

'Ah.' He bit his lip. 'That wouldn't be me, would it?' A hint of a cheeky smile.

'It might be. If you *want* it to be.'

'Well of *course* I want it to be! How can you say that?'

'Because every time we get anywhere near each other, you back away.'

He shook his head. 'Hooli, Hooli. What we have… is much too important to be rushed. You've been discovering about your mother, and then meeting your father – and I too have… had to get used to who you are, I must admit. Then both of us have been working hard – and on top of everything else we suddenly have a whole script to learn. Come here, you little sharpshooter.' He put a hand out and pulled her over towards him until she was in his arms, her back against his chest. Like Annie against Frank in the train carriage, pondering how wonderful it would be to fall in love.

She turned towards him in disbelief. 'I wasn't sure you…'

He squeezed her. 'Don't you realise how once we're together, it'll be hard to think of much else?' he said with a laugh. 'After the show, okay?'

'Okay! Oh, and you promised to come with me to Puddle Beach.'

'Of course. And if that's where you want to make love for the first time… Whatever you want, all yours!'

'Oh God!' she said, putting a hand to her face.

He took hold of both her hands. 'Don't worry, everything will be fine. Just promise to me honest with me. No more lies, okay?'

'I promise.'

TWENTY-TWO

DAY 65

Juliana bobbed around on her lilo, a passing boat much further out making some little waves on the lake-like sea. It was one of those days when it was so calm that it was safe to hand-paddle round the rocks to the next bay… and the next. The village beach was heaven – and one she'd soon be sharing with Josemi.

She stopped paddling, put her head down on the lilo pillow and closed her eyes. Smiled to herself as she remembered them kissing yesterday and then laughing as they prised themselves apart to let him get on with his ridiculous workload. It wasn't always as crazy as this, he'd assured her, just June and July, getting ready for the summer holidaymakers and second-homers wanting more paintings than he could possibly produce. Even come September, when she'd be down from her Granada TEFL course for the weekends, he'd have Sundays off for whole days at the beach… or in bed.

The thought of that set her tingling and melting all over. She slid off the lilo into the water – barely any less warm than herself but enough to bring her out of her dazed state. With her arms over the lilo, she slowly swam back to the main beach. A little sting on her forearm reminded her you couldn't always be sure about who else was enjoying the water. A purple jelly blob floated past. 'Well thanks for that, mate! All yours, I've had my bit of heaven for the day.' She needed to run through the script before the rehearsal later – the last before the dress rehearsal on Saturday. Although that too – unless she made too many mistakes – would be heaven, with all those funny and romantic scenes with Josemi.

It was getting too hot for walking to and from the beach. Josemi was right: she needed to get a bicycle, like he had. She wasn't good at pretending she'd probably be renting Arturo's house. She couldn't wait to tell him about how it would actually be hers if she met the conditions, and it annoyed her that she'd blabbed this to Toby, but couldn't tell Josemi. But only for a few more weeks. In which she just had to do Playa del Charco – Puddle Beach – and perhaps find a bit of proof that she and Dolores were getting on okay, and the house would be hers.

She was just thinking this when she got back, so couldn't believe her eyes when she opened the little envelope that had been slipped under her door: a note from Dolores, asking her to come to *merienda* at 17:00 the next day! She'd been invited to tea! She'd even left a phone number for her reply to. Whether this was a one-to-one or a gathering of Dolores's friends and neighbours, it was nothing short of a miracle, when the image of the person she'd named Miserable Bag on that first encounter came to mind. She grinned and couldn't wait to share it with Arturo – not just as proof for the condition, but because she knew this bizarre achievement would make him chuckle too.

She was getting sand from her feet and the lilo all over

the living room floor. At least she'd learnt not to bother with a sand-laden towel; she never got cold enough to need it, and she was dry minutes after coming out of the water anyway. If she was going to sit on the beach as well as swim, she took her Níjar animal-design sheet like the locals did. Odd that she'd entered by the front of the house, though; normally when she came back from the beach she came in through the terrace, so she could hose herself down a bit first – but if she'd done that, she might not have discovered Dolores's note for hours.

She delved around in her bag for her phone, took a picture of Dolores's note, and WhatsApped it to Arturo with an emoji of laughing and a thumbs-up. '*I don't know what I did right! But I'm pleased, because I like her – she's quite a character – and her son and I have just become novios!*'

What a good word that was, *novios*. So much easier than saying, girlfriend and boyfriend. Except that it also meant fiancés, so people were left to figure out which you meant. She smiled to herself. Arturo would wonder, as she just did, whether they might end up married. Who knows? But if it hadn't been for him, they would never even have met.

Right. Downstairs for a shower, lunch, and then the script in the shade before she and Josemi left together at four. She put her phone down – but noticed there were five missed calls. Damn, it would be Dad; she'd forgotten his Thursday calls had switched to mornings. But only one was from him. The other four were from Arturo, and three voicemails had been left during the last hour or so. The first was just noises like he'd dropped the phone. The second sounded like María José, saying something she couldn't catch and then being cut off. The third had both her and Arturo talking at the same time, asking her to come over. Had she missed a lunch? She thought they'd settled on Monday, with her confirming after today's rehearsal. Maybe there'd been a misunderstanding.

She called Arturo's phone, and it was answered after one ring – by María José. 'Hooliana. Can you come here now? Arturo wants to see you. He's not at all well…' She could hear Arturo being indignant in the background. 'He says there's nothing to worry about, and to please drive slowly and safely.' More words from Arturo. 'But come now.'

'I'll come over right away, and don't let him worry; I drive like a snail.'

She put the phone down and bit her lip in thought. There was something odd here. He'd never before asked María José to call on his behalf, and she'd called *four* times. That felt… *urgent*. She might drive like a snail, but she'd leave at once. No shower, just change her short beach dress for one of the market ones, grab her things and go.

Starting up the car, her phone pinged a message. It was Arturo, replying to hers with a dragon, teacup, artist palette, blue heart, thumbs-up and a smiley face. He was using his emojis; if he'd managed that, he couldn't be in too bad a state. She replied with a laughing face and a kiss, and set off.

As she drove, slowly and carefully, she realised how much – bar the moments of facetiousness – she'd become accustomed to listening to Arturo's advice and following it. She was like the most obedient of daughters; Dad wouldn't believe it. Even without the house, look what doing so had opened up for her – life in Spain, hopefully a wonderful partner, a new career, rediscovery of her enjoyment of drama, a mother who hadn't deserted her after all, and a biological father who was not only lovable but whose existence explained the way she'd spent her whole life feeling… foreign. She wished she could think of a way of thanking

Arturo for how much he'd done for her. For now, all she could do was drive slowly and carefully as he'd asked.

María José had said he *wasn't at all well*. Was there something he wasn't telling her? Once parked, she found herself running down the promenade – joining the joggers hugging the shady side. Finally nearing Arturo's apartment building and getting her breath back, she could see María José on the balcony, waving to her and saying something, presumably to Arturo inside; it seemed she'd been looking out for her.

When she got out of the lift, one look at María José's tired, red eyes set her heart beating. She pulled Juliana close to her in the hall and held her arm. 'He's very ill, very weak today. I'm so sorry, my dear, he insisted he didn't want you to know, but today you really have to.'

'But… has the doctor been? Should he be—'

'He doesn't want the doctor, and definitely not the hospital. There's nothing more they can do for him; the cancer is everywhere now.'

Cancer. Everywhere. No. She tried to take this in. Her head reeled.

'You know I'm a nurse?' María José asked.

'Yes… I mean, no… I didn't.'

'He's comfortable, and now that you're here, we only need Miguel, who's flying in and will be here soon. Come in, he's so looking forward to seeing you.' María José rubbed her arm. 'I'll get you some tea with sugar and a little to eat.'

In the living room, a smiling Arturo seemed tiny in what looked like an enormous semi-reclined throne, his usual peacock-blue armchair pushed to the side. He was dressed in one of his pale linen suits, a handkerchief folded at the pocket, and from the entrance to the grand living room, looked surprisingly well.

'Antoñita…'

Her heart thudded. Had he become confused?

'...would be so proud of you, Hooliana. I keep forgetting to tell you that.'

She smiled with relief. 'Uncle, you *have*, and many times. Don't worry.' She went over to him and thought she could hear him sigh as she kissed his cool papery cheek. Close up, his eyes looked sunken into his face, but bright as ever. 'How are you feeling? Are you in pain? Why didn't you tell me you...' She felt her voice start to catch.

María José came in with her tea and a plate of bite-size cheese sandwiches and tiny biscuits that she put on a small table next to her. The usual coffee table, she now noticed, was behind Arturo's throne, also pushed to the side, and covered in the bowls, bottles and packets of a nurse's trolley.

'I'm feeling... okay. I didn't tell you because I didn't want to waste time talking about...' He waved a vague hand over his body. 'It would have coloured our time together – which I thought would be longer, but...' He plucked at the neck of her turquoise-and-palm-tree dress. 'This is pretty, but from the market, so make sure you hand-wash.'

'I know,' she said with a smile, having heard this several times too.

A vague finger stroked her forearm and then went to his dry lips. 'You have brought the sea with you. How lovely. How could I have left you in London so long? I should have had the courage to bring you over here before.'

'But, Uncle, you *did*, that's what's important! And look at all you've—'

'No, no, look at what you've done for *me*.' He grimaced and rubbed his shoulder.

'Can I get you anything?'

'No, no.' He pointed at her tea and plate. 'Eat, drink.'

'Okay.' She wondered about offering to share it, like they

usually did – as the Spanish do, he'd told her – but as Arturo sipped a tiny amount from a beaker with a straw, she remembered how he'd often eaten like a bird at restaurants. She should have realised something was wrong.

'You have a rehearsal?' he asked.

'Yes, but I can miss it, it's okay.'

'I'm sorry I'll miss the play.'

'Oh...'

He shook his head, making himself cough. 'It would have been wonderful... but so would another swim, another concert, Miguel and Susana's baby... inviting you and Josemi here together, maybe *your* child... but there it is. I can't complain, when my Rosita was taken by this so many years ago. I can just hear her saying, "You can't control *everything*, Arturo!"'

María José came in and told him Miguel and Susana were on their way from the airport. He beckoned her over and kissed her hand, told her she was too good for him. She smiled and said she'd look out for them.

'Now, Hooliana, I have one more request. You have completed all the others?' he said with a twinkle in his eye.

'Just *Playa del Charco*, with Josemi, then yes. What can I do?'

'Please look after Miguel.'

'*Miguel?*' Confident, charming and successful Miguel – or so her cousin had seemed when they'd had dinner when he was in London a few years ago.

'He'll be angry I didn't tell him I was ill, feel guilty he hasn't seen me more. Maybe jealous of you – not because of the house, but... the time we've had, my affection for you. But keep in contact, forgive him. He's not so different to me – with time, your cousin could become a good friend. At the moment, he's just young for his age and a bit spoilt. Father-hood will be good for him.'

She smiled. 'Okay.'

He smiled back. 'O-kay,' he said in English, then lay back on the pillow and closed his eyes. Winced again.

Juliana watched anxiously. 'Something's hurting. Let me get María José.'

He didn't complain about that, so she went off to the kitchen, where María José was chopping salad.

'He may need a top-up…' María José said. 'He's stub-born, determined to stay awake. Maybe once he's seen Miguel, he'll…' She went off to attend to him.

He'll be more relaxed? Let go? Alone in the kitchen, the reality of losing Arturo… in the next few weeks, or maybe days, spread like a terrible pain through her body. She propped herself against the wall, half bent over. But if he was holding on, she would too; she'd cry all she needed to later. *Later*… she had the rehearsal. She couldn't do it. Or maybe she could – Arturo would want her to – but she'd have to be late. Drive from here. She sent a message to Josemi, and he replied immediately, supportive, sending love.

María José came back, with the plate of toddler-type lunch Juliana had left in the living room. She pulled out a chair at the kitchen table and made her sit down in front of it. 'Take a little rest, my dear. Eat and drink, keep your energy. Miguel and Susana are just coming up, give them a little time with him, then I know he wants you back.'

She could soon hear their voices, Miguel's rather loud, Susana's in quiet bursts, awkward. She emptied the plate and stopped feeling so dizzy. Finished her tea.

María José came back and insisted on making her another. Then Miguel came in, and she stood up to embrace him.

'He wants us all, together. María José, you too. And… would you believe it, a Raf tomato. It's not the season! What the fuck are we going to do?'

'Well I've got *these*,' María José said, pointing to a bowl. 'They must be hybrids, but sadly – or fortunately – I doubt he's up to telling the difference now.'

'Thank God.'

'Chopped or whole?' she asked.

'No idea. Some of each?'

They went in with the red-green offering. Susana was holding Arturo's hand and talking about the baby, while he gently nodded and smiled, eyes half shut now.

'Ah,' he said, on seeing the tomato. María José held the plate on his chest. He stroked the shiny, comically ridged form of the whole one. María José had to help him put one of the segments into his mouth. He groaned with pleasure, but took a while to swallow.

'Heaven,' he said in English, tapping Juliana's arm and waving a limp hand over at the bookcase.

They all followed his gaze, Miguel offering to read to him, María José asking what he wanted. The hand fell, impatiently, his face pained with frustration.

Juliana went over to the CD player on the bookcase. 'Er… Bee Gees?'

She thought she saw a little nod.

'"Too Much… Heaven"?' she said, her voice cracking.

Miguel put his face close to his father's, then turned to her and nodded.

The caressing harmonies filled the room. Arturo lay there motionless, his eyes closed, but with a little smile on his lips again. And then, with Miguel and Susana holding one hand, Juliana and María José the other, he left them.

TWENTY-THREE

DAY 72

'I'm sorry, can't tell when this is going to happen,' Juliana said, pulling another tissue out of the box Dolores had put beside her and blowing her nose.

'Normal,' Dolores said. 'It comes and goes, comes and goes; this is the way.'

It was calm in Dolores's small-windowed little living room, with its odd mix of old and new: a flat-screen TV on the wall behind the homely old sofa and armchairs, some of Níjar's more modern ceramics on the lace-covered dark wood sideboard. Checho, resting his head on his paws, looked up in sympathy from his bed. The mantelpiece clock ticked timelessly on.

This time last week, almost exactly, Arturo had died. In England, she'd probably be at his funeral today, but in Spain, funerals happen very quickly. Often in twenty-four hours, like Arturo's. While you're still so in shock you can hardly cry. Now Arturo was in San Rafael, with his parents and sister – in the *nicho* she'd photographed in the cemetery and shown him, like an idiot, way back at their first meeting here. Even though she still had *Arturo lunch?* on her calendar for tomorrow. It was all so impossible to believe; he'd looked old for his years, yes, but so full of life. She'd thought she would have years of lunches with her crazy, caring uncle; but now – despite the diary, the scrapbook and the blog – she didn't even have a photo of him.

Her throat painfully constricted again. She could do with getting back to the house and having one of those awful sobbing events best done on her own. But Arturo would be chuffed she was having *tea with Dolores,* and the Not-so-Miserable Bag had taken trouble to spread the little table with savoury snacks, homemade lemony biscuits and an almond-and-honey cake.

'Can you remember anything else?' Juliana asked, taking another biscuit while Dolores topped up her mint *infusión.* She'd already had a description of Arturo as a young chap with natty clothes that he'd picked up in the market and altered.

'Oh yes. When he and Antoñita were quite young teenagers, they had this puppet theatre they used to take to children's parties. They taped the play with music, using different voices, they had lighting, bought more and more puppets with their earnings. And Arturo, he was like a... circus master!'

'Ha, I can just see that! And there's a photo of them with a puppet theatre in the house!' She would have to have that as her photo of him. 'Then later, of course, he got into amateur dramatics.'

'Yes.' She sipped her tea and put down the cup. Shifted her solid, navy-clad body in her seat. 'Talking of drama, this is one of the reasons I wanted you to come over. I want you to know that... it's not a problem for me if Fran comes to the show.'

'Oh… Well that would be… He said he didn't want to cause any upset and wouldn't come, but—'

'No, he shouldn't miss it. Maybe he wants to avoid *me*.'

'No, no…'

'I blamed him for taking my sister off to Tabernas, where she was never going to be happy. And yes, for having an affair. But I never blamed him for the accident. That was down to María Carmen. She was always a very self-centred, reckless person – and with the drinking…'

'I… wondered if you blamed my *mother* for everything, and that was why…' Why you were so horrified at the sight of me on my arrival.

Dolores put down her cup, waited a moment. 'You have to understand… it was a shock when Josemi and I first saw you, and instantly realised that your mother must have returned and conceived you with Fran – you look so like him. We knew my sister was manically upset to hear that her rival had been blessed with a child when she hadn't been, but now we wonder if she could have known you were *his*.'

Juliana shook her head. 'Fran never told her. He'd only just found out about me himself. Eight years after they bumped into each other in San José, she took me to Tabernas, wanting to show me where she'd worked – although maybe hoping Fran still worked there, I don't know.'

She nodded slowly. 'Your poor mother, taken so young. And now the brother and sister are together again. I'm sorry, it's not the time to talk about this.'

'I'm glad we have. As Josemi says, we can't pretend it didn't happen.'

'But we can move forward. I will say hello to Fran at the show. I liked him once. When he was courting María Carmen and I was still a child, he was quite rude to my father, telling him he shouldn't force me to do riding just because the rest of the family loved it!'

'I can imagine that – he got annoyed at the idea of my dad having forced me into drama.'

Dolores laughed and patted Juliana's hand. 'But the difference is, I'm still scared of horses, but you're no longer scared of drama.'

'It's different. I'm more myself here, despite the language. And I'm lucky to have the most wonderful co-star!'

She smiled. 'He's lucky too. Finally! There have been too many girls who have lied to him, tricked him…'

How had they got onto that? Had he told Dolores about the little lie *she* had told him? Maybe the Miserable Bag was trying to warn her. But no, she was smiling and putting a slice of cake on her plate.

Dolores looked out of the window and grinned. 'Look at that. My son never fails to sense the moment a cake is being sliced!'

She opened the door and Josemi came in, kissed them both, made a fuss of Checho and sat down. 'Perfect timing!'

'You've been in Almería all day?' Dolores asked him.

'Yes. Paintings, this and that…' He turned to Juliana. 'How are you doing today?' He looked at her more closely, saw the red eyes and stroked her arm. 'Oh, poor thing… but you're eating better, I hope.'

She nodded, and took a small mouthful of cake. Its honeyed and nutty sweetness exploded in her mouth; it was the first thing she'd enjoyed in a week. 'Mm, this is amazing.'

'Good! You'll need the energy for the rehearsal,' Dolores said.

They chatted about the play for a while, then Juliana thanked Dolores profusely, and she and Josemi went back to their houses to get ready to leave.

Sorting out her bag, she noticed some unread Whats-Apps: Dad and Kim, bless them, both asking how she was doing today, even though she'd only spoken to them both last night, and Toby asking the same but following it with a further message about when he could phone her. When he'd called at the weekend to say a publisher was considering their proposal, she'd told him Arturo had died and she wasn't up to talking. She'd put him off on several days since. She quickly replied to all three, saying she was surviving and about to leave for the rehearsal.

She went downstairs and changed into the T-shirt she wore under the Annie dungarees. Putting the other one in the laundry basket, she saw the sea-salty dress she had been wearing when she was with Arturo.

'*Can I call?*'

Toby. No, he couldn't. Even if he'd been quite sweet with his messages and sent a CS Lewis quote.

'*I've got some news!*'

It would be quicker to talk than write messages. She tapped the phone sign.

'Jules! The publisher wants it! And you for the ghost writer! I'll email all you the details.'

'Oh brilliant!' Not least because – if the house became hers – the sooner she found the amount for the inheritance tax, the sooner she'd be able to come back to it.

'So, it's okay?'

She realised that with the distraction of putting the dress to her face and breathing in the polished-wood scent of Arturo's apartment, she hadn't been listening to what the publisher particularly liked. 'Now we just have to get to work!' she said.

'But… what I said about the narrative, regarding us. D'you mind looking like the girl who dumped me?'

Who wouldn't mind looking like the only girl who'd ever turned down Toby Campbell-West? How cool was that? She *had* turned him down, there was truth in this – even if what he'd offered was only a three-month friends-with-benefits thing.

'Okay.'

'Great. Well, *not* great, but you know what I mean. Obviously I'll keep asking, because…'

She couldn't follow him. Tea with Dolores, despite having gone surprisingly and deliciously well, had somehow taken a toll. It would have been better to put Toby off a bit longer and have a lie-down for half an hour. 'Sorry?'

'If you have to wait a bit for your house, you could always stay with me.'

'*No*, Toby.'

'How's it going with the house? When does the executor make a decision?'

'Some time after the ninety days. The solicitor called me in on Tuesday. He wouldn't tell me who the executor for the house conditions was, but I glimpsed Miguel's name on the papers.'

'Miguel?'

'Arturo's son.'

'But is there a reason he might he not want you to have it?'

'I don't know. If I don't get it, the proceeds of the sale go to a long list of Arturo's favourite charities. Look, I know it sounds weird, but I'm fatalistic about the house. Arturo has already given me so much, one way and another. D'you know, I was just feeling sad about giving the car up, when I got the documents out of the glove compartment and found I wasn't driving his "car he didn't use anymore"; he bought it a week before I arrived and put it in my name! I remember him saying it was like my Fiat in England – he'd obviously specially chosen it for me. I never even said thank you.' She could feel herself getting choked up again.

'But he sounds like a guy who didn't need to be thanked all the time.'

She suddenly noticed Josemi on the terrace, admiring one of her cacti. How long had he been there? She looked at her watch.

'Oh God, I've got to go. Dress rehearsal, wish me luck!'

'Ah, okay – break a leg!'

She went out to Josemi. 'Sorry, not quite ready.'

'What've you been *doing*? Come on!'

'Somebody called. I'll just be a minute.'

She went back inside and tried to concentrate on collecting her things rather than wondering what Josemi might have heard; she didn't want him to think she expected to inherit the house.

'I thought you'd stopped your dad ringing just before every Thursday rehearsal,' he said in the car.

She could have said she hadn't been completely successful in that, made out she'd been talking to him. Not mentioned Toby. But... no more lies.

'It was Toby. The publishers want the book, and I've got the ghostwriting job. To be honest, I'm going to have to re-find my enthusiasm, but the money will be handy for... for this and that.'

'Good! Congratulations!' He patted her back. 'I know you took some time over that proposal. And will there be a documentary too?'

'Yes. Just one programme – not a series.'

'And will you be involved in that?'

'No! That's nothing to do with me.' They bobbed over

the blind summit and had miles of precipitous coastline in front of them. 'Wow – this gets to me every time!'

'He should have chosen San Rafael, or somewhere else in the natural park. There's nowhere more beautiful.'

'There really isn't. But I don't want the Brits to know about it.'

'True, and if he was filming here, we could get caught up in his story – nightmare!'

'Quite!' she said, but tried to remember what Toby had said. She *was* sort of in the story, as the girl who'd turned him down. She'd have to make it clear that didn't mean being filmed or photographed. But then, he would have mentioned that, surely. She'd be mentioned as someone who'd rejected his advances – which was sort of prologue, rather than being in it. Surely Josemi wouldn't mind that.

TWENTY-FOUR

DAY 82

She could have been driving to San José to meet Kim at the weekly expat bar – except she was in Annie's tatty plaits, and next to her, Josemi's hair was tightly ponytailed and slicked back into 'swollen-headed' sharpshooter showman Frank Butler's.

'You should have let me drive,' he said.

'You always drive. Anyway, it gives me something else to think about.' She glanced over at him. He looked outrageously handsome – all the more so for not being bothered about it – and deceptively calm. 'How are *you* doing?'

'Not good. But I'll be better once we're there, and fine once the music starts. You?'

'Kind of sick. I'll be fine once it's *over!*' Actually, she wouldn't be, because it wasn't just the show she was nervous about. There was Dolores meeting Fran and Josefa, and Toby meeting Josemi. Thank heavens Dad and Olivia couldn't come. Then later there'd be just her and Josemi, which was wonderful but also butterfly-inducing to think about.

He patted her thigh. 'Don't say that, just enjoy it. So what if we get the verses muddled in "Anything You Can Do" again? Half the audience probably won't even look at the Spanish translation of the lyrics on the screen.'

'Er… *we?*' He'd come seriously a cropper in the dress rehearsal.

'Okay, *me,* but you made up a line in our love song, a far greater crime. So that's *at least* one miss each,' he said with a grin.

'Oh my God, we're turning into Frank and Annie. Surprised you haven't tried teaching me how to drive.'

He put his hands up defensively. 'I've shown such… restraint!'

'What?' she said with an indignant laugh.

'But I suggest you pull over and let me do the parking – I know all the places.'

When they came into the village she pulled into the entrance of a hotel with horses that Fran had told her about. They swapped places, and Josemi asked if she could reach his water bottle on the back seat. She hauled his rucksack onto her lap. 'Good God, what have you got in here? A load of extra rifles?'

'Don't open it,' he said quickly. 'Bottle's just in the side pocket.' She pulled it out and gave it to him. 'And what's in yours? It looks about to explode.'

'*Any bag you can pack, I can pack fatter,*' she sang. 'A towel. Just in case we… have a dip in the sea afterwards.'

He smiled and pulled her over to him. '*Eso,*' he said. *That.* He'd obviously thought the same. That's what they'd be doing. That and more, she imagined, when he kissed her so passionately that for a moment the show and the nerves disappeared.

———

230

It was nearly time. The sound check had gone well, the lighting and the translating screen put through their paces, and the choir and orchestra were already up on the stage. The two women backstage supervising the four overexcited kids struggled to give Juliana some peace, but fun with her stage siblings was a welcome distraction.

Juliana and Josemi peeped out from behind the stage at the growing audience filling the rows of chairs or queuing at the refreshment stalls. In the daytime, the park was a slightly tatty area with a playground, adult exercise bars, a paddle ball court and a cycle track, but for tonight it had been swept to perfection, and the eucalyptus trees, strung with coloured bulbs, looked magical against the backdrop of fuzzy hills surrounding the village.

Josemi nudged her. 'Look, about tenth row, next to the aisle!'

She could see Elise and her husband, and Dolores next to them. And next to her... Fran and Josefa, nodding and smiling at something Dolores was saying!

'Well! That's a relief!'

'Who's the chap in the row in front, turning around to talk—'

'Miguel and his wife! They must be down to start sorting out the apartment. I told them about the play, but I really didn't think they'd come.' She tried not to remember her hurt at having her offer to help with the apartment so firmly turned down. 'Oh look, Ben's here with his latest girlfriend.'

'No, that's Nerea's daughter. Whatever he did wrong, he's obviously been forgiven. Ah, and looks like the whole of the Rafaelarte group have come.'

'Oh yes, there's Gabi.' She then recognised the pretty red-headed artist '...talking to Pili.'

'Kim and the expat group in the front row for you!'

'God, Juan Luis, the gas boiler man has a *huge* family… There's the chap from the *ferretería*… the pharmacist…'

'Is there anyone who *isn't* here?' Josemi asked.

There *was*: Toby. He'd messaged yesterday to say he'd arrived in Spain and would be coming, but maybe he'd over-done working on the house in this heat. Much as she'd quite like to have his feedback on her first stage role for over a decade, it would be a relief not to have to introduce him to Josemi.

'That's got to be Toby,' Josemi said. 'A professional actor in the front row – that's all I need.'

Oh. She'd forgotten that Toby always made a last-minute entrance, minimising pestering from fans. He was already being absorbed by the expat group, members further down the row nudging each other as they recognised him. He was also turning a lot of Spanish female heads. Pili had broken off her chat with Gabi to go over to him, and looked delighted, as they did the double kiss thing, that he seemed to have remembered asking her for the road name when he came to San Rafael.

'He's a *television* actor. Hasn't got your gorgeous singing voice,' she said, tapping Josemi's smartly jacketed chest. It was true: Josemi's voice was untrained but had a beautiful tone and expression – like his harmonica playing. The ensemble was getting ready to go on for the first scene. 'Looks like we're off. Oh God!'

He squeezed her and smiled. 'You *are* Annie. Enjoy it! Promise?'

'Absolutely promise.' He was right. What was the point in all those rehearsals – all those years of drama training, in fact – if she couldn't enjoy the show? *A por ello*. Go for it. And yes, she could *be* Annie. Maybe that was the difference; it was the first time she'd thrown her own feelings into a role.

After some words from the mayor, the show began with the big ensemble piece introducing Buffalo Bill's Wild West Show and its spangled, red-and-white suited sharpshooter, Frank Butler. Josemi was frighteningly good at portraying the swaggering pride of the star, but pleasingly less successful at flirtation with the adoring girls.

On initially wobbly legs she went on with the kids and enjoyed her last time singing 'Doing What Comes Naturally' with her equally scruffy stage siblings. Then Annie met Frank, and the bit that used to annoy her − being all floppy-armed, mouth-open besotted-at-sight with Frank − was easy fun and got lots of laughs. She was soon on her own singing 'You Can't Get a Man with a Gun' − although this show and its plastic rifles had definitely helped get hers.

Once she'd been persuaded there was 'No Business Like Show Business', she was off for a quick change out of dungarees into a skirt and cowboy shirt. She was now a show partner with Frank − and, starting to fall for her, he asked if she'd ever loved anybody. Juliana *thought* she had − and he was sitting in the front row − but it wasn't like this. 'They Say It's Wonderful', they sang, and she was so wrapped around by Josemi's arm and the slow rapture of the melody that she almost forgot she was on a stage in front of hundreds of people.

After a change into a sparkly white sharpshooter costume, there was the scene where Buffalo Bill congratulated her on her new shooting trick, and Indian Chief Sitting Bull was so impressed that he put much-needed money into the company and adopted her as his daughter. Just before the interval, it turned out that Frank, unhappy to be overshadowed, was leaving to work with another show. Sitting Bull − portly Lolo, who ran both the tyre-mending place by the roundabout and the dog rescue centre −

comforted her and, Arturo-like, pretty much told her to ride it out.

Lolo patted her shoulder when they came off stage. 'You're splendid tonight, Annie – I mean, Hooliana. How proud your uncle would be. He was very good too. The wizard in the *Wizard of Oz*, the emcee in *Cabaret*…'

'Thank you! Oh – I can just see him in those roles!'

A quick hug and a piece of Elise's new fig *bizcocho* with Josemi in the interval, and she was back on stage. Annie was on a European tour, missing her man – as *she* would be, back in England in a week's time; it wasn't difficult to act this, or the delight when Buffalo Bill told her they were going back early.

Then she braced herself for the swanky reception scene where the two Wild West shows and their star shooters are due to unite, but her larger collection of medals sparked the competitive and lyric-nightmare 'Anything You Can Do' song with Frank. It had all been going too well; there wasn't a prayer of them getting it right. But when she mixed up one of the lines and they both started laugh-singing, the audience laughed with them and cheered.

It was then an easy roll to the 'There's No Business Like Show Business' happy ending. The applause, screams and shouts at the end were something she'd never known; you'd think they were stars touring a sell-out West End show, not a mixed-age bunch of rural amateurs with a creaky wooden stage and no scenery.

Buffalo Bill – who sold tomatoes to Almería's central market – thanked the directors, orchestra, cast and all the people who'd helped behind the scenes. When he'd finished, Juliana asked the audience to dig deep in their pockets so that this wonderful organisation could give drama, music and dance lessons to even more adults and children who couldn't afford them. Everybody should have the chance to have this much fun being in a show!

It was time to say hello to everyone. Dolores was tearfully delighted, and agreeing with Fran and Josefa about Juliana and Josemi's connection on stage. Elise was thanked for producing cake that had got them through the shows. Miguel brought a lump to Juliana's throat by mentioning how Arturo would have loved it. Josemi's Rafaelarte artist friends couldn't understand how he'd had the time, and the keyboard player from the band he'd played harmonica with at the cactus place said he'd being doing some guest vocals next time – with Juliana too, if she liked. The expat group were full of congratulations, as were English visitors who'd come along.

One English visitor, however, appeared to be holding back. Toby was talking to a long-faced chap who, despite the sunburn and prematurely receding hair, she recognised as his old friend Giles from drama college. Over the years, she'd heard that Giles had had little acting work, so he'd tried teaching, writing, and now, by the look of his massive camera, photography.

'So... Toby, and then... can we disappear?' she asked Josemi.

'We can! I've already excused us from the after-show party.'

'Oh well done!'

'Do I *want* to meet him?' Josemi asked.

'Maybe not, but he's coming over.'

It wouldn't have been Toby's style to have to wait in a queue to hug and talk to her. He was smiling, but looking a bit tired in the heavy evening heat. 'Jules...' He hugged her a bit too tightly. 'You were... fantastic. I always knew you had it in you.'

'No, no, the thing is that I'd forgotten I could enjoy it!'

'That's great.' He pointed to his friend. 'Remember Giles?'

'Of course, how're you doing?' she asked him.

Giles held out a sweaty hand and mumbled something.

'We've taken some lovely shots for you,' Toby said.

Hadn't he noticed there'd been a local photographer there, as well as someone from the English language *Olive Press* newspaper? 'Oh, brilliant.' She took Josemi's arm and introduced him.

Josemi shook their hands thoroughly, Giles looking like he might fall over.

'Great performance,' Toby said. He looked Josemi up and down, possibly glad to see the slick 'swollen-headed' sharpshooter now in beach shorts and a plain white T-shirt.

'Thanks, it was a lot of fun,' he replied in English.

'I bet. Jules has always loved cowboys.' He turned to her. 'Have you still got that Woody doll I gave you?'

'Of course. I'll be bringing him back here with me.'

Josemi nodded. 'And he can be seat-ed for watch my DVD of *Story of the Toy.* I love this film. *Especialmente* the girl cowboy!' He put an arm round Juliana and squeezed her.

Giles looked at Toby with concern. Juliana now remembered that Giles was another person in an unbalanced relationship with Toby: they'd been Jules and Giles, the adoring sidekicks. It didn't look like Giles had moved on from that.

'How's the house?' Juliana asked him. 'Don't forget I expect to see some first diary entries next week!'

The thought of the house seemed to cheer him. 'It's... magical. I've already cleared up the shady terrace and tended the plants, so I've got somewhere lovely to sit and relax with a beer between tasks.'

'Ha! Good idea. I look forward to an invitation when I come back from England.'

He opened his mouth as if to say something, then nodded and smiled.

'So-rry, we are going for something to eat… somewhere quiet, relax,' Josemi said. 'Thank you for coming from Vera to see the show.'

'My pleasure,' Toby said, looking back on form.

After a further round of hugs and handshakes, Josemi and Juliana picked up their rucksacks from the dressing rooms, hugged a few cast and orchestra members doing the same thing, and wandered off down the road to check out the water.

Arriving at where the road bends to follow the sea, a line of pretty beach houses on one side, some restaurants and bars – including the expat's one – on the other, Josemi pulled her arm to follow the road.

'There's a better beach? Or d'you want to eat first?' she asked, back in Spanish.

He grinned. 'A better beach.'

They passed another path going off between the houses to a beach. 'No?'

'No.'

They were nearly as far as the smart beachfront hotel where Dad and Olivia had stayed for their visit. The next beach was Playa de La Calilla, about another fifteen minutes on. It had super-soft sand, but the rocks might be a bit creepy at night…

He pulled her into the hotel reception. 'What? Josemi!' she said, as the laughing receptionist handed him a key.

'We deserve it!' he said, as he took her past a dining room looking out over the sea towards the marina, then along the corridor, looking at names on the doors. 'And don' worry of the clothes,' he said in English. 'I took some from your line, *incluso* some *bragas*!'

She laughed. 'You *stole* my knickers?'

'Yes! Here we are, room of the *faro*.' He unlocked the door.

'The lighthouse room. Oh... Oh my God!' A blue-tiled bedhead with lighthouse bedside lamps, huge white bed, a chunky blue Níjar rug, windows looking out on to the sea, and a door to a balcony that... ended in steps going down to their own tiny beach! 'This is...!'

He hugged her. '...what we deserve! Swim first?' Out of his rucksack came their beach towels, a bikini, a market dress, and a hairbrush and pack of hair ties from the pharmacy.

'Yes. Oh wow! But...'

Already having put a bikini on, she pulled the dress off over her head.

'*Ay, mi* Hooli...' He ran his hand down her side, then took of his T-shirt and pressed his body against hers, kissed down her neck...

She gasped, her legs not wanting to hold her up... She wanted to be on a flat surface with him, as soon as possible.

'Ah... But we've waited this long... Come on, quick swim first!' He took her hand and led her on to the balcony, helped her down most of the steps, then picked her up in his arms and carried her down the beach, wading into the mild sea until she felt it gently swirling around her... 'Under!' He let he go and leapt like a dolphin into the water, emerging a little further out among the ripples tipped with their red and green lights from the marina across the bay. She followed him, her body caressed by the water as she sped through it. Then she was with him again, their hair sleeked back form the water, laughing as they wiped the last of the Annie and Frank make-up away, then exploring each other's bodies with their hands... and pulling their swimsuits off. Another kiss, his tongue pushing inside her mouth, and then she pulled at his arm and made him race out of the water with her, padding up the soft warm sand and up the wooden steps… in and out of the shower to lose the sand, almost leaping on to the bed together.

There was kissing and licking of salty bodies, then arms wrapping around each other as they made love slowly and gently, and then more intensely, until she cried out with a stinging ecstasy she'd never known before, and as he shuddered with his own pleasure, the song came back to her, the one about how wonderful it would be, to hold a man in your arms, to fall in love.

TWENTY-FIVE

DAY 87

'I could get used to this. Great way to start the day.' Josemi lay back on the pillow and pulled her onto his shoulder.

'Mm.' An early morning swim followed by making love. 'Is it still warm enough to swim in October? People keep telling me different things.'

'Of course! Not a bath, but lovely. I swim in the sea into November. After that, I'll introduce you to a lovely indoor pool in Almería.'

'Okay!'

He reached for his phone. 'So you're on the course in Granada… 2nd to the 27th September?'

'That's right. So maybe I'll come and see you the weekend of the 7th?'

'Yes! Let's see that's…'

'Six weeks.'

He squeezed her. 'It's nothing. We'll chat, keep busy, and after another four weeks you'll move back in next door again.'

'If Miguel lets me rent the house,' she remembered to add.

'Of course he will.'

The lie stuck in her throat. What harm would it do to tell him now? 'Actually…' She raised herself up on one elbow and met his eyes. 'He told me not to tell anyone, but I'm sure he wouldn't mind, and since it's you… Arturo's left me the house, as long as I've completed a little list of conditions in my three months here.'

He looked puzzled. 'Conditions?'

'Yes, doing the house and terrace, being in the play, that kind of thing. Nothing that hasn't been a pleasure to do. I'm just waiting to hear from the executor for the house that I've met the conditions… but I know I have.'

'Who *is* the executor?' he asked, closing his phone and reaching for his water on the bedside table.

Why was he asking that? It seemed odd that he wasn't pushing her for more about the conditions, like Toby did. If it were her, she'd want to see the whole list.

'I don't know. I'm not supposed to know, for some reason. But as it happens, the lawyer was flipping the papers about and I'm pretty sure I saw Miguel's name, which sort of makes sense.'

'Really?'

'Yes! Although it really doesn't matter who it is; he and the lawyer will look at all my photos and scrapbook and that'll be that.'

'Ah.' He put his water back on the table and turned to her, patted her arm. 'Well… that's quite something! Congratulations!'

'My uncle was very generous, and adored my mama.'

'And you too, Hooli – that was obvious. You certainly earned this with the play! Did you see the pictures in the paper? Look.' He got up and fetched his iPad, brought the article up onto the screen. 'We should buy the paper and keep this.'

'...*There was a record high in donations, probably due to the bravery of the talented leads stepping into the roles less than four weeks before the show,*' she read. 'Great!' She pointed to a group shot with a folded-arms Sitting Bull. 'Ha – look at Lolo in that picture! Such a sweetie. Did you see him chatting with your mother after the show?'

'Was he? Ah, but probably just talking about Checho – we got him from the dog rescue centre he runs. Let's not get too excited!'

'Yeah, but he's on his own, with a grown-up son, loves dogs, funny and kind...'

'I know. But my mother's so, so fussy...' She'd flicked on to a picture of them singing 'They Say It's Wonderful'. 'Aw!'

'Giles has done a similar one. I put it in my blog yesterday,' she said.

'Toby's friend?'

'Yes. Look.' She went to her blog and showed it to him.

'It's great! Did he send you others too?'

'Yes, but... they're too centred on us rather than the whole show. Weird. Maybe he thought that's what I wanted.'

'Let's see.'

She opened the file. There were the duet photos, including close-ups that made them look like they were in a film; a few group shots; and then several of them laughing with friends after the show.

'Hm, looks like he's practising to be a private detective!'

She laughed. 'Either that, or he's smitten with you!'

'Or he's taking them for *Toby*, who's smitten with *you*.'

She stopped laughing. 'Oh *please*.' She closed the website and noticed the time. 'When's your client coming?'

'Still got an hour.'

'Coffee?'

'Please.'

She got up and had a quick shower, put on a new market dress – more cacti, but the tie-dye background in orange hues for a change. Arturo had loved orange; she'd been going to wear it for her next lunch with him. She cheered herself by thinking how he'd be happy she was seeing Fran and Josefa before she went back to England.

Josemi was watching her. 'Seriously though, you must have noticed that Toby looked... *gutted.*'

She turned to him. 'No, I didn't. He just looked like most newly arrived Brits – tired and dehydrated.'

Josemi shook his head slowly. Lying to him about that day Toby took her to see his house in Vera, even though they'd cleared that up, seemed to have left a scar.

'Look, Toby's never felt gutted in his life,' she said. 'I think he'd almost *like* to feel gutted. It's part of why he's doing his Spanish house; he wants to find the real Toby. Personally, I'm not sure such a creature exists.'

He was frowning.

'Josemi! I've got a day and a half left before I go, and don't want a minute more of it taken up talking about Toby! It's *work* for me, and really... a bit *boring*, to be honest.'

He laughed. 'Okay, okay! You're right.' He got out of bed and put his strong brown arms around her and squeezed. 'Ah, my Hooli. *Sorry,*' he said in English. 'You make the coffee, I shower and think about what maybe we will do tomorrow – after the usual start to the day!'

———

Fran wiped his mouth on the crisp Fort Tabernas Studios napkin and smiled at her. He was still a cowboy – checked shirt, tight trousers and cowboy boots, hat on the tablecloth – but in his cowboy best. 'We've only ever been in the smart restaurant for Christmas staff parties!'

Josefa nodded. 'We should do it more often!'

'It's such a treat. Thank you so much for all this,' Juliana said. He'd shown her part of Jill's house that wasn't open to visitors, all three having tears in their eyes when the music came on; they'd thanked Paco the barman for telling her to ask Fran about her mother, and seen his surprise when they told him they were father and daughter; and Fran had pointed out where he and Juliana had first met by the stable, when she was seven and a half.

'We know you must want to get back to your Josemi, so if you don't want to stay for the Wild West show and a swim, we'll understand,' he said, patting her hand.

They were so sweet about Josemi, especially now they'd seen how happy their relationship made Dolores.

'No, no, I want to do the whole thing. Anyway, he's working hard so he can have time off on my last day tomorrow before I fly on Sunday.'

'Ah, okay. And then you won't see him – and us! – until…?'

'The odd weekend while I'm studying in Granada – although my friend says it's intensive and I'll have lots to do in the evenings and weekends. I'm back from there on the 29th September.'

'We'll miss you,' Josefa said.

When Josefa excused herself to go to the ladies', Fran looked pensive a moment, sipped his wine, then patted her hand again. 'Hooliana, I want you to know – and Josefa knows about this – just before my accident, I was planning to end my marriage to María Carmen. Her behaviour had become… It is hard to say this, as a man, but… she used to throw things at me, hit me.'

'Oh my God, how awful.'

'It was. It couldn't go on. But then I had the accident, with no way of contacting Antoñita. I hoped she'd wait, have the courage to believe in me. But very sadly, she didn't. Obviously, I eventually found a soul mate in Josefa, nearly twenty years ago now, but for Antoñita… I'm telling you this, because… Be careful with England, that you and Josemi don't lose your trust in each other, that you have the courage to believe.'

———

Juliana put a finger on Arturo's glassed photo in the plaque. 'I hope you don't mind being here rather than with Rosita in the Almería cemetery. But I suppose you must have talked about it with Miguel. Shame you didn't discuss the photo.' It was a rather formal one, like something for a business convention. 'Anyway, they've arrived! All my orange flowers! I've also got gerbera, ranunculus, tulips… loads! The blue ones are taking longer. Thought we'd start with these…' She put the plastic orange calla lilies in the vases and stood back to see the effect. 'What do *you* think, Mama?' She smiled tearfully; there was quite a Sixties vibe going on, with Mama's purple and Arturo's orange. Then she kissed her two forefingers and put one on each photo. 'I'll just have to talk to you both from England, okay?'

She started walking back. It was about seven, but the heat still bore down – and up from the orange earth track, and across from the rock of the hillside next to her. She walked slowly, swigged from her water bottle, kept to the shady side of the path. She loved the enveloping heat here, now she knew how to go with it. How she would miss this scenery – particularly at this time of the day, when the shadows lengthen on the burnt-orange, fuzzy hills, sending them into the surreal three-dimension relief of Josemi's paintings.

Her phone buzzed in her bag. She thought it would be Josemi, asking when she'd be back, but it was Kim.

'What's he *thinking* of?' Kim said.

'Who?'

'Haven't you *seen*?'

'Seen what?' Toby must have left a stupid remark on her blog. She could delete it and have a word with him.

'Oh, Jules… Toby's got this story about how a Spanish amateur actress has dumped him for one of her own kind, and he's building a house in Spain to get her back.'

She stopped dead. '*What*? Where?'

'Er… everywhere. Several English papers… they must have nothing else to—'

'Oh for *fuck's* sake!'

'It's a small article, picture of him and you – a selfie somewhere in golden Spanish light – then a close-up of you and Josemi from the show.'

'Uh… Why—'

'Oh *no*. I've just seen it's in the *Olive Press* too.'

'*God*… I need to talk to Josemi. Thanks, Kim. And thanks for not even asking if there's any truth in it.'

'I don't need to. Let me know if there's anything I can do. Talk later.'

She speeded up her walk. Bloody Toby, how could he do this? Okay, he thought her relationship with Josemi had only just begun, so maybe didn't think this would do any harm. But to tell the world *he'd* been having a relationship with her, when in fact it was over between them eleven years ago, was outrageous. How *dare* he?

She stomped on, her head starting to throb with the inescapable truth that this was her fault too; why in hell had she agreed to being any part of the 'narrative' of his project? She should have thought about how this could go; *turning him down, dumped*… Once this was out of Toby's control and with the programme makers, agents, publicists… the difference between these two terms seemed to have been lost.

Once in the road, she noticed Dolores's house had all its shutters down. Maybe she'd gone to stay with her friend in Almería, coming back before Sunday afternoon for her and Josemi's drive up to his Uncle Pepe in Madrid.

She stopped outside Josemi's house and could hear the familiar sounds of display stands squeaking as they were moved about the floor. She took a big breath and let it out slowly; she needed to get this sorted out and over with, so they could enjoy their last little bit of time together.

Rodri answered the door – Josemi's reliable and serious eighteen-year-old assistant, shortly off to art college. 'Hello, Hooliana. He's not here. I'm getting the gallery ready for tomorrow.'

'Ah – of course.' Josemi had arranged for him to cover the Saturday gallery so he'd be free for their last day. 'So glad you can do it! When will he be back?'

He scratched his head. 'Thursday or Friday. Before next Saturday anyway, as he doesn't need me then.'

Her heart stopped for a moment. 'No, no, I meant when does he get back *today*? I know he's off to—'

'He… doesn't. They've gone early.'

'Gone early to…?'

'Madrid.'

Her heart thudded. 'Why?' she managed.

'He didn't say. Maybe his uncle's unwell or something.'

Juliana nodded slowly. 'Yes… Haven't checked my phone…' She stood there wondering if she could ask anything else, like how Josemi had seemed.

'D'you want a drink of anything?' he asked. 'Since you've had a wasted trip?'

She'd met Rodri a few times, but he didn't seem to realise she lived next door. Or that she and Josemi were lovers. Probably thought she was a client, or another artist. 'No, I'm fine. I'll… let you get on, I can see you're…' There were lots of paintings still on the floor, and the gaps between the stands were narrower than ever.

He grinned. 'I know. Even with the gallery in San José as well, there's just not the space. He needs to buy the house next door and extend the gallery.'

'I thought he went off that idea.'

'Well, I heard the chap who owns next door has died, so it might be on again.'

'Ah.' He'd got it wrong, that was all. She put a hand up to say goodbye and left in daze. Concentrated on putting one foot in front of the other. Then she saw Nerea staring at her from across the road. Nerea the sour-faced busybody – who spoke English, and could easily have seen the *Olive Press* and told Josemi.

She opened her front door and saw it immediately, as if she'd known it would be there. Went over to the table and picked it up. His large loopy handwriting filled the page torn from his small sketch pad. Paper that should have had a likeness of Chica, or Puddle Beach. Not this.

Juliana,

I've left early for Uncle Pepe's. I'm driving and will arrive late, so don't call me today.

In case you haven't seen it, Toby has publicised your relationship, his heartbreak, and his intention of winning you back. You'll deny this – just like you denied seeing him that day, and denied his obvious feelings after the show. You're accustomed to denying everything about Toby – to others, but particularly, to yourself.

It's not that I don't trust you. Maybe I'm a fool, but I believe you've been faithful to me. But for some ten years, you missed and wanted Toby, were unable to have other relationships, unable to move your life forward – while he used you as his emotional prop, his private support artiste, always there for him. You are understandably bitter, and this is why you must have agreed to some part of this story being told. Or maybe you're confused; you can't believe he finally wants you, and you hope he'll win you round.

Juli, you have to work through whatever is going on between you and Toby, and I can't be with you unless you have. I love you and wish you well but, for now, it would be easier if we don't contact each other.

Josemi

How was she going to convince him? She didn't need time to work through anything. She just wanted to be with Josemi, in their next-door houses – maybe one day in the same house, or knocking them together, to have more space for paintings, children…

She collapsed onto the chair, elbows on the table, head in hands. Clicked on a couple of the links to articles Kim had sent her, looked at Toby's Instagram, Twitter… until she felt sick. On her blog, there were just kind words from Toby about her performance, nothing but a friend's support – but this hadn't been enough to reassure Josemi. What *would* reassure him? Her stopping the work with Toby? He'd never complained about that, and knew she needed that money to pay the inheritance tax for the house.

Rodri could be heard putting Josemi's alarm on and closing the front door. Out of the window, she saw him get into his car. At some point, she was going to have to go and get the things she'd left in his house – preferably without Rodri there.

'*How's it going?*' Kim buzzed in a WhatsApp.

'*Terrible. Somebody's shown him. He's gone to Madrid,*' she typed. Then '*Can't talk now xx*', because the screen had gone into a watery blur.

'*Oh NO. How about I come over tomorrow, around ten? Spend your last day with me.*'

'*Please.*'

'*Hang on in there xxxx*'

After picking up keys and a beach bag, she went downstairs, took the bank path onto his terrace and let herself in, sprinting upstairs to turn the alarm off. Then went down again to dash round the bedroom and bathroom, trying to somehow not think or see anything, telling herself this was temporary, only temporary. Her flute was upstairs; she had to go up again. She couldn't look at the paintings, just focused on the table where the flute was. Nothing upsetting there, just some unopened post… to *José Miguel García Moreno*.

Of course. Josemi must be one of those shortened names, like Juanfran for Juan Francisco. His proper name was José Miguel. For legal things like this; it was from *abogados* – lawyers. She picked it up and looked closer, her heart beating hard as she stared in disbelief. It was from *Arturo*'s lawyers. The *Miguel García* she'd seen on the papers wasn't her cousin Miguel – Arturo's surnames were Fernández García, but Miguel's second surname would be his mother's: Gómez.

What she'd seen at the lawyer's office were two middle names, and they were Josemi's. The executor for the house was *Josemi*.

She dropped the envelope back on the table, glanced over at the window. Supposing Rodri came back, having forgotten something? She needed to get out of there. She put the flute case in the beach bag with everything else, put the alarm on and dashed back downstairs, locking his door behind her.

Lying on her bed with closed eyes, she tried to calm down and think, felt her heart slow... and then they came to her: all those times when he'd asked her whether she was going to get the decorating done 'in time', or which beaches she was going to, or insisting – when more than once she'd said she might not bother – that she *should* go and meet Fran in Tabernas. His efforts to read her blog. The hand to his face each time he mentioned 'her house' by mistake.

She smiled to herself and shook her head, even as a tear rolled down her cheek. He'd been a truly dreadful spy, bless him, but then she'd been truly dim not to have realised that, of course, who better for Arturo to choose as the executor, to observe her, than her neighbour? *Get on well with your neighbours*. But they weren't going to be neighbours again for some time – maybe even *never*, if she couldn't explain this terrible mistake to him and put things right.

TWENTY-SIX
AUGUST

Dad and Olivia had apologised for the guest bedroom, saying its double-aspect windows made it much too hot in the summer. Too hot? Standing here with supposedly 'heatwave' midday sun streaming through both sash windows, she still had a cardigan on from this morning's walk on Ealing Common. It had been pleasant enough, but getting there involved crossing roads full of huffing buses and sharing pavements with far too many miserable people going on about the government, the heat, and Tube line closures.

She turned from the town-scene window to the garden one – an oasis of ignored hosepipe-ban green in which Helena and Hermione were laying the garden table and deciding where to put her. She was sure she heard one of them joking about putting her in the pond. Nice. At twenty-three, and having some success with their acting and modelling, shouldn't they have moved out by now? Anyway, in three weeks and three days, she'd be out of their golden hair and in Granada.

She flopped back onto the bed. *Granada.* Just two hours

from Josemi. She could visit him the first weekend, on the 7th, like they'd planned. What would he do, if she just turned up? If she barged in and flung her arms round him, saying: *Stop this. I adore you and couldn't give a stuff about Toby or any other man in the entire universe.* She'd tried everything else, and all she'd got out of him so far was: '*Please stop the messages, emails and calls. You're only making this hurt us even more. Think about what I've said, take care of yourself, get on with your life, and I'll see you in October.*'

She hadn't mentioned Arturo's house in any of her messages; she wasn't supposed to know he was the executor for it. The ninety days had been up nine days ago; surely she'd know soon. Perhaps he was having difficulty deciding. After all, why would he want her living next door, somebody who'd hurt him, when he and Gabi could now buy it as they wanted to last year? Every day that passed, it felt more likely that she'd lost the house as well as Josemi. Although completely losing Josemi was unthinkable...

She closed her eyes, her body inert. *Get on with your life*, he'd said. She'd seen Lucy and watched the video of their play; she was working through an English grammar book, preparing for the TEFL course; she'd cleaned up the Fiat and had a second-hand car dealer coming to look at it; she'd Oxfammed countless belongings. She'd spent some surprisingly quality time with Dad and Olivia, even if she hadn't yet had the courage to tell them about Fran, as she knew she must. And as for Toby – she'd had a thundering row with him on the phone that left them both in tears and promising to find a way forward – in her case, mainly for the sake of the book. She was definitely getting on with her life. Except for when the screamingly unfair loss of Josemi left her either weeping uncontrollably or catatonic with misery.

A knock on the door. 'Can I come in?' Dad asked.

'Yes,' she managed, trying to sit up.

'Bit quiet up here. Thought you might need...' He put a Níjar mug of tea on the bedside table. 'Oh, and...' He fished five Lindor chocolate balls out of his shirt pocket. 'Don't tell Olivia. She'll say I've—'

'Spoilt my lunch, I know! Thanks, Dad.' She smiled weakly. For nearly two weeks he'd treated her like a little injured bird. She'd never known him so gentle; he'd even listened to her talk about Arturo and Josemi and conceded that they weren't the crackpot control freak and arty lothario that he'd clearly imagined them to be.

'Oh, darling...' He'd noticed her tears, and sat down next to her on the bed and patted her arm while she blew her nose. 'It's still early days; it'll heal with time.' In contrast to Fran telling her to have courage and Arturo telling her to ride it out, Dad seemed to think her relationship with Josemi was now something to recover from. 'Poor Julie. But you've got lots to look forward to: studying in Granada, finding a little flat in San José, a new career, being back with your new friends... Such an exciting time for you.'

Her phone tinkled with the arrival of a WhatsApp message. She quickly glanced at it – forever hoping it was Josemi – but it was Fran. She'd get back to him later.

'One of your new friends again? They're obviously all missing you.'

'Yes.' She took a sip of her tea. Now wasn't the moment to tell him about Fran; she wasn't feeling strong enough, it was nearly lunch time, Olivia should probably be present... But when *would* it feel like a good moment?

He put a hand to his face and rubbed his non-existent stubble. 'You never told me if you went to that lunch with... the Tabernas cowboy and his wife.'

Jesus. Maybe it *was* the time. Her heart started to patter.

'I did, yes. They showed me some old filming photos with Mama in them.' She had copies, but one had Mama and Fran exchanging a look, so…

'So… *more* friends.'

'Well…' God, how was she supposed to… but was it her imagination, or was he already flushed and breathing faster? 'Are you okay, Dad?'

'And did he tell you he was your father?'

'Oh!' she said, gasping. 'Well… yes, he did.' She put a hand on his arm. 'But you're my *dad*. Nothing's going to change that,' she said quickly. 'You *knew*?'

He nodded, staring at the floor. He didn't seem to want to look at her. 'Your mother told me, as soon as she was pregnant. I was devastated, but we'd so longed for a child… We agreed to tell you when you were eighteen, or when you were ready to know… But she wasn't here to help me do that.'

So he didn't tell her. Just like he hadn't told her the truth about Mama's death. She let go of his arm.

He looked at her. 'You weren't ready to hear it at eighteen or nineteen, with Toby, the drama college…'

'True, it wasn't a good time.'

'And then… well, there was Olivia's cancer, turning our world upside down for three years. When you were having counselling for depression a few years ago, I wondered if I should tell you, if it would help you or make things worse, but I was worried about you rushing off to Spain on your own to find the cowboy, who might have denied or rejected you…'

'The *cowboy*?'

'Antoñita never gave him a name.'

'It was the same in her letters to her friend Teresa.'

'Letters?' His eyes widened.

'Yes… I'll show you them. She mentions your first date…'

'I'd like to see them… Look, I know I should have told you, Julie. I always meant to. I nearly did when you were staying here just before you went out to Spain, but…' He shook his head.

'But I was flustered, not listening to a word you said.'

'No, I wasn't listening to a word *you* said!' They smiled at each other, then he looked serious again. 'And you got on okày with…'

'Fran. Francisco. And yes, he is a cowboy. But a very kind and likable one.'

'Other children?'

'His second wife's son, who he's brought up as his own.'

He smiled at that. 'Blood isn't everything!'

'No! It's not!' She swung her legs down beside him and gave him a hug, and he squeezed her back, not at all like the usual Dad-hug gesture. 'And look, they met by accident at San José, when… I happened, and the only other time she saw him was that fateful day she took me to Tabernas Studios, maybe hoping he still worked there and she could show him her daughter. I don't know.'

'What? He was *there*?'

'He *had* been. We literally just said hello. I don't remember much. But apparently he was shocked afterwards and asked to leave early that day, so wasn't there when she… What I'm trying to say is, from what Fran says, and I don't think he has any reason to lie, she wasn't "gradually leaving you", as you told me.'

'Oh…' He pulled out a handkerchief to wipe his eyes.

Olivia's voice called out 'lunch!' from downstairs.

They looked at each other in alarm, and he wiped his eyes again.

'It's okay, you could just say it's hay fever,' she reassured him.

'I want to ask you more about him, if I can, and see those letters.'

'Of course. And we can tell Olivia, when we're ready, and Helena and Hermione.' *Although I doubt they'll be too bothered*, she nearly added.

They went downstairs, and when Juliana asked what she could do to help, the twins pointedly told her everything had been done. Perhaps it would be easier to remember to help if she ever felt like eating anything.

They sat down outside to a rather waspy quiche and salad lunch.

'Don't say it again, there were no wasps in Spain, blah-de-blah,' Helena said, grabbing the swatter.

'Well… there weren't. Not on my terrace, anyway.'

The twins raised their eyes to the heavens in creepy unison.

'But I saw two snakes on my walks – no, three, counting the one at Tabernas – and a wild boar trotted down the riverbed one night.' She watched the twins' horrified faces; that should put them off visiting.

'Why don't you do the TEFL course *here*?' Olivia asked. 'You don't know anyone in Granada, and you'd save on rent.'

There was another horrified look from the twins at the thought of having her in the house for a further month.

Juliana shook her head. 'Kim told me it's a fantastic course.'

'Why *English teaching*?' Hermione asked. 'After enjoying doing *Annie*, why don't you do a drama course there instead?'

'The mere thought of courses and auditions makes me start hating drama again. Oh, and Kim got back to me – she loves the idea of me running an English-through-Drama club at the school as an extra activity. I'll get to teach, write *and* do drama.'

'That sounds *brilliant*,' Dad said. 'And of course, every summer there'll be the big show. I wonder what they'll do next year? Next time, we'll definitely be there – whatever role you get.'

In the show again, with Josemi…

'If you want to do it again, that is,' Dad added, seeming to read her mind.

'Absolutely she will, and we'll *all* be there!' Hermione said, always the more generous twin.

Olivia nodded and smiled. Another slice of quiche landed on Juliana's plate, even though she'd only gouged out a bit of the filling from the first one.

Her phone buzzed in her pocket. She took it out and saw a WhatsApp. *Toby*. There was really nothing more to say to him – until the next part of the diary came to her. On the other hand, maybe something else was going to hit the papers that she needed to know about.

'Jules, I'm back in London for four days. Can you come over? Today? We could catch up with the writing, then go to a Thai place you won't believe. In taxi from airport. Call you when home xxxx'

She put the phone back in her pocket. It would be better to say no, right now on WhatsApp, than talk to him… but then, he'd probably still call. Maybe she could go for the work and then come back after a cup of tea. She took her phone out again.

'Hi Toby. Yes, would be good to catch up with the writing face to face. See you later.'

'Toby?' Helena was looking over Juliana's arm at her phone. 'You're "catching up" with Toby?'

Juliana put her phone in front of Helena's face. 'Catching up with *work*, see?'

Helena scanned it eagerly; she and Hermione were avid followers of Toby's *King Arthur* series. 'With a *working* Thai dinner?'

'I'll probably be back before that.'

'Why?' Olivia asked. 'It would be good for you to get out. Now that you and Toby are okay again, why not let him take you somewhere fancy? You deserve it.'

There was so much wrong with what Olivia had said, Juliana couldn't begin to answer.

Dad was keeping quiet, but had looked up hopefully.

The twins were trying to guess which Thai restaurant Toby had in mind.

'Where does he live again?' Hermione asked.

'Islington,' Juliana said, since this information would be available on Google.

'Quite a way,' Helena said. 'It would be only gentlemanly to offer a bed for the night.'

Hermione smirked and put a hand over her mouth.

Dad put down his knife and fork. 'Girls. You know what Julie's been through. She's not going to find that funny, is she.'

Bless him, saying that even though he'd probably be delighted if she got together with Toby, walking red carpets with him at the TV awards, producing beautiful child actors with him. She smiled at him gratefully.

She'd not been to Toby's place since that disastrous spending the night with him 'for old times' sake', years ago. It was the same Victorian mansion block, but he'd now moved up to the top flat – and could probably have moved much further up the property ladder, had he not decided to put money into his Spanish project.

She took the lift, stood in front of his door for a moment reminding herself to keep this professional rather than start screaming at him again, and pressed the button.

'Jules…' He beamed and gave her the two-kiss Spanish greeting.

He was all sun-kissed golden, freshly showered and cologned, and in his usual light blue; she was going to be subjected to the full charm offensive. 'Hi. How are you doing?'

'Good, good… Come through to the terrace. What d'you want to drink?'

'Juice with some ice, please.'

'Right you are. Take a seat out here.'

The terrace was so high up that most of it was un-over-looked, hidden by treetops. There was an impressive collection of shrubs, lavender and small trees, an elegant outdoor heater, a covered Jacuzzi. Taking a seat, however, posed a problem: should she sprawl like a pampered date on a sun lounger, or sit in the lovers' swing seat? She opted for a narrow wooden bench next to the wall, even though, further along, it declared itself as a ledge for plants.

'What're you doing?' he said with a laugh, coming out with a tray and putting it on the table.

A table that had chairs tucked underneath, she then noticed.

'Come and sit in the sun; it's gloriously tepid!'

'I know. *Heatwave*?' she said with a smile, and joined him at the table. 'This is lovely out here. How d'you…'

'I have somebody coming in. Romanian chap, studying to be a nurse – lovely guy. And there's his wife too. Such a relief, now I'm going to spend so much time in Spain.'

'Are you? Even when the project's over?'

'I've told you, it's not just a project, it's going to be my home for a couple of months of the year. I'll be there whenever I can – especially in the winter, when I'm not filming *Arthur*.'

'But Toby, you've only been there five minutes!'

'Two weeks. I know. But I seem to remember it didn't take you too long to decide you belonged there.'

'That's true. I suppose you always did have a thing about Spain.'

'We *both* always did have a thing about Spain,' he said gently, putting his drink down and looking at her steadily.

She took a handful of pistachios. She didn't want to be reminded of anything they'd shared; it felt like those things didn't matter a jot, after what he'd done to her relationship with Josemi. The sooner they got down to the diary, the better.

His eyes were still on her. 'So… are we good?'

She looked up. She wasn't sure that was the word. 'If you keep your promise never to pull anything like that again. Although obviously I can't just instantly put this behind us.'

'How's it going with Josemi?' he asked gently. 'Doesn't he—'

'It's not. And I really don't want to talk about that.'

He nodded slowly.

'How's the house coming on?' she asked, remembering why she was here and trying to lighten her tone. 'I want to see the next bit of the diary – you made such a good start.'

'The house is fantastic. Even if it does bite back occasionally.' He lifted a lock of hair to reveal a sewn-up gash on his forehead, and held out a hand with a plaster and a swollen thumb.

261

'Oh dear! What happened? No, don't tell me, let's *read* about it. Go and get it!'

He grinned and disappeared inside. She cursed herself for not having said up front that the Thai restaurant was definitely not going to happen; they might be 'good' – as far as that was possible – but they certainly weren't ready for extra-curricular activities. She sipped her juice. Half an hour, maybe an hour, and she'd leave.

He came back with a surprisingly thick wad of A4s for the second week of his adventure.

She started reading, Toby initially sitting there like a child with his homework being marked, then restlessly dead-heading a purple hebe. In the diary, there was more appreci-ation of the blue skies and balmy nights, a discovery of a local wine, and efforts to discover, as she'd tried to do, what bird made that downturned call as if it was sighing with the heat. There was a lesson learnt too late about how to remove wall tiles without damaging the plaster. A comical inadver-tent visit to Vera's nudist beach. Intriguingly, a purchase of two of Pili's paintings from her exhibition in a gallery in Mojácar.

And then… she put a hand to her mouth. 'Oh my God, this is *hilarious*!' The farmer's single-fingered reaction to Toby asking him to remove some old equipment that was spoiling his view from the living room, followed by, as far as Toby could tell, a lecture about how not to meddle in other people's business. Too right, *hombre*, you tell him! She guffawed, finding this funnier than she should have done. Unbelievably, only days later, Toby had fallen off a ladder onto the very same equipment, and the farmer had had to put Toby in his tractor's trailer to go to the local hospital. 'Are you making this up?'

'No, I'm *not*! And he still hasn't removed the bloody

vicious thing!' He sat down opposite her again. 'Why are you laughing? I could have been impaled!'

She shook her head. 'If we're going to end up with a book, you've got to be more careful, that's for sure!' She read on to the end and put the papers down. 'It's good, Toby. *Really* good. Keep putting everything and anything in there. Including – like you do here, about the house – your feelings.'

He looked pleased. 'That's how you felt... *feel* about your Spanish house? When will it be yours?'

'I don't know. But I'm not holding my breath, because it turns out that Josemi's the executor who'll decide whether I've met the conditions or not.'

'*What?*' he said, indignant on her behalf. 'But that's... conflict of interest or something, isn't it? Didn't you say he'd wanted to buy it with his business partner?'

She shrugged. She didn't want to talk about this either. What she *did* want was a cup of tea and hopefully something sweet – she was finally hungry, as if this was all taking unseen amounts of energy. Then she could go.

'Is there... no word from him?' he asked tentatively. 'At all?'

'No. Just that we'll talk in October.'

'Why October?'

'Because... I'll then be back there, starting work with Kim.'

'And applying for residency. That's what he's waiting for; he wants to see proof you're actually going to settle there... rather than just have the house as a holiday home.'

'Or maybe he just wants to clear the air at that point, since even if we're not living next door, we're bound to keep bumping into each other.'

'He's crazy. I don't know how he can just... *give you up* like this.' He put his hand on hers. Then took both her hands in his. '*I* couldn't, *ever.*'

If only she could record this and show it to all those lovesick Julianas of the past eleven years. She looked down at their hands and, gently as she could, withdrew hers. 'Toby. You've really got to stop this.'

'I would – if I felt you believed what I'm saying.'

'I believe what you're saying, okay? Or at least, I believe *you* believe what you're saying.'

He frowned. 'So you still think I just want you as a friends-with-benefits girlfriend substitute for the sake of the book and the TV programme.'

'Well… why else would you suddenly want me again now, after eleven years?'

'The Spanish house,' he blurted out. 'I've thought of you more and more over the years… but when you started that blog, when I… saw you wanting all the same things I want, so courageously achieving them, finding out about yourself… I fell in love with you all over again.'

She looked up. When he sounded like a bad actor who hadn't learnt his script, he was usually speaking from the heart. 'Toby. I love you dearly, you know I do. Always have done, always will. But what I had with Josemi… it was something quite different, something I had no idea was even possible. I haven't even started to give up hope that he and I won't be together again. I don't think I ever will.'

He looked down at the table.

'You and I need to move forward now, enjoy our friendship, write a cracking book. Or we'll lose those things too.'

He looked up. 'I don't want that.'

'Nor do I. So please, let's not talk about this again, okay?'

'Okay.'

'You promise?'

'I promise.' Those blue eyes were looking rather too shiny. If he started crying, they'd neither of them ever stop.

'Look… Got anything super-sweet to go with some tea? Even just toast with masses of—'

'I have!' He sprung to his feet and gave her a watery smile. 'Picked up some deli carrot cake for you, just in case you…'

In case she backed out of the Thai restaurant. 'Ooh, yes please! Let me come and give you a hand.' She got up, and gave him a quick hug. 'Then I want to see all the photos of the house, near-murderous farming equipment, paintings and everything else.'

TWENTY-SEVEN
SEPTEMBER

Juliana watched the countryside outside the coach window turn into the lunar landscape of Tabernas. She would have liked to see Fran and Josefa, but there wasn't going to be time for that. Time was already whizzing by. It was ludicrously comfortable in the coach, and with nerves already exhausting her, she could have just sat there gawping out of the window, but she had a teacher-observed lesson to prepare for Monday. Her elementary pupils would be learning how to talk about the future by just adding phrases like *this Monday* or *next month* to a verb in the present tense. It wasn't going to be difficult to engage them with this – who doesn't want to talk about the future? She'd encourage everything from the mundane to the fantastical. She was going to San Rafael, *this weekend*. But she did need to work on the lesson now; one way or another, she was unlikely to have much concentration for studying in the next couple of days.

She recognised the jolly Indalo Parking lady who'd handed over the car – *her* car, although she hadn't known it then, in May. 'Juliana! Back for your Pandita at last! Here he is,' she said, smiling and patting her arm; it looked like she remembered Juliana looking red-eyed when she dropped the car off.

'Thanks!'

She put her bags in the back and got inside, breathed out heavily in the enclosed heat, shut her eyes for a moment. If she wasn't careful, she'd be red-eyed again. *Pandita.* Little panda. She'd never been sentimental about cars, but this one was different; so many memories, and Uncle Arturo had chosen him for her.

She left the airport and was soon at the roundabout where she used to turn off to Almería to go and see him. In a few weeks' time, she'd be going to what was now Miguel's apartment; her cousin had invited her to join him and Susana when they were down from Madrid. It would be strange that Arturo wasn't there – although of course he *would* be, in a way, and pleased to see her and his son starting to become closer.

She took the coast road in the other direction, blue on blue dazzling beside her. The water was choppy and frilly in the wind, lurching to one side with an undertow. A yellow flag flapped above one of the beaches; swim with caution. She might be doing that later, but first she had to have *lunch* with caution, not letting herself get drawn into a rip tide of resentment for nearly two months of agonising—

There was a buzz from her phone, so she pulled over, opened the windows wider to let the soothing salty air in… but it wasn't him.

'*How's the coach?*' Toby was asking.

'*It was great. Already in the car.*'

'*Good luck!*'

'*How did you get on with the Bastard Bath?*' she asked him.

'*I finally cracked it! No, I mean got it plumbed in and working! More diary and pics soon. Drive carefully x.*'

The road turned away from the sea into the unbeautiful area with plastic greenhouses that Arturo used to applaud for deterring English tourists from driving on and into the unspoilt natural park beyond. There were very few cars, it was an easy road she knew, but she was struggling to concentrate. She put some music on and turned it off. Turned the air con off and opened the windows. Got blown about and closed them again. Remembered to sip her water.

The *invernaderos* stopped. She was back in the natural park, with its friendly rounded hills, rocky and red-earthed mountains in the background. She smiled to herself and took the turning to San Rafael, drove along the high coast road, tipped over the blind summit until San Rafael and its glorious dinosaur-worthy valley was laid out beneath her.

Down she went, through the derelict old miners' cottages where Arturo and Mama had once lived, over the *rambla* that could have taken her life. She stopped at the supermarket on the corner, drove past Elise's, and then into her old road. No sign of Dolores, thank heavens. She wondered yet again what she made of all this. She liked to think Dolores had been telling Josemi he was being a stubborn fool, but maybe that was expecting too much of a protective mother.

The keys got dropped in her excitement again, just like the first time – but now, of course, she knew which was the one for the front door of the house. *Her* house.

She opened the door and flicked the electricity switch. The fridge buzzed into life; the ceiling fans cranked into action. She took in these familiar sounds, the smell of old, dark wood, and felt like the house was welcoming her back. In the kitchen, she put away the groceries, drank a glass of peach juice. Then she opened all the wooden shutters, letting in the sunshine, the view of the valley – and Josemi's terrace. Her heart started patting away – good God, just the sight of it was setting her off, even though he'd said in his message that he'd be busy in San José setting up an exhibition with Gabi, and would be going to the restaurant from there.

She looked around the room, her eyes meeting the bowl of pebbles, the Chica and the lavatera ones on the top. The chair that had supported Uncle Arturo when he'd sat here going through the conditions with her, telling her how happy she'd made him. The sofas, where she and Josemi had practised the play, and where they used to flop down in a cuddly tangle in front of the fan. Downstairs there'd be the shower, the *bed*. She often found herself still thinking of her and Josemi as a couple, just… floating apart for a while. But she was now struck by the real possibility that might not be the case, and imagined for a moment how she would feel living here if… She sank into Arturo's chair, hoping it would hold her up as it had done him. This house she'd so wanted, so needed, so loved and worked for, could become a purgatory – if she couldn't make Josemi trust and love her again.

Of course, there would be new friends, new memories made in the house. Maybe even a new love – but that seemed so utterly far off in the distant future, a mere speck of a possibility. How many people meet two perfect soulmates in a lifetime? Her mother and her uncle certainly hadn't.

She looked at her watch. If she got ready quickly, there would be time to go and talk with them first.

———

She had the cemetery to herself. She could talk as loudly as she liked… but oddly, once standing in front of the *nichos* for Mama and Uncle Arturo, she didn't know what to say.

'Bit dusty, but I've got just the thing – the Spanish version of Windolene wipes.' She pulled some of them out of the packet in her cotton cemetery-visiting bag, polished the black marble and the glass covering their photos. Then put the dusty purple and orange plastic flowers in the bag to take home later for washing, and took out the new ones.

'Blue today, I felt. Blue for honesty, trust... God, hadn't thought of that. How appropriate. Or *in*appropriate. Well, for me, anyway.' She divided them into the vases. 'How are you two doing? Sorry, I forgot to ask.' She giggled. What was the matter with her? These were the two people she'd loved most in the world. Well, two of the three. But she wasn't hearing them today. It was almost as bad as that first time she came, when she was nearly only able to think about Mama's bones. Maybe she just didn't *want* to hear them – their disappointment in how she'd hurt and risked losing Josemi, and Arturo admitting that he might not always be right, after all.

'I'm sorry. I love you both so much. See you soon,' she whispered, with a finger on each photo. She walked back to the gate, but turned to look at their *nichos* again before she left. The other possibility was that she wasn't hearing them because they had nothing to say; they were confident she knew what to do. Like some transcendental satnav, they were silent because all she had to do was go *todo directo*, as they say in Spanish, straight ahead, onwards.

She got back in the car, starting to feel dazed with nerves as she went through what she might say to Josemi. Distracted, she missed several small turnings off the narrow road – any of which could have been the one. She pulled the car into an entrance to a field of agaves and picked up her phone to check where she was. There was another message from Toby, with a fingers-crossed emoji wishing her luck with Josemi, but Google wasn't working. She reached over to the pocket in the passenger door and pulled out the treasure-hunt-like map of the area, which mercifully included a little knife and fork sign where the place was, but she had no idea where *she* was on it. She carried on, almost until she was coming into the pebble-beached village of Las Negras. This was how she'd found the place, driving back from beach explorations. She pulled over again and turned the car round... and finally she saw the sign, more visible from this direction.

She swayed and juddered down the meandering bumpy road until she reached what must have once been an old farmhouse and outbuildings, but was now a special little restaurant.

At the reception, with its bubbling tank showing leggy sea creatures people might want to eat, a middle-aged American couple were asking the receptionist to repeat something. Juliana looked through to the restaurant terrace. Just one of its tables was occupied – by a couple holding hands; she wasn't late – or she *was*, slightly, but not as late as *he* was.

The receptionist was still trying to give English directions for the old mine at San Rafael.

'Can I help?' Juliana asked in Spanish. 'They're getting confused because you're saying *all right* instead of *keep right*.'

They all thanked her.

'Are you English?' the receptionist asked.

'I'm English and Spanish,' Juliana replied, not thinking, but decided to adopt this from now on, in preference to the usual half this and half that description that made her sound both conflicted and cobbled together. She gave her name and was shown through to the terrace.

It looked out over rolling hills of esparto grass and *palmitos*, a herd of goats and, in the far distance, the skeletal remains of the old mine at San Rafael. The breeze was picking up. The tablecloths flapped and pulled against their clips; a wooden lover's bench squeaked as it blew to and fro. Visiting the ladies', she saw a rather anxious-looking and crumpled coach traveller in the mirror. She brushed her hair, and tied the front bits back so she didn't spend the whole lunch pulling wind-blown strands out of her mouth. Pulled at her seahorses-on-tie-dye-turquoise dress. Went back to the table. Ordered a *mosto*. Read the entire menu without taking in a word of it. Heard a car, but it was the arrival of a laundry van. Where was he?

A distant three-note call of an ambulance came to her across the valley, cutting into the Elton John playing on the sound system. What if he'd had an accident? The wind buffeting his car, a moment's distraction, an impatient driver overtaking him…

'Any news of your companion?' the waitress asked, offering her another *mosto*.

'I'm… sure he'll get here soon.'

The ambulance had stopped its child's-keyboard wailing and now started again, fainter as it rushed off in the direction of Almería. Her heart began to pound; it was so unlike him to be so late.

Then suddenly he was standing there in front of her, looking almost as startled as when she first met him over a goat and a crumbly wall. 'I'm so sorry, I couldn't find it. There was no signal…'

'I know, I couldn't either, even though I've been here…' She got up to exchange the two-kiss thing, took in that familiar paint-and-rosemary smell, wanted to hug him, but he sat down, still looking perturbed.

'I thought it would be nice to meet somewhere we won't get interrupted,' she explained, just as the waitress turned up to ask what he'd like to drink. He didn't look happy about the venue, but he'd put on a short-sleeved shirt rather than his usual T-shirt, and pale chinos instead of shorts. Once the waitress had gone, he ran a hand over the strands of wavy hair blown free from his ponytail and looked at her. Tried to smile. 'So you wanted to—'

'I hoped you'd—' she said at the same time.

They stopped and laughed nervously. He put a hand out to encourage her to speak first.

'I wanted to thank you for telling the lawyer I met the conditions for inheriting the house.'

'You already have,' he said, a little impatiently. 'Aren't you doing your course in Granada?'

'Of course. One week to go, and I'll be qualified.'

He smiled. 'That's great.'

'The lawyer pushed it through for me to be sent the house keys earlier. Today was a study day, so I thought I'd come down.'

'Ah,' he said, not looking too surprised; maybe the lawyer or Miguel had told him.

'So... it's good to be able to thank...'

He put up a hand. 'You don't have to keep saying it. How could you have thought for a moment that I'd say you *hadn't* met the conditions?'

'Well, the bit about the neighbours... I let you down, even though I never meant to. You could have argued that—'

'*Have* you let me down?' he asked quietly, looking concerned.

Maybe she hadn't used the right words in Spanish. Anyway, it was time to explain, as best she could. 'I let us *both* down, by not listening to Toby carefully enough, so allowing him to say things to the publicist that... were inevitably going to come out wrong. I was furious with him, but I know it was my fault too.'

The waitress was back, asking for their orders. The

menus were still in the holder. In a moment of telepathic complicity, they decided to share the house salad – whatever it was – and go along with the girl's suggestion of a side of chips.

'But...' she continued, determined to say it. 'You've let *me* down too, by not listening to me or believing—'

'But, Hooli...'

Hooli. How she'd longed to hear him say that again. That gentle, loving version of her name.

'You lied about where you were. We talked about it, you lied again,' he said. 'Once trust has gone, it's hard to get it back. Often impossible.'

Her heart thudded. He was talking gently now because maybe he *was* going to let her down. Let her *go*. 'But... not *totally* impossible,' she managed, with a croaky voice.

The salad and chips arrived, and there was a fuss about dressings she left him to deal with. She tried to remember what she'd planned to say, but it had all been wiped from her head by the word *impossible*. The music had moved on from Elton's greatest hits to those of Simply Red. Into the silence between her and Josemi, as they both stared at their lunch, came Mick singing about all the jealousy he'd caused, and how he wanted to fall into somebody's arms.

'Oh... Why do they always have to play *English* songs in this kind of restaurant?'

Seeing his mouth twitch into a smile for a moment gave her a little courage.

'Look... about *Toby*. You were right, that did need sorting out. My anger with him, his feelings for me. He genuinely *did* want to get back together with me, and I'll admit that was quite something to hear, after eleven years. But I had no problem turning him down, told him it was never going to happen, because I'd never be able to feel for him what I...

274

Well… anyway, we've moved on from that, so we can be friends.'

'And so you can still do the book?'

'Yes. Which has turned out to be mostly about his unlikely friendship with the farmer who's been working his land for forty years, not past or present girlfriends.'

He smiled and nodded, making a warmth spread through her; maybe things weren't going to be *so* impossible… 'And he's back in England now?'

'In a week or so.'

Her phone buzzed on the table, and Toby's name floated across the screen.

Josemi frowned. 'How often does he message you? That's the second one.'

'Is it?' She hadn't noticed.

'Well, *look.*'

'Okay.' She went into WhatsApp – and up came a photo of a bare-chested Toby in a bubble bath, holding out a glass of champagne to her with a big grin.

'That is *not* what you send a *friend*,' Josemi said, eyes fiery.

'No, no, it's… It's because he's been working on this—'

'You can't have a friendship like this, if I'm ever to trust you again.'

'*What?*'

'What would you think if Gabi sent me a photo like that?'

'If she'd been installing—'

'No, no, *no*. I can't have this.' He put up a stop-sign hand.

No Toby. Probably no Ben. Heaven help her if she took on a male private student. 'Now look here. You can be all macho *guardia civil* with me about safety around the *rambla*, drinking enough water, my driving skills and a few other things. But you can't start telling me who I can be friends with and who I can work with. I can't bel—'

'I didn't mean—'

'Toby's been struggling to install this bath for ages, he's celebrating. He's as bubbled as possible, there's nothing wrong here – other than his timing. Look,' she said, pushing the phone towards him again. 'Where's this jealousy getting you? If you're so bothered, if I mean that much... why don't you just *have* me?' She winced, hoping that came out better in Spanish. 'I mean... I'm completely all yours, always have been.'

'Except when receiving photos of beautiful men in bubble baths,' he said, but the anger seemed to be calming down.

'Oh for heaven's sake... Read *all* the messages and you'll see. Hang on.' She scrolled back.

She watched him read, his eyebrows unfurrowing. A slight smile at one point, probably enjoying the picture of a grubby Toby surrounded by pipes. Then spotted his own name. 'What's this?'

'He's wishing me luck with you. And dear God, am I needing it.'

The music had changed to the Bee Gees, the annoying More-than-a-Woman track. It was probably the *Greatest Hits* album, so only a question of time before...

He was still staring at the message. 'Okay. I'm sorry. It was just such a shock, after all we've...'

'Yes, I suppose!' she said, returning his smile when he looked up.

'I'm sorry I'm so...' He took her hand.

Then it came on, as she knew it would. The brass intro to 'Too Much Heaven'.

Josemi put his other hand in the air and looked up to the sky. 'Arturo, I'm getting there, okay? Give us a chance!'

She laughed, her heart fit to burst.

He turned back to her, his hand tightening on hers. 'Hooli, Hooli. Okay. Please… We'll have to be careful with each other for a bit, we've both been hurting, but… can we start again?' He stood up, pulled her to her feet, and then she was in his strong arms, dazed. 'What d'you say?'

'Oh…' she said through her tears. 'What d'you think? *Yes*!'

TWENTY-EIGHT

JANUARY

'Honestly, I think January is my favourite month here,' Juliana said. They were arriving back from a walk round the old castle at the beach and through the green valley now speckled with yellow and purple wildflowers.

'You say that for every month!' Josemi replied.

'I know!' she said, untying the thin cardigan from round her waist. 'What a gorgeous day. Think I'll do my edits in the patio until I go off to the school. But coffee first.'

'Yours or mine?' Josemi asked, pointing his finger at one front door and then the other. This was a frequent question, although some patterns had emerged: cooking was mainly done in Juliana's less cluttered front room – but by the more multi-tasking Josemi; clothes washing was usually done at Josemi's, but by the more careful Juliana; they tended to sleep at Juliana's when she came home after teaching Monday to Thursday evenings, but otherwise at Josemi's. Shopping and cleaning were haphazardly shared. Dolores, happy to see them together but still insisting she wanted to help, had a regular morning in which she could sweep both houses –

278

even though they were neither of them that bothered – and be taken off for an El Minero lunch to thank her.

'Both. I've got those croissants, but I'm out of coffee pods.'

'Okay. I'll get the coffee on and you bring them over.'

Half an hour later, Juliana was set up with her laptop under an umbrella in the middle of the terrace, with plans to look up and rest her eyes on the clumps of yellow-flowering albaida on the bank, and periodically get up and do some re-potting or clipping at her plants.

Josemi had also decided to work outside, and had put up an easel right by his pebble collection next to the wall between them. As the morning went on, his humming of some unknown song had become annoying, but then so, probably, had the clatter of a dropped trowel and the sweeping up of a broken plant pot. Returning to another bout of editing, however, Juliana found herself accompanied by a Spanish radio channel intent on playing Rolling Stones and other ghastly Seventies favourites of her dad's. Hoping Josemi would soon be sick of it too – wasn't flamenco, jazz and blues more his thing? – she got up to do the watering, and tried to work out what the equivalent of the snarky English "d'you *mind?*" would be in Spanish. Then, just as she was getting a really good idea for how she was going to address one of the changes the editor wanted, on came 'You Can't Always Get What You Want'; she hung up the hose and took her papers and laptop inside.

Toby's book had turned out to be such an unexpected delight. The romantic narrative he'd hoped for hadn't mate-rialised – until *after* the shooting of the documentary and most of the diary had been done. At some point after he'd introduced Pili's paintings to an art gallery in Chelsea, their relationship had begun – in a slow, private and non-narrative kind of way. She and Josemi were delighted for them. Meanwhile, the book had turned into a beautiful story about the initial distrust – and eventual unlikely friendship – between him and the farmer who'd been working Toby's land since long before the 'spoilt blonde English rich boy' was even born. The latter parts of the book reminded her of the relationship she'd had with Uncle Arturo...

'Hooliana!' Josemi shouted, crossly. She looked out of the window – and saw that she must have released the handset and put it back on the hook but forgotten to turn it off at the tap – causing the hose to explosively snake up into the air. She dashed out and turned the handle, getting herself a drenching – one that had clearly already happened and wasn't going down too well next door.

'Oh dear, sorry about that! Although if you must blast me with "You Can't Always Get What You Want", expect to get what you don't—'

'Just come round here.'

'What?'

'Just come round and look at what you've done.' He jerked his head towards the bank path.

She went down the path and up again, much quicker these days, with the well-worn earth and the little steps they'd added, and the plants no longer in leg-scratchy summer mode...

'Come on!'

'I'm *coming*!'

She went up on to his terrace. He was pointing at a large watercolour that had – well, taken itself a little too literally. Apart from a spray that had given the sunny Mediterranean scene an English hailstorm, the hose's spurt had dealt a fatal blow to the wooden fishing boat, dragging the front of it down into the sea.

Juliana put a hand over her mouth.

'Are you *laughing*?' he said, all fiery eyes.

'I'm sorry, I really—' The hand couldn't contain it; she was overtaken by wobbling shoulders.

He turned to the painting. Put his head on one side, as if following the boat's doomed trajectory. His mouth twitched. Then he picked up a paintbrush, clarified the boat's demise, and added a person on deck with a huge shocked mouth. Juliana picked up a small paintbrush and added a row of three shark fins. Josemi added a giant crimson octopus with an arm around the horrified mariner and a big grin on its gob, but after that they were shaking too much with laughter to carry on.

They wiped their eyes and groaned.

'Another coffee?' Josemi managed.

She nodded, and while he went inside to make them, she got the paper towel roll from his studio to wipe up the flood on his table.

He came out with a small tray including some of Elise's spicy Dutch biscuits.

'It wasn't for Madrid, was it?'

'No, no. A chap in San José. It's not an urgent present or anything. He's got a sense of humour – won't mind the delay.'

'All the same, I *am* sorry,' she said, sipping her coffee and avoiding looking at the painting in case she spluttered a mouthful everywhere.

'So you should be. And I'm going to hang it in your bathroom, as a reminder to be more careful with that hose! Once we've both signed it of course.'

'Great,' she said with a chuckle, and tried one of the biscuits. 'Oh... delicious.'

He wasn't eating them. He'd gone pensive, biting his lip.

'Actually, I've been meaning to tell you. I've got a plan for how we could manage our… outdoor privacy.'

'Oh? A rota? A double-stoned sound and waterproofed wall?'

He chuckled, but still looked a bit intense. He got up and came over to give her a squeeze. 'I think the answer is for us to have a… *choice* of outdoor rooms.' He pointed upwards. 'Roof terraces.'

'Of course! I love the idea of that. But I've got some saving up to do first.'

'Well… it doesn't have to cost you anything. I have a plan. Come, I'll show you.'

They went round to Juliana's terrace and he pointed to the area beyond the gas bottles where she hung her underwear.

'You'd have to hang the *bragas* somewhere else. What we'd do is, take the wall down between us there, and put in a spiral staircase… with a gate from both my terrace and yours. Since you'd be losing the space, I'd pay for it.'

'Oh *wow*! But what? I think I should contrib—'

'Have you seen up there?'

'No. Have you?'

'Yes! I'll show you.'

Back they went to his terrace, and then halfway up his side path. She watched him stabilise a ladder to the roof. 'Up you go.'

'Oh Gawd.'

'It's okay, really.'

They climbed up and walked on to his roof, and then over a low wall onto hers.

'Oh my God!' she exclaimed. 'You can see *everything* from up here – the sea, the church, the botanical gardens… Chica! I can see Chica! Sweetie! You can watch her with her friends… Amazing. Don't know how much work I'd get done up here though.'

'Just think of all those extra plants you could have. You'd have a hosepipe up here too of course – God help me!'

'Yes! And tables and chairs, sunbeds, a little shaded area…'

'There's Elise!' Josemi said, giving her an exaggerated wave and getting one back. 'Would it be rude to shout down a lunch order?'

'I'm sure my roof's bigger than yours.'

'That can't be. It's just that I've got this old defunct air con unit taking up space here – that would need chucking. Obviously, we'd need to put up a little fencing, so we don't fall off. Like they have over there,' he said, pointing to a roof garden further along on the opposite side of the road.

'Maybe mine looks bigger because it's whiter than yours.' She broke into song. '*Any roof you can make, I can make nicer!*'

'*I can make any roof nicer than you!*' he sang back.

They laughed, and then he cast his eyes over the two roofs and put an arm round her. 'Of course, we could just have… one *big* roof terrace. Get rid of the wall.'

That somehow sounded like a *step*… but maybe she was getting carried away. She turned to him – but he was now looking down at their crowded little terraces below.

'Maybe get rid of *that* wall too, put *both* terraces together…'

'Why not?' she said, laughing, but keeping her eyes on him, her heart fluttering.

'In fact, how would you like to… er…' He put his arms round her and was smiling widely, but seemed lost for words.

'Put our *houses* together?'

'Yes!' he said, squeezing her. 'What d'you say?'

'Oh! Well… *yes*, of course!'

They hugged each other tightly, tears pricking their eyes, had a salty kiss… and heard applause and excited shouts from below. Elise, worried there was a problem, had dashed over, and a crowd had gathered – her husband, Dolores and two of her friends, Kiko and his wife, even the usually sour-faced Nerea – who'd obviously been watching them from below. Dolores astounded everyone with a loud wolf whistle, prompting more laughter and shouts about a show and an encore – so they waved and then kissed again.

EPILOGUE

FIVE YEARS LATER

A last calming cuddle with Chica, and they left the terrace to go through the gate and up the steps to the road.

'We *could* just be going to the botanical gardens,' Juliana said to Josemi, as they reached the end of their road and turned up the hill.

'What? We *are* going to the botanical gardens... Hm, but to dress up as the King of Siam and the headstrong English teacher. How are you doing?'

'Feeling pretty sick, to be honest. Why do we put ourselves through this?' she said, smiling between trying to steady her nerves with long, slow breaths out.

'Maybe some year we'll manage to say no.'

She saw the church up ahead, uplit and golden in the fading light. 'D'you think? Even our wedding was no excuse – delaying our honeymoon for three weeks!'

'Yes, but we couldn't miss *We Will Rock You* – and the opportunity to *not* be the leads! Uh, we love it really – just not the first night!'

'True.' They were passing the church now, and Juliana gave him a wicked grin.

'Don't!' he said, holding up a warning finger. She liked to tease him about the 'Oh!' he let out when he saw her walk up the aisle.

She mimicked his shocked face, then laughed and took his arm. 'But then, you poor thing, you'd never seen your woman in a decent dress.'

'You were *stunning*. But I also love you in tie-dye pineapples,' he said, nodding at her latest six-euro *mercadillo* dress and squeezing her.

Kiko and his wife stopped them and gave them a kiss, saying the whole Rafaelarte group had tickets and would be coming. 'I don't know – tickets, a specially renovated amphitheatre, *six* performances in four villages now,' he said. 'Your drama group is going up in the world!'

The old San Rafael amphitheatre opposite the botanical gardens had been renovated by volunteers and donations, but he had a point. The village – its historic mine site, art group, restaurants, house renovations, small hotels – had also developed, but luckily the *ayuntamiento* was keen to protect it from expanding into the valley or losing its peaceful charm.

They'd arrived at the elegant terracotta-coloured botanical building, where gardener Ben was checking names against a clipboard list of people involved in the show. He was helped by Florrie, a friend from his Sussex horticultural college days who'd finally decided to join him in San Rafael and was apparently now happily shacked up with him – much to the disappointment of many girls in the village.

A shout of Juliana's name went up when she went into the female changing room that the Cabo De Gata Fauna and Flora display rooms had become. Many of the kids, playing the royal children learning English with her in the play, were also pupils from the English-through-Drama groups she ran with Kim.

'How's it going?' Juliana asked Kim, who'd volunteered to be one of the chaperones controlling this overexcited lot.

Kim laughed. 'Fine! Glad to be out of the house and leave Mum to deal with Daniel having a tantrum about wishing he was in it after all! But under-fives who can cope with this are rare... Elise did your hair? Looks great!'

'Yes! Is there no end to that woman's talents? Anyway, better get my big dress on...'

As the director called thirty minutes, she met Josemi in a little room where you could peep out of the window at the audience queuing outside the entrance to the amphitheatre opposite.

'Oh look at that, Olivia and the twins have obviously sent Dad out to queue for the best seats while they finish doing themselves up,' Juliana said.

'And he seems to be trying out his new Spanish on Fran and Josefa.'

'Oh God, so he is. I always thought he was only okay with Fran because they couldn't speak to each other, but maybe I'm wrong... Ah, there's Miguel, Susana and little Rosa...'

'And Lolo.'

'Miss having him in the play this year.'

'But then, can't complain about him putting his love life first.'

'Well quite – especially when it's taken us five years to get him and your mum together!'

Josemi smiled; he was so happy for his mother to have found love again after so long. 'Ah... and Pili's come with the baby!'

'Oh yes!'

The long queue at the barrier started to flow into the amphitheatre; Juliana felt her stomach turn, and beside her, the King of Siam breathed out heavily and swore. She turned away from the window, slid a hand under the red silk jacket to his firm warm chest. 'You've got nothing to worry about. And in case you hadn't noticed, you look outrageously hot in that.'

He laughed and kissed her. 'Well, you *definitely* shouldn't worry; you *are* Anna!'

They broke apart when they heard others come in, including Toby – all grey-haired and moustached for playing his cameo as British envoy Sir Edward Ramsay, an old flame of Anna's.

'Toby, I didn't think Pili would come!' Juliana said. 'Have you got a name for that gorgeous little girl yet?'

He grinned. 'Rafaela. After the village where we first met!'

'Aw, that's lovely!' she said, and Josemi gave him a thumbs-up.

Ten minutes was called.

'Right. Need to find that big son of mine.' She smiled at Josemi and Toby and, warming her voice up as she went, caught up with nervous-looking 'Louis', a bright eleven-year-old who'd been coming to English-through-Drama since they started it.

Before long, she and Louis were on stage, starting their Thai adventure. Nerves fell away as she started to enjoy all her favourite moments – and one of those was near the beginning: 'The March of the Siamese Children' to that haunting music. Each little prince or princess was led in by a nurse, bowed to their father the king, touched their forehead to the hands of their new teacher Mrs Anna, and then sat down with their royal wife mother. The orchestra's brass section gave quite a fanfare for Crown Prince Chulalongko-rn's entrance, then after that, the smaller children came on, and finally the very smallest... three-year-old Arturito. He was led on stage by Dolores − making her acting debut, for the sake of her grandson. One of his nursery school teachers was playing his mother and waiting to put him next to her − or remove him from the stage, if necessary.

But Arturito had been studying Chulalongkorn's regal bearing and scene-stealing performance. On he came, dismissing his nurse − and beloved grandma − to get every minute of his solo regal march. The audience sighed. He looked both his parents in the eye as he bowed to them, and then, taking everyone by surprise, fixed the audience with his fiery brown eyes and bowed to them too − to a riotous applause that made him smile at last and run and sit down. Juliana exchanged a grin with Josemi, and just managed to remember to say her words about not returning to England, wanting to stay.

Juliana's life was here now, with her Spanish family − and with the return of the passionate craving for Raf tomatoes she'd had when expecting Arturito, she strongly suspected there could be a new little family member on the way.

ACKNOWLEDGMENTS

The Spanish House was written when I was trapped in England during the first UK COVID-19 lockdown, so I'm grateful to the inspiration genie for letting me transport myself back to my own Spanish life. Luckily, the story had started coming to me when I was there the previous month, so I'd visited the local cemetery, and I already had experience of nearly everything else, such as the annual local musical production, the Tabernas film studios, and a patient local teaching me about the worrying-looking orange gas bottles!

Special thanks must go to next-door neighbours María José Martín and Paulino Espigares, for all the glorious hours walking, talking and introducing the *inglesa* to all things Almerian. *Os quiero!*

I'm also grateful to Spanish friends Juan del Pozo, for both the inspiration from his paintings (www.juandelpozo.net) and for being a useful source of English language mistakes (*"qué dice este hombre?!"*), and his teacher wife, Marta Rodriguez, for picking me up on my Spanish ones. *Hasta pronto!*

Two of the books I couldn't have managed without were the glorious *Once Upon a Time in the West: Shooting a Masterpiece* by Christopher Frayling, and the engaging and uniquely informative *Flamingos in the Desert: Exploring Almeria* by Kevin Borman.

I've never written a novel with such happy absorption, so big hugs for my husband Phil (my staunchest supporter but a brilliantly brutal critic), and sons Jack and Robin (who both promise they'll actually read this one) for putting up with me during this time.

Then came the running of the literary agent submission gauntlet, despite promising myself I'd never do this again - but I finally found my literary soul mate! Many, many thanks to Kiran Kataria (Keane Kataria Literary Agency), for her invaluable guidance and calming of my angsty author moments.

Also, a big thank you to my wonderful editor Hannah Todd, cover designer Leah Jacobs-Gordon, copyeditor Helena Newton and all the team at Aria Fiction (Head of Zeus) for their painstaking hard work, enthusiasm and turning of my story into a beautiful book.

Thank you to all the encouraging friends and generously supportive fellow writers - particularly Beverley Harvey, who is basically an angel.

Last but not least, I can't forget my half-Spanish mother's part in this - and she would have loved it.

LOCATIONS IN THE SPANISH HOUSE

As anyone who's been to the Cabo de Gata-Níjar Natural Park in Almería will quickly realise, 'San Rafael' is basically the old gold mining village of Rodalquilar. Apart from wanting to add a couple more shops for Juliana's convenience, I couldn't bear the thought of the name, so beautiful in Spanish, being read as 'Roddle-killer'! All the other villages and towns exist, and although the film studio theme park, restaurants and gardens have fictitious names, they are all inspired by real places here. Come and see for yourself!

ABOUT THE AUTHOR

CHERRY RADFORD has been a keyboard player in a band, piano teacher at the royal ballet school and a post-doctoral scientist at London's Moorfields eye hospital. She began her first novel in a coffee break at a scientific conference.

She writes uplifting novels about identity, renewal and finding soulmate romance when you least expect it. Having inherited a love of Spain and its culture from her half-Spanish mother, all her novels have a Spanish connection or setting.

The Spanish House is the first of three stories set in the starkly beautiful and unspoilt Cabo de Gata region of coastal Andalusia where she now lives. She is married to a musician and has two sons.

Website and blog:
www.cherryradford.com

Hello from Aria

We hope you enjoyed this book! If you did, let us know,
we'd love to hear from you.

We are Aria, a dynamic fiction imprint from
award-winning publishers Head of Zeus. At heart,
we're committed to publishing fantastic commercial
fiction – from romance to sagas to historical fiction.

Visit us online and discover a community of
like-minded fiction fans.

You can find us at:

www.ariafiction.com
🐦 @Aria_fiction
📘 @Ariafiction